D1785396

SPECIAL MESSAGE TO READERS

This book is published under the auspices of

THE ULVERSCROFT FOUNDATION

(registered charity No. 264873 UK)

Established in 1972 to provide funds for research, diagnosis and treatment of eye diseases. Examples of contributions made are: —

A new Children's Assessment Unit at Moorfield's Hospital, London.

•

Twin operating theatres at the Western Ophthalmic Hospital, London.

•

A Chair of Ophthalmology at the University of Leicester.

•

The establishment of a Royal Australian College of Ophthalmologists "Fellowship".

You can help further the work of the Foundation by making a donation or leaving a legacy. Every contribution, no matter how small, is received with gratitude. Please write for details to:

**THE ULVERSCROFT FOUNDATION,
The Green, Bradgate Road, Anstey,
Leicester LE7 7FU, England.
Telephone: (0116) 236 4325**

**In Australia write to:
THE ULVERSCROFT FOUNDATION,
c/o The Royal Australian College of
Ophthalmologists,
27, Commonwealth Street, Sydney,
N.S.W. 2010.**

I've travelled the world twice over,
Met the famous: saints and sinners,
Poets and artists, kings and queens,
Old stars and hopeful beginners,
I've been where no-one's been before,
Learned secrets from writers and cooks
All with one library ticket
To the wonderful world of books.

©Janice James.

The wisdom of the ages
Is there for you and me,
The wisdom of the ages,
In your local library

There's large print books
And talking books,
For those who cannot see,
The wisdom of the ages,
It's fantastic, and it's free.

Written by Sam Wood, aged 92

McLEAN AT THE GOLDEN OWL

Inspector McLean has resigned from Scotland Yard's CID and has opened an office in Wimpole Street, where there is a small gilt owl on a bracket over his door and a brass plate inscribed 'Robert McLean, Private Investigator'. With the help of his able assistant, Tiny, he solves many crimes, including cases of kidnapping, murder and poisoning. He also investigates the conspiracy against him which led to his resignation from the Yard, and seeks revenge against the man who framed him.

Books by George Goodchild
Published by The House of Ulverscroft:

THE DANGER LINE
McLEAN DISPOSES
THE LAST REDOUBT
THE EFFORD TANGLE
NEXT OF KIN
McLEAN INVESTIGATES
COMPANION TO SIRIUS
SAVAGE ENCOUNTER
FALSE INTRUDER
DEAR CONSPIRATOR
TIGER, TIGER
LADY TAKE CARE

GEORGE GOODCHILD

◆

McLEAN
AT THE
GOLDEN OWL

Complete and Unabridged

ULVERSCROFT
Leicester

First published in Great Britain

First Large Print Edition
published 1997

The right of George Goodchild to be identified
as the author of this work has been asserted
by him in accordance with the
Copyright, Designs and Patents Act, 1988

British Library CIP Data

Goodchild, George
    McLean at the Golden Owl.—Large print ed.—
Ulverscroft large print series: mystery
1. English fiction—20th century
2. Large type books
I. Title
823.9'14 [F]

ISBN 0–7089–3665–2

Published by
F. A. Thorpe (Publishing) Ltd.
Anstey, Leicestershire
Set by Words & Graphics Ltd.
Anstey, Leicestershire
Printed and bound in Great Britain by
T. J. Press (Padstow) Ltd., Padstow, Cornwall

This book is printed on acid-free paper

1

FOR some time past pedestrians in the neighbourhood of Wimpole Street had noticed the redecoration of a tall, slim house, and the more curious of them had been puzzled by the erection of a small gilt owl on a bracket over the door. In due course appeared a brass plate, and on this was inscribed the legend — Robert McLean, Private Investigator.

It was a quiet street, and in the usual way not suited to any business office, but McLean did not rely upon the casual client. What business he did came to him entirely by introduction from various sources — Scotland Yard not least. The sign of the owl was a mere whim on his part, and it certainly did strike a note of mystery in a thoroughfare of private houses.

On the ground floor were a dining-room and a waiting-room. On the floor above was a large chamber which he termed 'lounge' and in which he beguiled most of his spare time. Behind it was a laboratory. The second floor contained some four bedrooms. There was also a half-basement, but this was the sanctum-sanctorum of Mrs. Kelly, who was responsible for the domestic arrangements. The only other person in the house was Tiny — late 'page' at a West End hotel, whom McLean had singled out at once as being a youth of bright intelligence. Tiny did not take much persuading to give up shouting room numbers for the more noble profession of assistant to a Private Investigator.

The decorating was completed to McLean's satisfaction, and he was now admiring the effect of some new wall-paper panelling in the dining-room. He rang the bell and Tiny appeared as if by magic. Knowing his master's mania for punctuality he could judge the time of his summons to the second. He was attired in a brown uniform with many buttons down the front, and he looked as clean and neat as a new pin.

"Morning, sir!"

"Good morning, Tiny. What is going to win the Derby?"

"Mrs. Kelly has a fancy for 'Blue Magic,' sir, but, I've got a bob on 'White Heather' meself."

"You are probably wiser than she. No — no porridge this morning. That ceases on the first of June. I will attack the eggs and bacon forthwith."

"Yus, sir."

McLean waved his finger admonishingly.

"Not 'yus,' Tiny, but 'yes.' Y-E-S."

"Yus, sir — I mean, yes."

"You are improving."

Tiny grinned and went off like a rocket. He reappeared less than a minute later with the food on a tray — also two letters. McLean dealt with the latter first.

"Oh, Tiny, Sergeant Brook is calling early — probably in a few minutes. You can show him in here, if he arrives before I have finished breakfast."

"Yus — er — yes, sir."

"That is all. Vanish!"

McLean read the morning newspaper as he ate. He frowned at a letter which had reference to a recent police

3

scandal, and in which his own name was mentioned, and his gaze lengthened into space as he recalled certain facts. He was still in a brown study when there came a knock on the door.

"Come in!"

The door opened and Sergeant Brook entered. He was in plain clothes and his big face relaxed into a smile as he saw McLean. They gripped hands and Brook seated himself on the couch.

"Am I too early?"

"Not a bit. I have just finished. Well, what do you think of my new quarters?"

"A bit better than the 'Yard.'"

"A little more peaceful. How are things in that neighbourhood?"

"Pretty dull. Of course that business is still the reigning topic. Everyone is taking sides, but the whole of my division is with you. It was nothing more or less than a dirty frame-up."

McLean's face tightened, though his eyes continued to smile.

"A clever piece of work, Brook. I will admit that I under-estimated the credulity of the members of the Commission. Yet, in the face of the evidence, they could do no other than ask for my resignation. Of course all that money was planted, and the witnesses bribed. But proof of such a conspiracy was completely lacking. I was unable to explain things satisfactorily. The end was inevitable — for me."

Brook's big hands closed and unclosed.

"We all know that De Wynter was behind it. He swore he would get you — "

"And he did," cut in McLean. "I tell you frankly, Brook, I have an admiration for the fellow."

"Admiration!"

"Well, it isn't everyone who can pull off a big thing like that with complete success, and without stirring a finger himself. His name was never mentioned. It was a masterly stroke to bring about the resignation — I might almost say 'discharge' — of an officer who, I hope I may say with all due modesty, was in considerable favour at head-quarters. But this is all beside the point. One day I hope to square accounts with Arnaud de Wynter. In the meantime I am still interested in the ways of the unrighteous.

Now, what is it exactly that brings you here?"

"You know the name of Sir George Benson?"

"At the Admiralty?"

"Yes. He is in trouble, and we can't help him much at the moment. In short, he has made an ass of himself, and dare not face the music. Last night, after dining not wisely but too well, he came upon a woman in distress. She was young and very attractive, and Sir George undertook to see her home, in a taxi. During the journey he was robbed of a certain important document. He discovered the loss before he left the taxi and gave the woman in charge. The case is to be heard at Marylebone Police Court this morning."

"Well?"

"The trouble is that Sir George dare not face it out. He gave a false name to the inspector on night duty, hoping that a search would reveal his wallet containing money and the document in question. But there was nothing found on the woman but a few pounds."

"Who is the woman?"

"She gave her name as Gladys Spring — married and living with her husband. We have nothing against her, but it is pretty certain she is a bad case. Sir George is downstairs at this moment. I suggest you hear his own version. I will introduce him and then I must get back to the Yard."

McLean nodded and Sir George was shown into the room. Brook introduced him and then made his departure. The visitor was obviously deeply perturbed. He looked as if he had not slept a wink all night.

"Sergeant Brook has told me a few details," said McLean. "I understand you do not intend to put in an appearance at the court?"

"I — I dare not. No one would believe that I offered to take that woman home out of chivalry — call it a zest for adventure if you like. She was at the Savoy and — and encouraged my attentions by subtle glances. I admit I had — er — dined well. I danced with her, and then she pleaded faintness. I — I undertook to escort her home, and she was grateful. In the taxi she changed

7

seats with me — insisted on doing so. I did not understand her motive at the time. Later she said it would not do for me to be seen getting out of the taxi with her — near her apartment. She begged me to leave at once. I agreed, stopped the taxi, and went to pay the driver. But she intervened and said she would pay the fare. She even offered me the money, but I declined it. I was short of change, so felt for my wallet. It was gone. Then I realised why she had changed seats. My wallet was in my hip pocket — the left side, and when I entered the taxi she was on my right. She wanted to get near my hip pocket."

"Obviously. What did you do then?"

"I saw a policeman on point duty farther on, and told the taxi-driver to stop close to him. This he did. I then told the woman that I knew she had stolen my wallet, and that if she gave it back to me I would let the matter drop."

"She was indignant?"

"Very. She called me every name under the sun, and threatened me with proceedings. Well, I decided to take the risk and asked the constable to accompany us to the nearest police station. There I charged her."

"You gave a wrong name?"

"Yes. She tried to queer my pitch by hinting that I had agreed to go to her lodgings — the usual sort of thing. I realised that she could make things extremely uncomfortable for me at home. Doubtless I was indiscreet, but there is no truth in her allegations. I hoped that a search would reveal my wallet, but apparently it did not, and this morning the case will be dismissed."

"Was the taxi searched?"

"Yes — outside the police station."

"Then she must have disposed of the wallet elsewhere. Can you remember exactly where you first stopped the taxi?"

"Oh, yes. It was at the end of Cadogan Gardens."

"You got out?"

"Yes."

"She must have disposed of it then. The thing you lost is of some value?"

"The money is nothing — fifteen pounds or so — but the small document is of the utmost value. I would personally

9

give a thousand pounds for its recovery."

"That may still be possible. I should like you to accompany me to the place where you first stopped the taxi."

"I am ready."

Tiny called a taxi and the pair drove in the direction of the Marylebone Road. Sir George located the spot easily, and the taxi stopped. They got out and McLean looked about him. In the centre of the road there were gardens, enclosed by high railings, and the taxi was exactly level with the end of these. McLean walked to the gate and entered the gardens. A search produced no satisfactory result. After some delay it was evident that the wallet was not there.

"Retrieved," he said. "We must start on a new trail. At what time was the case to be heard?"

"Ten-thirty."

"There is just time. I will go to the court. It will be better if you are not seen. Tell me where I can communicate with you?"

Sir George gave him a card, and then left him. McLean instructed the driver to go to Marylebone Police Court. In the plaintiff's absence the case was dropped, but McLean was afforded a lengthy view of Mrs. Gladys Spring, and was not surprised that Sir George had been guilty of an indiscretion. The woman was round about thirty years of age, and particularly fascinating. She seemed to be perfectly at ease, apparently knowing that there was not a scrap of real evidence against her. Ultimately she was told that the case was dropped, and she shrugged her shoulders and left the court. McLean followed her.

★ ★ ★

It was ten o'clock in the evening, and a man sat smoking in a small apartment off St. James's Square. He was a middle-aged man, of handsome features and immaculate dress, and it was obvious that he was expecting someone, for every few minutes he consulted his wrist-watch and sighed. At last there came a ring at the bell. He flung away the end of his cigarette and went to answer the summons. The woman known as Gladys entered.

"Thank God!" sighed the man. "I began to think the whole thing had gone wrong."

"It didn't. He had the courage to charge me, but he funked the public appearance at the last moment."

"Good! What happened?"

"I hooked him all right. We danced together and I faked illness. He volunteered to see me home. I saw Charlie in the vestibule and gave him the tip. He took the next taxi and followed us. Well, I located the paper eventually, and got it. But he discovered the loss of his wallet when I gave him the hint to go. There was a policeman farther up the street, and I overheard him tell the taxi-driver to pull up near the cop. Charlie was close behind — watching. I flung the wallet over the railings of Cadogan Gardens."

"You think he saw you?"

"Yes. He signalled."

"Have you been to the spot since?"

"Yes — on being released. The wallet wasn't there. I'll wager Charlie has it."

"The appointment was for ten o'clock, and he isn't here."

"It is only five minutes past ten. He'll come all right."

"If he double-crosses me — "

"Don't be a damned fool. The paper's no use to him. Guess he'll be glad to get rid of it."

A few minutes passed and then the bell rang again. The owner of the flat breathed a sigh of great relief, and almost ran to the front door. He returned with his visitor — a tall, slim man, with a cast in one eye.

"Hallo, Charlie!" greeted Gladys. "Did you get it?"

Charlie grinned and tapped his inside pocket.

"You bet your sweet eyes. Say, I saw the cop get into the taxi. Did he take you?"

"He did, but that's all over. Where's the wallet?"

Charlie produced it from his pocket, and handed it to the handsome man — his chief.

"It's just as I found it, Denny," he averred. "I only had a peep inside it. There's money and some papers."

Denny nodded, and was soon busy

removing the contents of the big wallet. There were fifteen pounds in notes, some visiting-cards, two letters, and a blue document folded several times. Denny left the notes lying on the table and consulted the document. It contained about half a dozen different plans and drawings in colour. He nodded.

"Good work, that! You've earned your reward. I said fifty — didn't I?"

Charlie inclined his head and lighted a cigarette casually. Denny took out his own wallet and counted out ten five-pound notes. Gladys, too, held out her hand, and received a similar sum.

"What about the other money?" she inquired.

"You can share that between you."

"Thanks!"

They divided up the notes. Gladys kissed hers as she stowed them away in her handbag. Denny now took the wallet and the other oddments and flung them into the blazing fire. In a few minutes nothing was left of them.

"What's the plan all about?" inquired Charlie.

"That's my business. Well, that little

job is done. Let's go to Moulding's and celebrate."

His companions concurred. They waited for him to don a coat and hat, and then accompanied him into the street. As they entered a taxi, a tall form vanished into a passage opposite them. It reappeared immediately the taxi started, and moved towards the house. It was McLean, and he had shadowed Gladys ever since her dismissal from the court. When Charlie had arrived at the house it was immediately clear to McLean that here was the solution of the mystery. Charlie undoubtedly had the document and was on his way to deliver it. The question now was — whether the conspirators had gone out with a view to doing business with another party, or whether their excursion was nothing more than a celebration of their victory. He was inclined to accept the latter view, and decided to examine the flat while he had an opportunity.

It was not difficult to force an entry, for McLean was equipped with excellent tools, and the ground floor flat was apparently empty. Within five minutes he was inside the flat, without having caused any injury to the lock. It contained a sitting-room, and three bedrooms, two of which were very small and barely furnished. The largest bedroom was undoubtedly the occupant's, for there were clothes in the wardrobe, and a suit of pyjamas spread across the pillow.

McLean started a thorough search, replacing everything exactly as he found it. At length he was assured that the document was not in the bedroom. The sitting-room underwent a similar search, but with no more satisfactory result. It appeared to be certain that the owner of the flat had the paper on his person. The fire had been allowed to go out, and in the fender was a charred fragment that was still smouldering. McLean picked this up with the tongs, and was satisfied that it was the remnant of a leather wallet.

He was still searching in the hope of finding correspondence that would inform him of Denny's intentions regarding the stolen document, when he heard a taxi draw up outside, and also the sound of voices. Quickly he made out of the sitting-room, and concealed himself under the large double bed in the bedroom, leaving the communicating door slightly ajar.

Very soon the outer door was opened and the flat was illuminated. All three of the recent occupants had come back, and one of the men, at least, was the worse for drink. He heard the clink of a glass and then raucous laughter — a toast and a hiccup.

"You two can stay here tonight," said Denny. "Accommodation isn't exactly palatial, but I had the bed-clothes aired this morning. Say 'when,' Gladys."

"Well, here's jolly good health, old bean," said Gladys. "I pulled this thing off well, didn't I?"

"You certainly did."

"But how did you know he had that paper on him?"

"I have ways of getting that sort of information. Government clerks are not all angels, and some are very badly paid. Have another spot, Charlie?"

"No — hic — no, thanks. I'm dead tired, I am. Where's that room you were mentioning?"

"Second door on the left along the passage. Gladys and I will have a 'final' before we turn in — "

"Not me," said Gladys. "I've had enough for one night. I'm for sheet lane. I can't stand your pace, Denny."

Denny laughed, and a few minutes later his two confederates retired for the night. A quarter of an hour passed before Denny himself sought his bed. McLean crouched well under the top part of the bed, and in due course he saw a pair of bare feet disappear. He waited patiently and Denny's breathing became more regular. At last McLean decided to move, and crawled out of his hiding-place. Denny now appeared to be sleeping soundly, and from an adjacent room came the unmusical sound of snoring. McLean flashed his electric torch and brought to light Denny's clothing. The coat was hanging on the back of a chair, and McLean's hands went through the pockets in a few seconds. In the left inside one he found a strong linen envelope. It was gummed down lightly, and across the face of it was written: *J. Denny — Private and confidential.* He managed to unseal the flap and brought to view the stolen plans.

He was turning to go, when his sleeve touched a vase on the dressing-table. It turned over and fell on the floor with a resounding crash. There was a movement from the bed, and then a sudden blaze of light. Denny was sitting up, rubbing his eyes.

"By Gosh!" he ejaculated. Then raising his voice: "Charlie! Charlie!"

McLean made to pass him, but a hand appeared from under the pillow and gripped in the fingers of it was a pistol.

★ ★ ★

"Got you!" snarled Denny. "If you move an inch I'll shoot you — you dirty thief!"

He crawled out of bed, still keeping McLean covered. Again he called for his confederate, and at last Charlie came into the room — half dressed. He opened his eyes wide at what he saw.

"Feel inside my coat — left side," snapped Denny. "I've got a notion of what this fellow is after. Hurry!"

Charlie found the coat and did as he was bid.

19

"Nothing there," he said.

"I thought so." He advanced on McLean. "Hand over that envelope, or — "

McLean stood quite still. There was a pistol in his pocket, but he knew that any movement towards that would be fatal. The envelope he still held in his hand.

"Take it, Charlie," ordered Denny. "You'll find another gun in the bottom drawer of the wardrobe — yes, there."

Charlie found the weapon and slowly advanced on McLean, holding out his left hand for the envelope.

"One minute," said McLean. "I think you are under a misapprehension. This envelope contains nothing but — "

He suddenly kicked the pistol from Denny's hand, and made a lightning leap at the electric switch. As he reached it Charlie fired. McLean felt an acute pain in his arm as he pressed down the switch. The room was reduced to blackness.

"Guard that door!" shouted Denny. "Don't let him get away. I'll find a match."

McLean was feeling strangely weak. His arm — just below the shoulder — was aching badly. His keen eyes saw but one thing — a very faint ray of light from the window. He crawled across the floor and reached the window curtain. His hand travelled upwards and found the window latch. Slowly the casement window opened. There was a small veranda outside, and a drop of twelve feet into a kind of court. A match flickered.

"The window!" cried Denny. "It's open."

McLean did not hesitate. He swung himself over the railing and then dropped — to meet a stone pavement with a painful concussion. He lay there breathless for a few moments. The two men stared down at him from the veranda above.

"He's out," said Denny. "There's blood — here. He's wounded. We can get him yet — hurry!"

McLean dragged himself to his feet. His left sleeve was saturated with blood and the pain was considerable. He judged that the two men would approach him from the right, and accordingly he made in the opposite direction. But progress was slow, for he was growing weaker and weaker. At last he emerged on a very quiet street. From behind came the sound of running feet . . .

Denny and Charlie appeared a few minutes later. They saw McLean stagger and then fall across the pavement. There was not another soul in sight, and Denny was soon by the side of the prostrate man. In his right hand was the linen envelope. Denny snatched it.

"Look out!" whispered Charlie. "Someone is coming up the street. Have you got it?"

"Yes."

"Good! Quick, there isn't a moment to spare."

They dived back into the passage.

★ ★ ★

McLean reached his home at close upon one o'clock in the morning, through the good offices of a late pedestrian. Tiny was shocked at the sight of his master, but McLean was able to assure him that his injuries were slight.

"A little brandy, Tiny," he said, "and a

long bandage from the medicine chest. I have been enjoying myself immensely."

Tiny tied the bandage under his master's instructions and made quite a fair job of it. An hour later McLean was sound asleep. To Tiny's amazement his master came down to breakfast the next morning at the usual time. His arm was in a sling, but otherwise he looked quite normal.

"Fine morning, Tiny."

"Are you better, sir?"

"I've a quart of blood to make up. I think I will have an extra egg."

"Yes, sir. Oh, and a gentleman has been ringing up. He said he was Sir George Benson, and must see you immediately. I told him you were not well but he said he would come round at once."

"I will see him. Has the post come?"

"Not yet, sir. A little bit late this morning."

McLean was making a praiseworthy attempt to eat his breakfast with one hand when Sir George was announced.

"Show him in here," said McLean. "But take the tray away first, and bring

23

in the post immediately it comes."

Sir George was shown in. He was breathless and excited.

"I heard you were not well," he said. "Why — you have hurt your arm?"

"A slight accident. It will soon be better. You have something to say to me?"

"Yes. I received a letter this morning. Perhaps I had better read it to you:

"*Dear Sir, the writer is able to lay his hands on a certain document which you had the ill-fortune to lose. He is prepared to deliver this safely into your hands for a payment of £10,000. He will telephone you at 10 a.m. to hear your decision, and to arrange necessary details. He takes this opportunity to warn you that any communication made to the police will merely result in placing the document in the hands of certain people who would not hesitate to pay even a larger sum for it.*"

"Posted last night," mused McLean.

"Yes — last post."

"What do you intend to do?"

"I have no alternative but to pay up. For the sake of my reputation I dare not refuse. I want you to arrange the matter for me."

"It is a large sum."

"I know — far more than I can afford. I thought — I hoped you might be able to help me, but now I am up against time. There is little more than an hour left."

McLean smiled and stroked his wounded shoulder.

"I have never known the post so late," he said. "I am expecting an important letter — "

"But this business is of the greatest importance. I must ask you if you are willing to act — "

There came a knock on the door and Tiny entered.

"Post, sir. Threepence to pay on one — this one. Shall I pay it, sir?"

The letter in question was nothing more than a small roll, held together by a strip of stamp-edging. It bore McLean's name and address in pencil.

"Pay it, Tiny," he said. "And give the postman a tip. It is well worth it."

He then removed the piece of stamp-edging, and unrolled the contents. Sir George's roving eyes fell on it, and a gasp left his lips.

"Why, — why, that is — the document — the plans!"

"Yes. I regret the spot of blood, but the addressing and dispatch were done in difficult circumstances."

"Thank God! Then you — you went after it?"

"Yes. There was rather a — a rough house. I had to leave in a hurry. Fortunately I came upon a post-box in my unsteady flight. There was just time to do what was necessary — and carry out a somewhat exaggerated faint. The man who wrote you that letter will doubtless have suffered a bitter disappointment by this time. I very much doubt if he will telephone you as arranged. The only thing he has to sell is a batch of quite useless press cuttings."

Sir George produced his cheque-book, while McLean was busy tightening a knot in his sling with his strong and useful teeth. When Sir George left he was whistling softly to himself, and he made

Tiny his life-long champion by slipping a ten-shilling note into his hand.

"Tiny," said McLean later, "I think we will take the day off and go to the Zoo."

2

SIX months had elapsed since the career of Inspector McLean of the C.I.D. received the check which culminated in his retirement from Scotland Yard, and more than three months since — under the sign of the owl — he had started as a private investigator. In that short time the world of law-breakers had come to realise that although the smart police officer was no more, the alert criminologist was very much alive.

McLean found himself in considerable demand, and it was somewhat gratifying to reflect that, despite the unfavourable finding of the Commission, there were many persons who were presumably content to give him the benefit of the doubt. A big private detective agency had put up a suggestion to him, but McLean scorned the idea of figuring in dirty divorce cases — of playing spy to jealous husbands and wives. Almost every post brought letters pleading for his services in cases which left him cold. It became necessary to have a slip printed — 'Mr. Robert McLean regrets . . . '

"We may have had a slight fall, Tiny," he confided to his adoring 'page.' "But we have fallen on our feet — more or less."

Tiny merely grinned. He knew that 'something' had happened at Scotland Yard which had removed his 'boss' from office, but as that removal had the result of getting Tiny inside the wonderful world of crime, that ingenuous youth was more inclined to bless the occasion than otherwise.

Among the letters one morning was one which caused McLean to stroke his chin reflectively. It came from the north of Scotland and was brief and to the point.

Dear Mr. McLean,

You may recall meeting me at the Caledonian Dinner three years ago. I am in great trouble — as you doubtless know. I implore you to come to my help. I would come in person, but I

29

am so distressed I could not endure the long journey to London. Wire me that you will come.

Helen McNaire.

McLean recalled the writer. Someone had introduced him to her and he had found her both charming and intelligent. She had taken a great interest in his work, and later he was told that she lived in a great house, and was exceedingly well-placed financially. But the name signified more than this. He went to a file and turned up the recent issues of a daily newspaper. At last he found what he sought.

TRAGEDY IN A SCOTTISH MANSION
MYSTERIOUS DEATH OF A WELL-KNOWN BARONET

During the next half-hour he had read all the known details of the case of Sir Angus McNaire, and within an hour he had dispatched a telegram to the writer of the letter, informing her that he was on his way north.

The Scotch express was not well

patronised that morning, and McLean was able to secure an empty compartment. The train was about to start when his solitude was cut short by the entry of a short, clean-shaven man, of about forty years of age. He deposited his suit-case in the rack and sat down immediately opposite McLean. A glance passed between the two men, and McLean nodded.

"How do you do, Datchett?"

Inspector Datchett smiled in his customary cynical fashion. During McLean's last year of service at the Yard, Datchett had gone out of his way to annoy him. He was the most cantankerous man alive and disliked by most of the men in his division. Nothing had pleased Datchett more than the news of McLean's resignation.

"Homeward bound?" he inquired.

"Not exactly."

"Business perhaps?"

"Shall we call it business and pleasure combined?"

Datchett lighted a cigarette and pushed the end of it into a long holder.

"I thought you had grown tired of the

unsophisticated south."

"On the contrary, I find London very interesting."

"We miss you at the Yard."

McLean did not miss the thrust and what it implied. It gave Datchett great pleasure to recall the past.

"I ought to feel flattered, but somehow I don't. I presume you are on business bent?"

"Yes. Your Scotch friends thought they were capable of handling a certain case; now they find they can't and have sent out an SOS for help."

McLean's eyes gleamed at this remark.

"The McNaire case?" he asked.

"A pretty good guess. They should have called us in at the start, but their pride prevented them. Now precious days have been wasted. The idiots!"

"Interesting case, that," mused McLean. "I suppose you hope to shed some new light on the matter?"

"That is very possible."

After the first exchange of conversation the two travellers spoke but little. Datchett carried a huge pile of newspapers, and McLean was reading a delightful work by Fabre on mason wasps. They lunched at different tables, and in due course the train reached Edinburgh. Datchett seemed to expect McLean's departure, but this did not take place.

"Going farther?" he inquired.

"Yes. Kingussie, in fact."

"Kingussie! Why, that's my destination."

"So I understood."

Datchett's mouth became a little hard. "You're going to Dorland Castle, eh?"

"Well, yes, to be truthful."

"I wish you wouldn't interfere."

McLean raised his eyebrows.

"Interfere isn't quite the word, my dear Datchett. I come by special invitation."

"From whom?"

"Miss Helen McNaire."

"But you must know that the police have the matter in hand. You have no authority, and I wish you would be good enough to leave the matter to us."

"It was a case of *noblesse oblige*. A young lady implored my — interference. I could not decline."

"She had no right to do anything of the kind. This is a case calling for — "

"For you?"

33

"For purely official investigation. We are in possession of certain facts."

"You are welcome to them. I fancy there is room for both of us. I presume you would have no really rooted objection to my finding the murderer?"

Datchett frowned and handled his newspaper savagely. It was perfectly clear he resented McLean's interest in the business, and that he would do all he could to place obstacles in his path. McLean was more amused than annoyed. He had not a very high opinion of Datchett's abilities.

In due course the two men reached their destination. Datchett went to the police station, and McLean took a conveyance to the great mansion. It was very early in the morning, and the country-side was sweet and fresh, and musical with the song of birds. Dorland Castle was a vast pile situated amid wonderful scenery. It had a splendid deer park, and a magnificent natural lake. Outside the precincts of the place the undulating moorland stretched away in all directions. McLean handed his card to a servant, and a few minutes later saw the niece of the dead man.

She was about twenty-five, a well-built woman, with deep brown eyes and abundant hair. Normally she possessed a good complexion, but now it was pallid. An expression of relief passed over her features when she saw McLean. She held out her hand and he gripped it.

"I was overjoyed to receive your telegram," she said. "Are you tired?"

"Not a bit. I slept quite well."

"You know why I begged your help?"

"I think I can guess. As a matter of fact, I travelled up with an old colleague — an Inspector Datchett."

"I heard last night that the local police had called in Scotland Yard. I suppose the inspector will come here?"

"Undoubtedly — and very soon. I am in possession of some of the facts, but I should like you to run over the points."

"Yes — yes. Perhaps you know that I have lived here with my late uncle since my mother died six years ago? He was somewhat of a recluse — hated society, and spent nearly all his time reading — chiefly philosophy. He has been very good to me. At times he was inclined to be quick of temper, but it soon passed, and I have had no cause for complaint. He was rich but very thrifty — some called him parsimonious. He hated modern things — cars, cinemas, and such — and what exercise he took was in horse-riding. About a week ago — last Wednesday night, to be exact — he sat up rather late, reading in the library. I retired to bed about ten o'clock and went in to him to bid him good-night. That was the last time I saw him alive. At eight o'clock the next morning his valet knocked on his bedroom door. There was no response, and in due course the valet entered the room. The bed had not been slept in. Later my poor uncle was found dead in the library. There was a bullet wound in his heart, and the doctor stated that he had been dead at least eight hours."

"The local police have dealt with the case until recently?"

"Yes. They failed to discover a single clue. The library windows were closed. There were no footprints — no sign of a struggle. Nothing to shed any light on the tragedy."

"Did no one in the house hear the sound of a shot?"

"Presumably not. All the servants were questioned."

"I should like to see the place where the body was found."

She bade him follow her, and escorted him into a huge oak-beamed room. It was lined with bookshelves all laden down with books. Near the great fireplace were an easy chair and a small table.

"He was found there — on the floor, with his head close to the chair. There is the stain — on the carpet. His heart was close to that."

"He had no enemies so far as you know?"

"I think not."

"Was the bullet found?"

"Yes. It was extracted from the body. It is now in the possession of the police."

"You have not seen it?"

"No."

"H'm! I should like to get a glimpse of that, but I fear that Inspector Datchett will not do me that favour. You are sure that nothing is missing from the house?"

"Quite sure. Everything has been checked twice. The motive could not have been burglary, for there were many small things that a burglar might have taken with him — unless he was scared by what he had done."

"Your uncle was rich?"

"Yes. His estate totals over three hundred thousand pounds."

"Do you know who will benefit under the will?"

"Oh, yes. There was no secret about that. My cousin Andrew is to receive a thousand a year. There are gifts to charities amounting to ten thousand pounds. The residue comes — to me."

"Where does your cousin live?"

"In Dunblane. He is twenty-nine years of age and single."

"He was on good terms with Sir Angus?"

"Oh, yes; but we saw very little of him. It was his custom to visit us for a week or two in the summer, but he did not come this summer — not until he heard of the tragedy. He is in the house now."

"I will see him later." He ran his finger over the mantelpiece and removed it — covered with dust. "I conclude the room has not been touched since the time of the tragedy?"

"Scarcely. The police requested it should be left as it was — for the time being. All the servants did was to remove the stain from the carpet as much as possible."

"Good. I should like to spend some time in this room."

"The house is at your disposal. I have had a bedroom got ready for you, and I trust you will stay here until you have solved this mystery. I cannot rest until I know that justice will be done."

She left McLean probing into everything.

★ ★ ★

Inspector Datchett put in an appearance two hours later. He spent some time with the servants, and McLean ran into him in the garden. Datchett stopped and glared at him.

"So you are staying here, McLean?"

"Yes. Any objections?"

"Personally, no — professionally, yes.

It is obstructive to have amateurs butting in."

"Amateurs! Oh, yes — I had almost forgotten. But I promise you I shall not steal your thunder. I am, in fact, enjoying a quiet rest. Just look at those roses."

"Damn the roses. Look here, McLean — this position is impossible. Miss McNaire had no right — "

"There we disagree," retorted McLean. "She has the right to take any conceivable step that may lead to the arrest of her uncle's murderer. Why not let us work together — swap theories, clues — "

"You can keep your own theories. As for clues, there are none worth mentioning."

"Oh, aren't there! I think I can produce three. But have your own way."

Datchett shot him a swift glance — a look in which doubt was mingled with curiosity.

"You have found something, eh?"

"Well — yes."

"What?"

"I'll make a bargain with you. I'll show you the thing I have found if you will let me see the bullet that was extracted from

Sir Angus McNaire's body."

Datchett hesitated for a moment and then inclined his head. He produced a small box and disclosed a small nickel bullet. On the base of it were five spiral marks made by rifling. McLean took out a small rule, and after using it made two notes in his book.

"Thanks!"

"And now — what have you found?"

"This."

A small cylindrical vulcanite object was thrust under Datchett's nose. The inspector blinked at it and then took it between his fingers.

"What the devil — !"

"You know what that is?"

"I'm blest if I do."

"My dear Datchett! But then I forgot that, like Sir Angus McNaire, you do not drive a car."

"Well, what is it?"

"A neon gas ignition tester. A finicky motorist would carry such a thing. It merely suggests that the man we want is a habitual motorist."

"Where did you find it?"

"Immediately outside the library

window — in the grass. I am afraid the local police are rather unobservant."

"But the windows were locked!"

"No doubt — after the crime. The murderer entered by the window I am convinced. Have you tried firing a shot in the library late at night?"

"No."

"Well, I have. The result is rather interesting. I should like to have that exhibit back — please."

Datchett got no more out of him, and McLean smiled as he went on his way. He preferred not to tell Datchett that the shot he had fired was through a pocket-handkerchief, and that no member of the household had been disturbed thereby. The discovery of the plug-tester had suggested to him that it might have been extracted from a pocket with a pocket-handkerchief, and the object of the pocket-handkerchief was to smother the report of the pistol. Why the murderer had locked the windows behind him he did not know, but he was convinced that that had been done.

On his perambulation back to the

house he met Andrew McNaire, who was still staying on, in order to keep his distressed cousin company. He was a reflective type of man with, as a rule, very little to say for himself. But on this occasion he stopped.

"Any developments, Mr. McLean?"

"Nothing conclusive."

"It is a strange and baffling case. I am certain that my uncle hadn't an enemy in all the world, and yet it is unquestionable that he was shot dead."

"He undoubtedly was."

"I cannot find the shadow of a motive."

"There was one notwithstanding."

"You have a theory?"

"Yes, but I should prefer not to discuss it at this juncture."

"I understand."

He was turning to go when McLean shot a question at him.

"Mr. McNaire, did your uncle engage in pistol practice at any time?"

"Not to my knowledge. But I used to do so. There is an old oak tree at the south end of the park where I used to hang a target."

"Thank you. I happened to see it yesterday."

Later in the day Datchett found the selfsame tree. McLean saw the inspector digging out bullets with a big knife.

"Another clue?" he inquired.

Datchett looked annoyed and nodded.

"You do not connect that with the crime?"

"I do. As a matter of fact it is possible I may make an arrest almost immediately."

McLean exhibited some surprise. Datchett, now apparently sure of his ground, displayed two nickel bullets. One was perfect in shape and the other was battered. Both were exactly the same size.

"Do you doubt they were fired by the same pistol?" he asked.

"The same make of pistol, you mean?"

"No, I mean the same pistol — this pistol."

To McLean's surprise he produced a small automatic pistol, and grinned with unconcealed joy.

"So you have found the weapon?"

"Yes. It was lying in a bush off the main drive. The murderer must have flung it away in his flight. In confidence I will show you something else. Look!"

He pointed to the wooden butt of the weapon. On it were inscribed the initials A.M.

"You think that stands for Andrew McNaire?"

"I know it does. I have ascertained from a servant that Andrew used to practise here with this weapon. The bullet that killed Sir Angus was fired from it — "

"Suppose A.M. stands for Angus McNaire and not Andrew?"

"I have considered that possibility, but it is ruled out by the evidence. Sir Angus was never in possession of a fire-arm. And then there is the plug-tester which you found near the library window. Andrew owns and drives a car."

"And the motive?"

"On the death of his uncle Andrew was to inherit a fortune of a thousand a year. He pretended he had not been here for over a year, but I am convinced he was here a week ago."

"You think you have sufficient grounds to arrest him?"

"No, but I hope to have soon. I am going to prove that Andrew was not in Dunblane on the night of the murder."

"Your conclusion seems a little bit premature to me," said McLean. "But you know best."

"Maybe you have a different theory?"

"Slightly different. But don't let that fact disturb you."

Datchett murmured something unintelligible and went away. A little later McLean saw him enter the house, and Andrew McNaire was informed that the inspector wished to see him. Helen came to McLean in a state of excitement.

"The inspector suspects my cousin," she said. "But it is all a mistake. Andrew would never dream of such a thing. What — what can we do?"

"Nothing — at the moment. You know that a pistol has been found?"

"No. You don't mean the pistol which — ?"

"Yes. I think there is no doubt it belonged to your cousin. He will have to explain that matter."

"But I can explain it. Andrew left the pistol and some ammunition in the old summer house, after he left last year. I saw it later, and put it into a box."

"Did you tell Andrew?"

"No. I forgot all about it."

"Well, it doesn't matter much. Now I regret to tell you that I must leave you for a few days."

"Leave us! You have not given up the case?"

"Oh, no. I am going after the man who killed your uncle."

Her eyes opened in amazement.

"You — you know who he is?"

"I think so. If and when I get him I shall hand him over to our friend the inspector." He smiled grimly. "Unfortunately in these days I have no power of arrest. Don't worry about your cousin."

"You will let me know as soon — ?"

"Immediately I am sure I am right."

★ ★ ★

McLean's quest took him to a small house in Glasgow. He asked for a Mrs. Linning, and after waiting for some time he saw the woman in question. She was

47

aged and dirty. Also she smelt of drink. She eyed the visitor suspiciously.

"What do you want with me?"

"I'm looking for Dan," said McLean with a disarming smile. "We were in the Seaforths together until — well, you know. I've been abroad for years and Dan once gave me this address. Is he living at home now?"

"No, the ungrateful snipe. After all I did for him he goes and leaves me in my old age. It was me that got him his job, too — when things were looking black. Who would take a man on — coming straight from prison? It was me who knew Miss Sandgate and aroused her sympathy. Now he is earning over three pounds a week, and never a bawbee does he pass on to his old mother."

"Maybe he will," said McLean. "Perhaps he is saving up to present you with a nice sum."

"Not him. He never was the sort to save up. Prison didn't do him any good. He was mad when he came out. Well, I've done with him. You can tell him I never want to see him again."

"I will — when I can find him. I've

owed him a pound for ten years. I'll tell you what I'll do — I'll give you the money to give to him. If you like to borrow it that isn't my concern. Maybe I won't have time to see him now. If you'll give me his address I'll send him a line, for old times' sake."

He passed over the pound note and a greedy claw snatched it. She gave him the address of Miss Sandgate immediately, and McLean was glad to get away from her. In due course he found Daniel Linning. He was filling the post of chauffeur to the wealthy Miss Sandgate, who was notoriously sympathetic towards jail-birds. Linning drove a fine car and was clad in a smart brown uniform. McLean ascertained that on the night of the murder Miss Sandgate was in London, and her chauffeur was thus free to do as he chose. It was also established that on the night in question Linning was out with the car until the early hours of the morning. A maid had heard the car being garaged, and had teased Linning about his taking a joy-ride during the absence of his mistress.

It took McLean two days to find

the opportunity he sought, and he was quite ready for it. Linning approached the big house in his mistress's car, to find McLean standing over a small vehicle which had apparently 'conked' out. McLean stopped him and craved his help.

"What's wrong?" asked Linning.

"Dud plug, I think. You don't happen to have a plug-tester?"

"Yes. Half a mo'!"

Linning searched in his pocket, but did not find the thing he wanted. Then he turned out one of the car pockets. The plug tester did not materialise, but the small box which had contained it did. While Linning was looking through the second car pocket, McLean captured the empty box.

"Must have mislaid it," said Linning. "But if you will drop into my garage — yonder — I can fix you up with a couple of spare plugs."

He drove his own car into the garage, and McLean followed him on foot. There was a box of spare parts on the bench, and in the box was an old handkerchief, now smothered in grease. McLean picked it up while Linning's eyes were averted. Near the centre of it was a jagged hole, *and the edges of it were burnt.*

★ ★ ★

McLean returned to Dorland Castle that evening, to find Datchett in the house.

"So you've come back?" he snapped.

"Oh, yes. Any luck?"

"No. I haven't yet proved that Andrew McNaire was not in Dunblane that night, but I am going to."

"You needn't waste time," said McLean. "I have found the murderer."

"What!"

"I am serious. My job is done. Yours is about to commence. His name is Daniel Linning, and he was once in the Seaforths."

"The Seaforths! That was Sir Angus's regiment."

"It was. Linning was court-martialled for a serious offence towards the end of the war. It was Sir Angus who sentenced him, and Linning never forgot it. Among some old papers I found a note. It is here. Read it."

The note was passed over, and Datchett read the awful scrawl:

I'll get you one day — you swine, if I have to swing for it.

"No signature," mused Datchett.

"No. He was too cunning for that. But here is some writing of Linning's. The two are identical."

"By Jove, yes!"

"I will now make you a present of the plug-tester — and this box which was found in the car he is driving. The garage which supplied it will state that Linning made a similar purchase a few weeks ago. Also, in the box at the end of the bench in his garage you will find the handkerchief which smothered the sound of the pistol shot. I left that there for obvious reasons."

"But the pistol — how did he get hold of that?"

"For some reason or other he went into the summer-house where it was left by Andrew McNaire. Probably he was seen by a servant and had to take refuge. Anyway, he found that weapon, and decided to use it. Why he did not leave by the window of entry I do not know, but that is a matter of no great importance. Now you had better get busy."

Linning was arrested the next day, but he made the fatal mistake of an attempted escape, and later, when he realised that everything was against him, he made a complete statement. McLean read the details in his sitting-room at the sign of the owl. There was a fulsome article on the excellent police work of Inspector Datchett, accompanied by a photograph of the great human sleuthhound. McLean smiled, and picked up the valuable platinum and gold cigarette case that was lying close to the box in which it had arrived. On the inside was inscribed:

To Robert McLean with deepest gratitude from Helen and Andrew McNaire.

He rang the bell and Tiny entered.
"Two eggs this morning, Tiny," said McLean brightly. "Never mind the expense."

3

ARNAUD DE WYNTER emerged from his delightful bathroom at the Park Hotel, looking the picture of health and contentment. He did not dress at once, but lay on a couch in his private sitting-room and let the morning sun play on the exposed parts of his well developed body. At this period he was thirty-five years of age, tall and fresh of complexion. He boasted a little toothbrush moustache under a rather large nose, and it pleased him to have his hair cut as short as a Prussian.

De Wynter had spent his boyhood in France, but later he had gone to an English public school, with the result that he spoke two languages perfectly. He now spent his time between London and Paris, and lived a life of comparative luxury. To outward view he was a cultured man — such a one as can be found in a dozen clubs at any time before lunch, and he possessed two entirely different sets of acquaintances. One set was beyond reproach; the other seldom came near Pall Mall.

If any man ever succeeded in living two completely detached existences it was de Wynter. In social circles he was the embodiment of sophistication and natural charm. In the circle from which came the sycophants which permitted him to lead a life of comparative ease he was the Devil himself. A dozen men had measured their brains against de Wynter, and all of them had gone down. The greatest of these had been McLean. It afforded de Wynter particular pleasure to reflect upon this fact. McLean had threatened his very liberty, and de Wynter had found the means to break him. It had been cleverly done. All sorts of tools had had to be employed — all kinds of strings pulled. But there it was. De Wynter could afford to preen himself.

It was curious that he should recall that success at this moment, for as he lay there gazing over the house-tops at the mass of traffic in the far distance, the telephone bell rang and he was informed that a Mr. Nidds wished to see him.

His brow became furrowed, and his eyes expressed his surprise — nay, anger.

"Send him up," he said.

A few minutes later there was a knock on the door, and George Nidds entered. He was a big individual, with enormous hands and feet, and he carried himself awkwardly — hat in hand. De Wynter scowled at him.

"What the devil do you mean, coming here?" he demanded.

"I got a bit of news. I bin trying to get you on the telephone for the last half-hour."

"I was in my bath. What is it you have to tell me?"

"The Lowrie girl has gone to McLean."

De Wynter's eyes narrowed to mere slits.

"How do you know?"

"Mike followed her this morning. She called at his office, and was with him for a quarter of an hour. Mike came to me at once, and I reckoned you ought to know."

"I'm glad I do. I didn't quite expect this. Did she leave McLean's place alone?"

"Yes."

"That means she has told him where the stuff is."

"But she swore — !"

"Tch! She would swear anything. She knows where it is and is afraid to go for it, because we are watching her. She has employed McLean to get it."

"What's to be done, anyway?"

"I want McLean watched. Bill can do that. If he knows where the stuff is he won't be long getting on the trail. You and Mike can get hold of the girl without delay."

"You mean — ?"

"Grab her — you idiot. Take her to Mike's apartment and keep her quiet."

"But I can't see — "

"Of course you can't. You haven't the brains to see anything but a mug of beer. Do as I tell you. Bill can get any assistance he likes. I want McLean's movements watched."

* * *

At that very moment McLean was perusing a sheet of paper which his client had left with him. He recalled the Lowrie case, and it had always been his opinion that Alice Lowrie had had no hand in the big Brixton robbery. But she and her father had gone to prison — the girl for three years, and her father for five. She had come to him now because she was afraid to go to the police. Until quite recently she had believed her father to be innocent of the charge for which he was convicted. Some of the jewels had been found in her handbag, but just before the raid on the house de Wynter had been with her father, and she was convinced that it was de Wynter who had hidden part of the booty when he knew the police were on the premises.

Upon her release from prison she had been met by Nidds and another man. They had made it clear to her that only half the booty had been recovered, and that the remainder had been hidden by her father during his flight from the police. They thought she knew the location and offered to get the stuff, dispose of it, and share up the proceeds with her. She protested she did not know where the booty was — that her father had never mentioned the matter. But neither of them believed her. Cajolery was followed by threats. She was 'shadowed' everywhere. The house was broken into several times, and her life was made most miserable.

Then had come a letter, evidently posted by a man who had served a sentence with her father. To guard against being cheated by the messenger, Lowrie had resorted to hieroglyphics, backing his daughter's intelligence to interpret them. But the girl was too perturbed to make an attempt. The daily 'shadowing' was getting on her nerves. She recalled McLean, who had been very kind to her during her trial — and she had gone to him in desperation. McLean was now gazing at the sheet of notepaper which she had left. It carried the following symbols:

McLean had expected that the girl would interpret the signs with comparative ease, since they were intended for her, but she seemed incapable of making any useful suggestions at that juncture. He had advised her to go home and compose herself, and promised to call on her that evening.

In the interim he had other work on hand, but no sooner was he in the street than he was aware that he was being followed. There were two men employed, and they gave him little rest. He came home to lunch, and saw one of the men turn the corner of the street as he entered the house.

"Tiny," he said to his 'page,' "run along to the post office and buy me a shilling postal order. On the corner you may possibly observe a man in a grey suit, black felt hat and loud tie. Just take notice."

Tiny came back ten minutes later.

"He was there, sir," he said. "I barged into him and he swore at me."

"Ah, I imagined he was no gentleman. You can keep the postal order, Tiny. That will pay for two attempts at cross-word puzzles. Now I will have lunch."

During the afternoon McLean gave his shadowers a little exercise. He felt he needed a walk, and took the Tube to Hampstead. For three solid hours he walked in the neighbourhood of the Heath, going round and round in ever-narrowing circles, until at last he rested under a tree. Here he took out a pocket-knife and probed in the soil. In the distance was a man apparently admiring the scene through a pair of binoculars!

McLean performed a few lightning tactics and ultimately came suddenly upon his 'shadower.' The man lighted a cigarette calmly and made to walk in the opposite direction.

"One moment!"

The square face came round.

"I hope I haven't tired you," said McLean. "You might tell de Wynter I propose walking to Brighton to-morrow, in which case he had better provide you and your friend with bicycles."

"What the — !"

McLean walked on, but still he was followed stubbornly until he reached home. He spent two hours indoors and then sallied forth to call on Alice Lowrie.

Upon reaching her home he found the maid greatly perturbed. Her mistress had gone out early that morning and returned about ten o'clock. She went out again at noon and stated she would be a little late for lunch, but would most certainly be home by two o'clock. Now it was seven o'clock, and there had been no message of any kind. What upset the maid was the fact that it was her evening out, and she had an appointment for six o'clock with her young man.

McLean said he would wait, and spent the best part of an hour in the sitting-room.

"You have a telephone?" he inquired.

"Oh, yes, sir."

"When Miss Lowrie returns, tell her to telephone me at this number."

"Very good, sir."

He sat at home that evening puzzling his brain over the black cat, the broken window, and the other signs. It was nearly midnight when the telephone bell rang, and a very agitated voice informed him that Alice Lowrie was still absent.

"De Wynter," muttered McLean. Then to the maid: "Don't worry — your mistress is quite all right."

He put up the receiver, and after a few moments' reflection donned his coat and hat. But before he left he rang up the Park Hotel and left a message to the effect that an old friend was coming to see Mr. de Wynter.

★ ★ ★

De Wynter was in the deserted lounge when McLean arrived. He displayed no astonishment when he saw the late victim of his cunning.

"I was told it was an old friend," he remarked. "The description is rather — humorous."

"Quite. I am glad to see you looking so well."

"I am always well — except after being kept up late at night. Have you come to discuss business?"

"I have come to tell you that removing young ladies by force is a serious crime."

"Meaning what exactly?"

"Alice Lowrie disappeared some time between noon and midnight. Hadn't you better let her go?"

"Lowrie! I seem to recall the name."

"I fancy your memory is equal to that effort. Lowrie pulled some chestnuts out of the fire for you, and his daughter was roped in too, though innocent."

"Very interesting. But even now I don't understand the real object of your very late and inconvenient call."

"Nothing more than I have said. I merely came to advise you to let that girl go. She cannot help you, and you are courting considerable danger."

De Wynter laughed amusedly.

"Your interest in my welfare is really remarkable."

"Quite natural, I assure you. I do not want you hurt or removed from society — yet. When you are removed — as you undoubtedly will be — I wish to have the self-satisfaction of being the instrument to bring that about. And I hope to make it permanent."

De Wynter's eyes flashed angrily, but he laughed off his displeasure.

"We are alone, and can afford to be frank," he said. "On a previous occasion you uttered a similar threat, but curiously enough it was not I who was removed, but a person associated with Scotland Yard. Do I make myself clear?"

"Perfectly. You won the first round, through a regrettable blunder on my part."

"Blunder! Does the great McLean blunder?"

"Oh, yes. I did not credit you with sufficient cunning. I was inclined to treat you with contempt. But all this is beside the point. Are you going to let that girl go?"

"I don't know what you are talking about. May I suggest this interview closes?"

"That is your last word?"

"Yes. I am now going to bed."

"Very well."

McLean got up and walked out of the hotel. Any doubts he may have had were removed now. It was abundantly clear that Alice Lowrie had been kidnapped on de Wynter's instructions, and that his object was to force from her the locality of the hidden jewels.

* * *

65

On the following evening three men sat in the living-room of a dilapidated and isolated house outside London, awaiting a visitor. He came at the stroke of eight o'clock — de Wynter. Michael O'Brien, who owned the house, waved his visitor into a chair, and Nidds and the third man waited for the oracle to speak.

"So you brought her here?" rapped de Wynter.

"Yes. The flat was too public. We ran her out here early this morning."

"Have you questioned her yet?"

"I should think I have, and not a blooming word will she speak — at least, nothing useful. She says she doesn't know where the stuff is — that the old man never confided in her."

"She lies. She would not have gone to McLean except to secure his help."

"Then why hasn't he located the stuff?"

"Because he doesn't know where it is — yet. It is highly probable that she was planning to go with McLean — to guide him to the place. He made an appointment, and that is why I took steps to make sure she did not keep it. Well, we are going to make her talk up — and at once."

His expression was devilish. The sophisticated de Wynter could be a fiend when his interests were at stake. He had come prepared to wring the truth from his victim, and he was clever enough to resort to more potent means than mere brutality or torture.

"Where is she now?" he asked.

"In the cellar."

"You can bring her up here."

O'Brien nodded and left the room. De Wynter produced a small box from his pocket and laid it on the table. It was little more than an inch and a half square, and what it contained no one but himself knew. A few minutes passed, and then O'Brien appeared with the prisoner. She was pallid and obviously scared, but she seemed to be relieved to see de Wynter there. He smiled at her and bade her be seated.

"Now, Alice," he said, "you must be reasonable. I regret the rather harsh measures that have been adopted. We know you know where your father hid the rest of the booty. I promise you half of it when we retrieve it. That will mean at least five thousand pounds in cash. I have a car outside. We can drive to the place now and get the whole matter finished. Come, be sensible."

"I tell you I don't know anything about it. I never even knew that my father was a crook until that night when the police came. It was not he who put the jewels into my handbag — "

"Never mind about that. Tell me what I want to know. Where did your father hide the rest of the stuff?"

"I don't know. I think he was going to tell me when I saw him in prison, but there was a warder within hearing. I — I know nothing. I swear I don't."

"Then why did you go to McLean?"

"You were making my life a misery. He was once kind to me. I wanted his advice."

"You lie. You intended to lead him to the place — because you were afraid to go alone. You are going to tell me where that place is."

Unexpectedly she displayed signs of courage. It was that or a complete breakdown, and she fought against the latter.

"If I knew I wouldn't tell you," she said. "You got my poor father to take all the risk, and then betrayed him. You got me sent to prison, although I was innocent. You can beat me — do anything you like — but I'll never speak."

"Ah, now we know where we are. Don't lie any more. You know, and you think you can defy me with impunity. There are various ways of inducing speech — confessions, and much depends upon the circumstances. Beating! Oh, no, I never beat women. You have quite made up your mind you will tell me nothing?"

"Yes."

"Very well. We must resort to subtler forms of persuasion."

He sighed and untied the strip of silk which was round the mysterious little box. Then he slipped on a glove and removed the lid. A horrible-looking insect came to view. It was hairy and bloated, and slow of movement. The onlookers gasped, and the girl's eyes became round with horror.

69

"Hold her, Mike," said de Wynter.

She was caught in a firm grip, and de Wynter undid the top button of her silk blouse with his free hand. A shriek left her palsied lips, but de Wynter only smiled.

"A tropical thing," he said. "Oh, have no fear, it is not really dangerous. It certainly bites, but — "

The struggling insect was near the white throat, held firmly in the gloved hand. The girl screamed again. Physical torture she might have borne, but this — !

"Wait! Wait!" she cried chokingly.

"A little nearer, Mike!"

"No — no — no! For God's sake — I'll tell you. Yes, yes — I'll tell you everything."

De Wynter smiled and withdrew the insect a few inches.

"Go on. Your father did confide in you?"

"Yes. But — but only yesterday. A letter came and it contained a message in symbols."

"Where is it?"

"I took it to McLean."

"What did the symbols mean?"

"I — I don't know. I swear I don't. I thought McLean would be able to interpret them."

"What were they?"

"A black cat, a broken window, a zigzag line, and the number 199."

De Wynter repeated this, and then to his victim's immense relief he put the insect back into the box and fastened down the lid.

"A pencil, Mike."

With the pencil he made a sketch of the symbols, and then stroked his chin reflectively.

"Take her away," he snapped at length. "I want to think this thing out."

The girl was led down to her filthy prison, and de Wynter got busy on the symbols. Mike came back, and he and his friends sat and smoked in silence.

"Where was Lowrie arrested?" asked de Wynter suddenly.

"Near Reading."

"The black cat must stand for a village, and perhaps the broken pane of glass too. The last syllable may be 'stone,' for there is an obvious connection between a broken pane of glass and a stone. Can it be Catstone?"

"Never heard of such a village," put in Nidds, who knew the country fairly well.

"Is the zig zag line a street and the number that of a house?" inquired Mike.

"Shut up!" retorted de Wynter testily. "One thing at a time, and the first thing is the name of the town or village. What we need is a good map. Nidds, you had better take the car and get a map of the district."

"The shops are all closed."

"Then get one by other means. Try an hotel — or the railway station. Hurry!"

★ ★ ★

It was two hours later that McLean was startled by the furious ringing of the front door bell. The faithful Tiny had gone to the 'pictures,' and the housekeeper had retired to bed early with a bad headache. McLean rose from his seat before a big atlas and answered the door himself. To his great astonishment it was Alice

Lowrie in a state of collapse.

"They — let me go," she gasped. "I — I —"

McLean escorted her to the sitting-room and compelled her to drink a little brandy.

"I have tried to find you all day," he said. "To-night I intended to enlist the assistance of an old police friend. I am pleased to know that that is now unnecessary."

"It was de Wynter. He got the truth from me."

"He ill-used you?"

"Oh, no — it was worse than that. He brought a terrible insect with him. I had to speak up or — I left them together for a time, but Mike O'Brien forgot to lock the cellar door. I crept up the stairs and heard what was said. De Wynter sent out for a map and he deciphered the pictures."

"Then he is cleverer than I imagined. The last part of the cryptogram is fairly simple, but the first part offers some difficulty. Where has he gone now?"

"To get the jewels. I heard him tell the others that the zig zag line was intended to mean telegraph lines, and the number was that of a telegraph post."

"He is right. Oh, he has brains. But where is this particular telegraph post?"

"Petstone — a small village near Reading."

"Not so bad. I hit upon that myself but am not at all satisfied."

"You think he is wrong?"

"I am sure of it. Your father had to send this message by a fellow-prisoner. It was necessary for him to frame it in such a way that you were at an advantage. Look at it well."

He placed the original document before her, and she perused the symbols.

"Regard the cat," he said. "It is badly drawn, but is intended to be black. Also I can detect only one eye. In the ordinary way a tail would be visible, but there is no tail. Therein lies the whole key. It is a picture meant for you. What does it convey?"

She gasped and became very excited.

"I think I understand. We once had a cat — a Manx cat. It jumped through a window and injured its left eye."

"Splendid. What was its name?"

"We called it Ben."

McLean consulted a sheet of paper on which were written many town and village names.

"We have it," he said. "The village is Benleep. Your father imagined you would remember the tragic leap of your pet. Here it is on the map — ten miles from Reading, where your father was arrested. Petstone is six miles distant. Are you fit to take an evening run?"

"Yes — yes. I should have thought of that before, but I was too flustered. Oh, let us go."

McLean got on the telephone to a hire-car company, and ordered a fast closed car to be sent round at once. His name and business were known at the garage, and the car was at the door within a quarter of an hour. McLean instructed the driver where to go, and then entered the car.

An hour later the car passed through the village of Benleep, now sunk in sleep. McLean stopped the driver on the outskirts and went to examine a telegraph post. It bore the number 117.

"Farther yet," he said.

As the car progressed he counted the poles, and at last reached what he believed was number 199, but it turned out to be 198.

"The car can stay where it is," he said to the girl. "Probably it is better so. I have a pocket torch and a big knife. Will you stay or come?"

"I think I will come."

They walked up the deserted road and were soon under the towering post. It was rooted in grass on a flat high bank. McLean flashed the torch, and noticed a piece of stamp-edging attached to the post about a foot above the ground. Across it was written 'Alice' in pencil.

"This makes our task easier," he said. "It indicates the exact spot."

He commenced to probe with the knife, and in a minute or two the long blade struck something hard. Up came a sod of earth and then another. A small oblong box came to view. McLean put his fingers down — just as the road became brilliantly illuminated.

"A car!" gasped the girl.

The vehicle came on, but stopped suddenly close to the post. Two men stepped out of it, and McLean's face grew tense as he recognised de Wynter — presumably on his return from an abortive hunt at Petstone. McLean extricated the jewel-casket and gave it to the girl.

"Run to the car," he said. "As fast as you can."

She started off like a hare. De Wynter saw what had taken place and did exactly what McLean wanted him to do. He sped after the agile form, shouting at her to stop. The second man was no athlete and merely ambled. McLean disregarded him and ran swiftly along the top of the bank. He drew level with de Wynter just as that worthy contrived to catch the girl's arm and interrupt her headlong flight. McLean leaped from the bank. De Wynter saw him and his right hand flew to his pocket. McLean measured the distance with marvellous accuracy. His left arm shot out with the force of a battering ram, and his knuckles rattled on the point of de Wynter's jaw. A poleaxe could not have felled him more completely. He just grunted and lay still.

"The car!" cried McLean.

The chauffeur had already realised that things were getting warm, and had started up his engine. McLean and his client were scarcely inside the car before it moved forward, gathered speed and went rushing through the night. They saw no more of the other car.

"Oh!"

It was a long exclamation from the girl. She had opened the box and was now gazing at a mass of brilliant jewels. McLean pursed his lips as his gaze went to them.

"What are you going to do?" he asked.

"I — I want you to take them to the police."

"But that is not really necessary. You have served your sentence and — "

"I couldn't keep them in the circumstances. My father probably meant me to do so, but I should always be unhappy. I hope to find work soon. Please — please take them."

"I think that is the right course. I admire your courage immensely, Miss Lowrie."

"How can I ever thank you, Mr. Mclean?

I can't even pay you a fee for your services — at least, not until — "

He pressed her hand, and then smiled as he noticed that two of his knuckles were bleeding.

"My fee is paid," he said. "That was Round Two in the combat — McLean versus de Wynter. We may go the whole ten rounds — but I think not. I think I had better take you straight home, or you will miss your beauty sleep — not that it is really necessary."

She laughed and shot him a swift glance, but he was nursing his knuckles reflectively.

4

MCLEAN usually found something in the morning newspaper to arouse his wrath or lend him amusement. Sometimes it was a murder trial, or an article on the need for the reorganisation of Scotland Yard. Not invariably it was a mere paragraph, inserted by a rather credulous sub-editor as a 'fill-up.' On this particular morning it was contained in a dozen lines and headed 'The Spectre of Manrose.' McLean read it and smiled.

"Some excitement has been caused among fishermen in the Outer Hebrides by the alleged appearance of the Spectre of Manrose. Manrose lies in the Sound of Harris, within a few miles of Uist. It is barely half a mile in length, by a quarter of a mile wide, and contains but one habitation — an ancient half-ruined castle now occupied by a Mr. Andrew Lee. A century ago

the castle was the scene of a tragedy
— the wife of its owner having gone
mad, and flung herself from the north
turret into the deep sea below, in full
view of her distracted husband. Since
then the spectre of the dead woman is
reputed to have been seen from time
to time by neighbouring fishermen
who occasionally pass the island. The
reappearance of the spectre, with her
long hair trailing behind her, has so
filled the superstitious natives with awe
that few will go within two miles of
the island. Mr. Andrew Lee, who is
a recluse, treats the whole thing as
pure imagination, and still continues
to occupy his isolated home."

★ ★ ★

During the next month McLean forgot
all about the Spectre of Manrose, but
when his annual holiday came round he
decided to make a tour of the West Coast
to revive some very pleasant memories. In
due course he reached Kilmuir in Skye,
and there something happened which
brought to mind the paragraph in the

newspaper. An old fisherman had a story of his own to relate. He had had occasion to sail to Harris the week before, and on the return journey he passed quite close to Manrose. There were two lights in the Castle, one downstairs, and one at a barred window in the tower. At the upper window he saw, with the aid of a telescope, the form of a young woman, clearly silhouetted. He clapped on every inch of sail and made away from the place.

"But why?" asked McLean. "It was probably Mr. Lee's wife or daughter."

"Mon, he has no wife nor lass. There's no one there but himself and a manservant."

"He may have a visitor."

"A visitor to Manrose — and at dark. No sensible person would dream of staying there. I'm no' a nervous man, bit I wouldna take my ketch there again for a bag of gold. It was the wife of McGill I saw — old McGill who has been dead a century."

It occurred to McLean that here was an excellent chance to see a well-established spectre. The weather was perfect, and the prospect of seeing Manrose again after so many years appealed to him strongly. He had an excellent camping outfit which could be packed into a haversack. On the following day he came to a decision, and hunted up his fisherman friend.

"When are you sailing to Harris again?" he asked.

"This very night it so happens."

"Would you take a passenger?"

"Meaning yersel'?"

"Yes."

"I'd be pleased to have your company."

"But I want you to drop me at Manrose."

The old man took his pipe from between his lips and projected his shaggy head forward.

"I'm not sailing to that Hell's garden. I won't go within five miles of it. But I'll take you to Harris and maybe you can find some venturesome fool who will pull ye across. There's Dundarrow who laughs at everything, including common sense. He'll do anything silly for a shilling or two."

"All right," agreed McLean. "I will

take my chance at Harris. At what time do you sail?"

"Six o'clock."

"I will be here."

The sea trip was a sheer delight, for the sea was unrippled and like burnished gold. The old man grumbled at having to use his auxiliary motor with petrol at so much per gallon. But as they drew near Harris a wind sprang up and sail was resorted to at once.

"That's Manrose," said the weather-beaten pilot, pointing to a blue hump up the strait.

McLean nodded as he remembered the characteristics of the small island. In due course they made their objective, and McLean decided to spend the night there, for it was beginning to grow dark, and was much too late to commence a search for the venturesome Dundarrow.

Early in the morning he found his man. Rob Dundarrow was young and owned a boat of his own. He possessed eyes that constantly twinkled and was, McLean learned, a bit of a bad character because he declined to take most things seriously. When it was suggested that he should run McLean across to Manrose, Dundarrow twisted his mouth into less than half its normal size.

"Ye'll ken it's no' a favourite resort these days?" he asked.

"I've heard some strange stories."

"Aye, and ye'll hear more if ye stay long enough. Why didna Murdoch drop ye there when he passed?"

"Murdoch has certain superstitions."

"It's a longish journey."

McLean knew what he was hitting up for, and promptly offered him a generous reward. Dundarrow smiled and nodded his head. Half an hour the little sailing-boat was beating up to Manrose, under the skilful hands of Dundarrow.

"Ye'll be staying with Mr. Lee?" he asked.

"No, I'm camping."

"But yon island is private. Mr. Lee bought it ten years ago."

"Then I must obtain his permission."

"I'm no' thinking ye'll get it. A sullen man that — has no use of the wor-r-ld at all. I'll run the boat in at the little beach yonder. Hold tight!"

The craft was run inshore, and

Dundarrow carried McLean on his broad back through some two feet of clear water. McLean gave him the promised sum of money, which Dundarrow thrust into his breeches pocket.

"Ye'll be wanting me to bring you back?" he asked.

"Perhaps. Yes, you might come over tomorrow afternoon. I expect I shall have had enough of it by then."

"You will," replied Dundarrow emphatically, and with a salute he splashed through the sea towards his boat. A few minutes later he was speeding away under a favourable wind.

Manrose was a perfect paradise under the warm morning sun. There were alluring little patches of timber close to the sea on that side, and numerous coves. Wild flowers abounded, and insects, as McLean had cause to remember, were in great variety. Remembering Dundarrow's remark, his first business was to call on the owner of the island with a view to getting permission to camp. Then it occurred to him that he had already burnt his boat behind him, and that with or without permission he would have to stay, unless Lee provided a means to remove him.

The castle lay over a green hill that went up at a precipitous angle. It was built on a vast rock, and its eastern side went down sheer to the sea. McLean saw the turret from which, it was rumoured, the wife of old McGill committed suicide in the long ago. It was bare and grim against the opal sky.

The main entrance was on the western side — an arch leading into a stone-flagged courtyard, in which were two heavy nail-studded doors. McLean decided on the left one, and rapped on it with the end of his stick. A few seconds passed and then the door opened. A huge freckled face came to view. The owner of the face was middle-aged, and sported breeches and stockings over which was a green baize apron. He stared at McLean as if he were an apparition.

"Is Mr. Lee in?"

"Y-yes, sir. But how — ?"

"I would like to see him. Is he available?"

"I will see, sir. What name?"

"Havelock. I am a total stranger to

him. I wish to ask a favour of him."

The servant nodded, and went away. He was absent quite a long time and then came back to say that Mr. Lee would be pleased to see the visitor. McLean entered the place, and was immediately surprised at the state of the interior. It was most handsomely appointed, with furniture in keeping with the building. In the big hall were many antiques and suits of armour. If the freckled man was the sole servant he must have been a perfect glutton for work, for everything was clean and orderly, and the furniture highly polished. McLean was shown into a room on the left of the hall, and there he was met by Andrew Lee. The owner of Manrose was an arrestive individual. He must have been about fifty years of age, with a great head of hair, and enormous sandy beard. On his nose was poised a pair of large horn-rimmed glasses, the lenses of which magnified his eyes considerably.

"Are you aware that you are trespassing?" he demanded in a deep booming voice.

McLean nodded.

"I am sorry," he added. "I did not know until I was here. Years ago I used to come here — when this place was more or less derelict. I came to the castle to ask if you would have any objection to my camping at the far end of the island for to-night?"

"Camping!"

"Yes. I am interested in butterflies and insects — Coleoptera."

Lee's eyes went to the big haversack, and lighted on the end of a butterfly net. He hesitated for a moment.

"Very well," he said. "I have no objection."

"Thank you. And may I use the well outside for the purpose of fresh water?"

"Certainly."

McLean thanked him again, and left the place. For the rest of the morning and afternoon he employed his skill in tracking down various insects, in which he had a genuine interest. While engaged in this he made an interesting discovery. It was a tortoiseshell comb such as a woman with long hair might use to keep her tresses in place, and it was in perfect condition!

It caused him to reflect deeply. Old Murdoch had sworn he had seen a woman on Manrose — a spectre. But spectres did not usually indulge in hair combs! Of course there was always the possibility that a woman visitor had come to the island. He was still gazing at his find when he saw the freckled manservant emerge from the castle and meander across to him. He put the comb into his pocket and became engaged with his poison-bottle. The servant greeted him civilly.

"Beetle hunting, sir?"

"Yes, here is a *lamprophonus tardus*."

"Eh!"

"A polite name for the common glowworm."

"Oh! Lots of them about here. But how did you find him in the daytime?"

"By knowing just where to look for him. A very beautiful evening."

"Very, sir. So you are camping here?"

"Yes. My tent is already pitched yonder. Just about big enough for one average human being — and no more. You must be very lonely here?"

"No — not now. I used to be when I first came."

"I suppose there are a few other servants?"

"Oh no — just me and Mr. Lee. My master couldn't stand a lot of gossiping, noisy people about him. He likes solitude, and I've got to like it too."

"How do you provision yourselves in this remote place?"

"We have a motor boat, and I can run across to Harris or Uist in quick time."

"But does Mr. Lee stay here always?"

"Yes — except when he takes a short holiday."

"A wealthy gentleman, I presume?"

"I imagine, so. Of course I have no means of knowing."

There was a brief silence while McLean extracted the dead beetle from the bottle and boxed it.

"There are strange stories about this island, aren't there?" he asked, looking up suddenly.

The freckled face tightened.

"Ah, you've heard that?"

"Yes — in Harris they say that the ghost of old McGill's wife still haunts the island, and there are some who swear they have seen it of late."

The servant shook his head.

"Superstitious people — the islanders," he added. "There's no such thing — of course not."

"That is a relief," said McLean. "I don't want her walking into my tent. I don't object to beetles, but lank-haired spectres with the salt of the sea all over them — ugh!"

The servant looked as if he were about to say something, but he turned his head and saw the figure of his master silhouetted on the hill-side against the setting sun.

"I must go," he said hurriedly.

McLean sought his tent, and after making a scrap meal he sat down outside it on a boulder and watched the afterglow. From where he was the castle was plainly visible, and as darkness fell it became more and more eerie in appearance. A great moon came up out of the sea and turned the landscape into a flood of silver light. The slight wind beat in his face, salting his lips. He was lighting his pipe when suddenly he heard a cry — borne faintly on the wind. It was low and pitiful — and undoubtedly a woman's voice.

"The spectre," he said to himself. "This is decidedly interesting."

Putting the unlighted pipe away he moved towards the castle, from which direction he was sure the sound had come. From where he approached there was no light to be seen but as he passed round the southern end two lights came to view. One was from a leaded lower-room window — the room in which he had interviewed Lee — and the other was high up in the main tower, at a window that was barred. He drew closer to the place and watched the upper window. Again came a sound — a convulsive sobbing. A form passed the window, and his heart leapt to realise that it was a woman. Then there was a bang and the light was obscured. Someone had closed the shutters from the inside. So there *was* a woman in the castle — exactly as old Murdoch had stated. At times she came out — that was pretty certain. Hence the comb, and the stories of the spectre. But who was she? And what was the meaning of this seclusion? He waited there for some time, but heard no more cries.

★ ★ ★

On the following day Dundarrow called in his boat, but McLean was not ready to go. He gave Dundarrow a few shillings for his trouble, and told him to call again on the following day. Then for the second time he visited Lee and begged to be allowed to stay on the island for another night. This permission seemed to be given reluctantly. Lee was obviously a little ill at ease — nervy and slightly irritable.

McLean spent most of his time in full view of the tower window, but the shutters remained closed, and nothing untoward happened during the day. Late in the evening the weather conspired to aid his plans. A storm gathered across the strait, and very soon thunder was booming, and lightning flashing from a black sky. Then came rain and a semi-cyclone. McLean took the opportunity to dismantle his tent and hide it among the rocks. Some time later he entered the courtyard drenched to the skin, and rapped on the studded door. The freckled servant answered the summons, and saw the dripping form of McLean.

"My tent has gone — carried away by the wind. Can you give me shelter for the night? I'm wet to the skin, and the storm seems like continuing for some time."

The servant appeared to have considerable doubts about this, and ultimately said he would inform Mr. Lee. McLean stepped inside out of the driving rain while the owner of the castle was informed of the circumstances. The servant came back later and told McLean that he could occupy a couch downstairs for the night.

"Thank you. By the way — what is your name?"

"Gilson."

"I am greatly obliged to you, Mr. Gilson. Perhaps you could find me an old coat or something to put round me while my clothes are drying?"

Gilson brought a large dressing gown, and lighted a big fire in the room where McLean was to sleep. McLean disrobed and laid his drenched clothing before the fire. An hour later Gilson came in with some sandwiches and coffee.

"I thought these might be welcome," he said.

"They are. I have had nothing to eat since noon. My food supply ran out."

"You are going back to-morrow."

"Yes — at least I think so."

Gilson shot him a glance.

"I should," he added briefly.

"Ah! I somehow feel that despite Mr. Lee's kindness he will be glad to see the back of me."

"Well — yes. He does not welcome visitors to the island."

"Why not?"

"Just a whim. He is a strange man."

"How long have you been with him?"

"Ten years — ever since he came here."

McLean put a few more questions, but the faithful Gilson did not answer them very willingly. At ten o'clock he left, after bidding McLean good night. The castle became very quiet, and the wind outside abated. McLean crept to the door and turned the handle. It was locked on the outside! He turned his attention to the window. That gave him outlet to the roof of what appeared to be an old dungeon. Over the roof scrambled thick ivy roots, and these ascended to a dilapidated wall under the tower, in which there was a narrow window, slightly open.

McLean found that his clothes were now quite dry, and quickly changed into them. Stepping through the window, he ran along the dungeon roof and began to swarm up the ivy to where the window was clearly illuminated by the moon. It was no difficult task to make entry, and he found himself in a corridor. It ended in a flight of steps which evidently went up to the tower room. Treading cautiously he reached the top. A window on his right told him that he was next to the room in which he had seen the feminine form. The door before him was all that separated him from the mystery of Castle Manrose. After a moment's hesitation he rapped on it. There was a dead silence. He rapped again. There was a slight sound from within, and a childish voice said:

"Is that you, Gilson?"

"I want to speak to you," he whispered.

"I can't — the door is locked. He always locks it."

McLean tried the handle and found this was true. He produced some tools from his pocket and very soon had the lock turned. The door was pushed open, and he found himself facing a tall, slim girl with exceedingly long hair. She was clad in a kimono of good quality, and the room was well furnished. What amazed him was her voice — it was that of a child of six or seven. At the sight of him she opened her mouth to cry out.

"S-sh!" he warned. "I am a friend. I think you are in need of a friend."

She edged away before him, but quickly put aside her fears, as it became clear to her that he meant her no harm.

"What is your name?" he asked.

"Nancy — Nancy Webster."

"Is Mr. Lee your uncle?"

"No. He was my mummy's second husband. My daddy was killed in the war. I know that."

"Is Mr. Lee kind to you?"

"Oh yes — very kind. But he locks me in sometimes. He says — he says that if anyone were to know I was here they would take me away and put me in an asy — something like that."

"Asylum?"

"Yes. What is an asylum?"

"Not a nice kind of place. But have you never been to school?"

"No."

"But you have books here?"

She smiled and nodded, then handed him a book from the book-case. It was a child's picture book.

"I can read that," she said proudly.

McLean gulped, as he realised what all this meant. This beautiful girl had been denied education — everything worth having to suit Andrew Lee's purpose. When anyone was about she was locked in the tower, but on other occasions she was let out into the sunshine. Gilson no doubt had been informed that her mind was deranged, and believed that story.

"Would you like to see the world?" asked McLean. "Many people, shops, animals — "

"Like the books? Oh yes — yes, but I must stay here. If anyone saw me they would put me away — "

"I don't think they would. Now there is one thing you must do. Say nothing about having seen me. I will lock your door again when I leave, but I will come and see you again in a few days. I am a friend who is going to help you. You understand?"

"Oh yes, I think I like you."

McLean went back to his room. The next day he thanked Lee for his hospitality, and when Dundarrow arrived with his boat the pair set sail for Harris. On the following day McLean was in Glasgow, and from there he got into touch with London. In less than a week a very interesting story had been pieced together. A Major John Webster had been killed in France in 1917, leaving a widow and daughter, also a considerable fortune. A year later the widow had met and married a man named Seager. Her second marriage lasted but three months, and a motor accident made Seager a widower. Her fortune was held in trust for her daughter, passing to the second husband in the event of the daughter's death. A year later the daughter — Nancy Webster — was missing, near Liverpool. Her body was subsequently found and identified by Seager. Three months later Seager — under the name of Lee — bought Manrose and furnished it.

"You've a photograph?" asked McLean.

"Yes — here."

McLean examined the print, and was satisfied.

"The same man. Evidently he did not get rid of the child. I imagine he is quite fond of her — in his queer way. Manrose doubtless appealed to him because of the legend. It would help to keep people away from the place. It will be interesting to know how he faked that drowning business. Anyway, we will pay a visit to Manrose."

That same evening McLean and a police officer put across to the sunlit island — this time on Murdoch's boat, the old man having been given a rather peremptory order. They found Lee at home, sitting before a pile of books.

"Mr. Havelock!" he exclaimed.

"I am a detective and my friend is a police officer," corrected McLean. "We have come to arrest you on a charge of perjury with embezzlement."

Lee tried to express complete bewilderment, but the sight of a pair of handcuffs convinced him that the game was up.

"I want the key of your stepdaughter's jail," said McLean.

"Stepdaughter!"

"Come — I have already seen her and spoken to her. Where is the key?"

Lee gulped and then inclined his head towards the bureau. McLean found two keys on a ring. The fair Nancy Webster was released, and she and her unscrupulous relative were taken away. At the subsequent trial Lee was found guilty and sentenced. Before he went away he confessed that he had had a confederate — a man whose child had died from some ailment. For the price of five hundred pounds this unnatural father had aided and abetted Lee. But he was now dead, and no action could be taken.

Nancy Webster was sent to the home of some distant relatives, and when McLean saw her a few months later she had already gained a considerable knowledge of the strange new world. But curiously enough, she was not embittered against her stepfather.

"I am glad to be free," she said. "But he loved me. When he comes out I must help him. Poor man, I don't think he quite realised what he was doing."

"Such is life!" mused McLean. "Ah well, a little touch of human sympathy is worth a ton of righteous indignation."

5

DOCTOR ARTHUR LOGAN emerged from his study into his sitting-room in a reflective state of mind. For days past he had been worried about a particular patient of his, and now his suspicions were such as to cause him considerable anxiety — not to say alarm. He sat by the fire and smoked for some time, then came to a decision and picked up the telephone. He gave the number, and a few seconds later heard a voice at the other end.

"Hallo! Is that McLean? Doctor Logan speaking. You may remember me in reference to — Ah, you do! Could you possibly call here this evening? I am worried about a patient of mine. It may be a matter for the police."

Half an hour later McLean arrived, and was shown into the consulting-room by the maid. The doctor joined him a few minutes later, and shook hands gravely.

"You were quick to respond."

"Things are singularly quiet at the moment. What is the business that troubles you?"

"I have a patient — a Mr. Mortimer Worrall. He is a wealthy man, and for the past year I have been treating him for bad kidney trouble. Of late curious symptoms have appeared. They might possibly be associated with his disease, but I doubt it. In fact, I have good reason to believe he is being slowly poisoned."

"Whom do you suspect?"

"That is a difficult question to answer. He lives with his brother Arnold — in Westbury Square — a very old rambling house. I think there has always been a certain amount of friction between the two brothers, but no real quarrel. Mortimer is nearly fifteen years older than Arnold, and made money in South Africa years ago. Arnold is comfortably off. The house is their joint property which accounts for their living together. A fortnight ago, I sent for Mortimer's son and daughter. The girl was in Canada and the boy in South Africa. The boy has not seen his sister for twelve years."

"Was that done at Mortimer's request?"

"Yes. He got the feeling that he was dying. The girl arrived two days ago, but Harry, the son, is not due for a week. In the meantime the old man has been getting worse. He scarcely recognises his own daughter, and he may not last until the son arrives."

"How does the will run?"

"The whole property goes in equal parts to his son and daughter. There is a quarter of a million at stake."

"Then Arnold Worrall gets nothing?"

"Not a penny."

"So we can rule him out?"

"I suppose so."

"Will the servants benefit?"

"In small sums."

"Tell me the grounds of your suspicions."

"It is a little difficult, because it rests chiefly with symptoms. Only a medical man would appreciate the position. I feel he is getting poison somehow."

McLean reflected for a few minutes. He knew Logan well enough to be sure that he would not have sent for him without very good reason.

"You say the son is due in about a week?"

"That is so."

"What age is he?"

"About thirty, I believe."

"And the girl may not recognise her brother after twelve years?"

"It is doubtful. She was but eight years of age when he went away."

"Then that gives us an excellent chance to keep an eye on the patient, provided he does not die before the brother arrives."

"I don't quite follow."

"I will impersonate the brother, and he can be told as soon as he lands. But in the meantime it is very essential to have the patient closely guarded. No, that is too risky. I must get into the house at once. It is possible to speed up the trip from Africa by taking an airplane at different stages. Has the brother said by what means he is travelling — ?"

"No. His cablegram merely stated that he was leaving immediately."

"Good. The brother will arrive to-morrow. If any subsequent message arrives from him it can be intercepted. Now about Arnold — is he likely to recognise his nephew?"

"No. He was abroad for many years, and Harry had left for South Africa when he returned."

"Splendid! The girl's name?"

"Grace. A charming girl."

"Why did she go to Canada?"

"Trouble with the old man. He is a bad-tempered fellow, and made Grace's life a misery. She had a chance to go out as a teacher eighteen months ago, and she went. He was furious at first, but has since forgiven her."

"Can you get me a photograph of Harry?"

"Yes — to-morrow."

"That will do. I shall arrive at the house to-morrow evening, but will wire during the afternoon from Southampton."

★ ★ ★

McLean received the photograph about noon the following day. Logan enclosed a note to say that it was taken in South Africa seven years ago, and it showed a good looking, dark young man, of cheerful countenance, dressed in drill coat and breeches. The question of make-up was not of great importance, in view of the fact that it was improbable that Grace would remember her brother with any clarity, and that the uncle was similarly placed. In the event of the sick man having any suspicion of an impersonation the situation could be explained. Notwithstanding, McLean played the part with his usual thoroughness, and shortly before seven o'clock arrived at the house in a taxi, with various articles of baggage. Arnold Worrall met him at the door and shook hands warmly.

"This is a pleasant surprise, Harry," he said. "We had no idea you could get here so quickly."

"You got my wire?"

"Yes. But how did you manage it?"

"A lot of it by air — and finally overland from Brindisi. But how is father?"

"Very bad, I fear."

All the time McLean's eyes were taking in details of the man he was talking to. He was about fifty, and built loosely. His clothes were shabby and fitted his lank form badly. The eyes were deep-set and surmounted by shaggy eyebrows. He stooped slightly and shuffled as he led McLean into the sitting-room.

"Grace is here," he said. "She was also sent for."

"By Jove, it's years since I saw her. I suppose she is quite a woman now."

"Oh, yes. She was excited to get your wire. Come in."

McLean entered a large room full of very old furniture and smelling rather musty. A big fire was blazing on the hearth, and an ancient parrot was dozing in his cage near the window. Arnold waved him into a chair.

"You've changed," he said.

"You think so?"

"I remember you as being rather slim."

"Sunshine sometimes fattens. But I must see father."

"Better wait. The doctor is with him now. Grace will be down in a moment. She went upstairs to change."

"What is wrong with father?"

"Old trouble — kidneys."

"It must be serious for him to send for me."

"I'm afraid it is. But since he wired

he has got worse. I doubt if he will know you. He didn't even recognise Grace, whom he saw less than eighteen months ago."

"Has he forgiven her for running away?"

"Yes. I understand that his will is in order, and that the estate is to go to you and Grace."

"All of it?"

"Every penny."

"But you — ?"

Arnold curled his lip a little cynically.

"I am the one he does not forgive. Curious how I have always got on his nerves! Well, I dare say I can manage. If the worst should happen I am willing to dispose of my interest in the house, which was left to us jointly by your grandfather."

"Oh, but we must not anticipate the worst."

The door opened and a young girl entered the room. She was dressed in a black velvet semi-evening gown which suited her admirably. She was fair, with a perfect complexion, now somewhat pallid as if from weeping. Her abundant hair was bobbed rather long, and gleamed like gold in contrast with the dark dress. She looked at her uncle and then at McLean.

"Harry! You are Harry!"

McLean stood up and offered her both his hands. She blushed as she took them, together with a brotherly kiss.

"It's — it's such a surprise," she said.

"You are the biggest surprise. A grown-up woman and in such a short time."

"It is over twelve years."

"As long as that. Tell me — have you seen father?"

Her mouth twitched and she nodded her head.

"That means — he is very ill?"

"Yes — dreadfully. I don't think he really knew me. He just — just smiled and — "

There was a knock on the door, and then Dr. Logan entered. He looked at McLean and then at Grace.

"Doctor — this is my brother Harry."

Logan and McLean shook hands, and all hung upon his report.

"No worse," he said. "But no better. If you would like to see him now you may.

I will come with you, as the day nurse is just retiring. The night nurse will arrive at any minute."

McLean nodded and followed Logan up the stairs into the sick-room. Worrall was lying back with his eyes closed, and it was at once evident from his ashen face that he was in a bad way. The doctor pursed his lips as he closed the door.

"He'll need watching," he said, "or he'll slip through our fingers. Someone is giving him dope — somehow."

"But the nurses?"

"That is the strange part. But of course there are moments when he is alone, and then — "

"There is only one possible culprit."

"You mean — his brother?"

"Yes."

"But why should he? He does not stand to gain a penny. On the contrary, he would lose, for he lives here free of charge. He knows how the will reads."

"Then we must look for another motive."

Low as their voices were they roused the sick man. He opened his eyes a shade and tried to focus them on McLean.

Then his voice came in a whisper.

"Is that — Harry?"

"Don't you know me?" asked McLean, drawing closer to the bedside.

"Yes, I think — I'm glad you've come. I've missed you, my boy — you and Grace. I've not long to live, but I mean to make things right — before I go."

"Nonsense! You are going to get well again."

But the grey head moved from side to side. There was no hope there. The doctor too seemed very doubtful and worried at his inability to explain the mystery. Shortly afterwards the night nurse arrived, and McLean and Logan went out.

"Here's a problem for you," said the doctor.

McLean nodded.

★ ★ ★

McLean was not long in the house before he established certain facts. One was that the servants were devoted to their master, and the other that the two nurses were doing their very best for their patient. Ruling out the possibility of an intruder, which in the circumstances was a fantastic idea, it left Arnold and Grace. Grace in turn was ruled out for obvious reasons, and the full weight of suspicion fell on Arnold.

But here the mystery deepened. McLean could find no kind of motive — except hate. Did Arnold hate his brother sufficiently to plot his death? He could find no grounds for this — no real cause for hatred alone. It was true they had never got on well together, but so far as he could gather there had never been any real quarrel between them. He tackled Grace on this point.

"Did Uncle Arnold and father continue to wrangle up to the time you went away?" he asked.

"They — they never agreed on any subject. Why do you ask that?"

"It is a little strange that uncle should not be mentioned in the will. Rather hard on him."

"Yes, it is," she demurred. "But — but must we talk of that? Isn't it possible father may recover?"

"Quite, but it would be foolish to try to

minimise the seriousness of his illness."

"I — I don't want to talk about it — please, please," she implored in a choking voice.

Her emotion surprised him, for it bordered upon hysteria. While they were together Arnold entered the room. McLean's back was towards him, but he had a good view of the intruder through the medium of a mirror. He saw Arnold make a rapid sign to Grace — a sign of warning. The girl went even more pallid, and her hand gripped the back of a chair. Then she met McLean's eyes and strove to smile through her tears.

"We — we must hope for the best," she murmured.

"Of course. He has every possible care. There may be quite a sudden rally. Ah, uncle, you are up and about early."

"I slept badly. Have you seen your father yet?"

"No. I think I will go up after breakfast."

Later he and Grace went to the sick-room together, but the nurse begged them not to attempt to speak to the sick man. He had had a bad night and had only just fallen into a sleep. Grace seemed tremendously affected.

"I — I can't stand it," she said.

"What?"

"This dreadful suspense. Is there anything the matter? I mean — "

McLean looked at her sharply.

"What do you mean?"

"I — I don't know. But the doctor seems puzzled — as if he wasn't sure what was really the matter. Is he — are you keeping anything from me? I must know — I must."

"You must trust the doctor to pull him through. There are complications."

She nodded and left him when they reached the downstairs hall. McLean found himself in a fog. One by one new features were creeping into the case. What had been the meaning of that undoubted signal that passed between Arnold and his niece? Why was the girl so strangely agitated, when she looked the type of woman who could display courage in adversity?

In secret he investigated the house, and in the back of an old cupboard he made a remarkable discovery. The cupboard was built into the landing and backed upon the panelled room in which the sick man lay. The back panelling seemed loose and upon closer examination he found that it was hinged on the inside and opened inwards. It was a secret entrance into the sick-room. Any person concealed there could spy into the room through a small crack, and enter it at any favourable moment. And Logan had suggested that there were moments when the patient was alone!

It was the first real gleam of light in the darkness, and McLean was favourably placed to take advantage of his discovery. His bedroom was on the opposite side of the landing — nearer the stairs. For his purpose he needed a warning signal, and he contrived to manufacture one by lifting the carpet and loosening two of the floor boards. On replacing the carpet he found that the loose boards squeaked every time they were trodden on — and it was almost impossible for any approaching person to avoid treading on one of them.

When Doctor Logan called he stated that his patient was still in the same condition, and gave it as his opinion that the poison or drug was still being administered. McLean had no doubt that this was done during the night, and decided to start his vigil that evening.

It was close upon one o'clock in the morning when he heard a squeak from outside. He went to the door and peered through the keyhole. To his amazement the figure of a woman was seen. It was Grace, attired in a kimono and slippers. She carried an electric torch in her hand and was moving with some hesitation. When she passed the door McLean opened it slightly and peered along the landing. He saw her halt before the cupboard door, then turn the handle quietly and enter.

He was about to follow her when she appeared again. It was evident she had not time to enter the bedroom. Again she hesitated and then moved forward — towards a door at the far end of the landing. It was the door of Arnold's bedroom! She stood outside it for a few moments, listening intently, and then tried the handle. The door opened, and she entered.

McLean scratched his chin in perplexity. Was it a rendezvous? No, he had to dismiss that idea from his mind. And yet here were these queer facts staring him in the face — for which at the moment he could find no explanation. A long time passed before Grace emerged. He closed his door, but heard the board squeak as she passed over it. A moment or two later he went after her and saw her enter her own room. Nothing more happened that night.

On the following morning Grace seemed quite calm. He asked her how she had slept, and she said she had had a fair night. Then the doctor came and stated that there seemed to be a slight improvement in the patient's condition. Grace was overjoyed, and Arnold expressed his satisfaction in a voice that did not ring with any great amount of sincerity.

That day certain information reached McLean. He had been pursuing inquiries in other directions in regard to the affairs of the two brothers, and what he now learned was of interest. Nothing was known against Mortimer Worrall, but

Arnold was a bird of another colour. He had been mixed up in some shady affairs in France and Germany, and had even served a sentence of imprisonment some ten years back. A man associated with him — named Robson — was now in prison. Arnold was reputed to be a desperate character — the sort of man who would stick at nothing to attain his ends. But what were his ends now?

McLean slept during the afternoon, in order to carry out another night vigil. The doctor arrived late, and again reported progress. He believed that Worrall would soon be out of real danger. There was no doubt about Grace's relief.

"I — I'm so glad," she said. "I began to think that he — he would not recover. Oh, I shall be glad to get away."

"Why?"

The question seemed to embarrass her.

"I — want to get back to my work," she stammered.

"Don't you think father will want you to stay on here?"

"Oh no — I couldn't."

There was fear in her eyes. Again came

a look from Arnold who was writing at the bureau.

"It looks as if I too shall soon be able to get back to my farms," said McLean.

"And you'll both be poor instead of rich," put in Arnold dryly. "Well, it was a shame to bring you both all this way."

Grace made no reply, and McLean merely shrugged his shoulders. That afternoon a telegram came from the real son of Mortimer Worrall. Fortunately McLean saw the telegraph boy approaching and secured the message. Harry was at sea and due to reach England the following day. McLean gave secret instructions for him to be met.

★ ★ ★

That night he resumed his vigil, and shortly after midnight the board squeaked. This time it was Arnold. He approached the cupboard stealthily and then entered it. Immediately McLean went round the corridor to the main entrance to the bedroom. He listened at the door and heard the nurse cough. There he waited.

A long time passed and no sound came from within. About three hours must have elapsed when the door opened and the nurse came out. She blinked as she saw McLean sitting on the top stair. He put his finger to his lips, and then approached her.

"Leave the door slightly open," he whispered. "Do as I tell you. It is very important. Now stay here as a witness."

Amazed, she did as she was bid. McLean stood close by the slightly open door. A few seconds passed, and then he heard a sound from within. It was the noise of a door swinging on a hinge. He waited five seconds, and then peeped round the door. Leaning over the bed was Arnold Worrall. He had a pad in one hand and was holding this over the nose and mouth of the sick man, who lay perfectly still, breathing rather deeply. McLean bounded into the room and almost swung Arnold off his feet.

"Got you!"

"What the — !"

"I am going to arrest you on a charge of attempted murder. Nurse, ring up the doctor. He may be needed. Then get on to Scotland Yard and say that Mr. Robert McLean requires two officers here at once."

Arnold Worrall had his back to the wall. McLean saw his hand go towards the pocket of his dressing gown.

"Hands up!" he snapped, and produced an automatic.

Arnold uttered a fierce oath, but did as he was ordered. McLean reached out and secured a revolver — and then the doped pad. Then he sat on the bed and waited for help to arrive. The two police officers and the doctor came at the same time.

"Hold him here for a few minutes," said McLean. "There is another factor in this affair."

He left the room and went to Grace's bedroom. Upon knocking he got no response. He pushed the button and found the room empty, but the bed had been slept on, and Grace's shoes and some other garments were there. A slight noise from the passage sent him outside, and he saw Grace in the vicinity of Arnold's bedroom. She had some papers in hand, which she made no attempt to conceal.

"Harry! I — I — "

"I am not Harry. I am a detective."

Her face went pallid and she began to stammer.

"Come downstairs," he said. "There are a few points to be cleared up."

"I — I can explain."

"You shall have a chance — in a moment."

They went into the library, and McLean had the prisoner brought in. He scowled as he saw Grace — and then gulped when his gaze fell on the papers she still held in her hand.

"Now," said McLean. "There is something between you two. I want to know what it is. Were you aware that your uncle was plotting to kill his brother?"

"He — he isn't my uncle."

"What!"

"My name is Robson — Eleanor Robson. A year ago my father was convicted and sent to prison for something he didn't do. He told me that the guilty man was named Arnold Worrall, and that he possessed documents that would prove father's innocence if they could be found.

125

I found this man at last, and came here disguised as a man in order to find the papers that might set my father free. I entered the house like a common burglar, after watching this man go out. But he came back at once for some unknown reason and caught me in the house. He believed I was just a daring crook, and I let him believe that. He said he could get me three years, but then made a strange proposal. His brother was seriously ill — dying, in fact. His niece and nephew had been called home from abroad, but he had just heard that the niece had been killed by a motor-car while on her way to the docks. He told me that there was a lot of money involved — that he could pass me off as his niece, and that his brother was too ill to recognise anyone. We were to share up the money — the daughter's share of the estate — between us."

"And you consented?" asked McLean.

"Yes, but with an ulterior motive. I knew he was a scoundrel, and had no desire to make a penny by such a mean impersonation. I wanted to get inside the house, to find the papers that my father swore were here. I didn't know that attempted murder was involved. I wanted to get the papers first, and then I intended to expose him. I scarcely expect you to believe me, but it is true. To-night I found the papers. They prove that my father was innocent. Please — please take them."

She handed them to McLean, who perused them quickly. They were most incriminating documents, and Arnold Worrall realised that nothing could now save him. Somewhat to McLean's surprise he did the decent thing.

"The girl is innocent," he mumbled.

"Better let her go. I'm ready to face the music. Mortimer has been a mean old dog with his money. The world would probably be better without him. Don't keep me standing here all night!"

So ended an intriguing double impersonation.

"You are free," said McLean to the distressed girl. "I feel rather sorry that our relationship is not what it purported to be."

She slipped her warm, slim hand into his.

6

MᴄLEAN's introduction to the amazing Naga case followed upon a conversation which he had with Sergeant Brook, in a tea-shop in the West End. McLean had met Brook quite by accident, and conversation led up to 'shop.'

"Have you heard from a man named Cornelius Conrad?" inquired Brook.

"No."

"I rather fancy you will. He called at the 'Yard' this morning and acted like a goat. Do you remember the Conrad case? It was about a year ago in Sussex. Joseph Conrad fell over the cliff on New Year's Eve, and was killed instantly. His brother — Cornelius — made certain allegations against a Jap named Naga, but there was nothing to substantiate them."

"What did he allege?"

"He swore that Naga had threatened to kill his brother on that very night — and he was positive that the cliff fall was no accident. Of course nothing could be done in the complete absence of evidence."

"What is the trouble now?"

"Cornelius swears that his own death is planned for New Year's Eve — this year."

"The same date!"

"Yes. There is a reason for it, according to Cornelius. So far as I could gather, he and his brother fell foul of Naga in Tokio about two years ago. What the trouble was about he is reluctant to confess, but presumably this Naga fellow is aching for revenge, and if we can accept Cornelius's story he has already taken part of it."

"What makes him think his own life is in danger?"

"Naga threatened him openly — before he left Japan for England. He swore to take his revenge in instalments — three instalments in all."

"That sounds a bit melodramatic. Who is the third?"

"Cornelius's daughter — a young girl of about eighteen. Of course she knows nothing about all this. Cornelius desires to keep her in complete ignorance of the threat."

"Well what is the result of these allegations?"

"What do you expect? He could produce no evidence against the Jap. We were bound to wink an eye. The Chief was inclined to treat it all as a hallucination, and yet the fellow seemed sincere. He was cute enough to realise that we did not take him seriously, and he asked after you. I told him where he could find you."

"Very kind of you," said McLean dryly. "What sort of a man is he?"

"Round about fifty — nervy — not too healthy a specimen. I believe he is wealthy — made a lot of money in Japan, in the rice business, I heard. I am not sure that the Chief isn't right — and that he is nothing more than a victim of hysteria. I wish you joy of him, anyway."

The sequel came much sooner than McLean expected. He returned home about two hours later, and was told that a gentleman was waiting to see him.

"What name?" he inquired.

Tiny handed him a card. It bore the name of Cornelius Conrad, with an address in Sussex.

"All upset he is," said Tiny. "I told him it was necessary to make an appointment, but he snapped me up and said he was determined to see you — if he had to wait all night."

"We won't keep him waiting as long as that. You can show him in in two minutes' time."

Later Conrad was shown in. He was lank and lean, and his face was like old parchment. All his hair was gone except a few strands on the left side of his head, and these were carefully brushed across the bald expanse. Cold as it was Conrad seemed to be perspiring at every pore.

"Please sit down, Mr. Conrad," begged McLean. "I understand you are anxious to see me on an important matter?"

"Yes. I have been to the police, but they can do nothing for me. They take me for an hysterical fool, but they will find that I am as calm and collected as any man. Just over a year ago my brother was murdered — "

"Are you sure?"

131

"Positive. In seven days' time it will be my turn. On New Year's Eve an attempt will be made on my life, and it will succeed unless — "

"Excuse me — hadn't we better have a few facts first? Why are you so sure this attempt will be made — and by whom?"

"A Japanese named Naga — now a curio dealer in London. It was he who killed my brother last year. It all started in Tokio over two years ago. My brother and I were in business there — the same type of business as the Naga family. We — we had a chance of getting their business. It was a fair enough deal — but Naga's brother didn't see it in that light. When the deal went through he committed *hari-kari*, after killing his wife and daughter. The surviving brother laid the whole blame upon Joseph and myself. He waylaid us on our journey to the port, and told us that he would take three lives for the three he had lost. Thank God my daughter was not within hearing at the moment."

"Did your brother take that threat seriously?"

"No. He was not like me. He had no nerves. He just laughed and told Naga to go to the devil. The last words Naga said were: "It will be on the same date that my brother died. Remember!""

"And you did remember?"

"No. I forgot all about it. We settled down in a big house on the coast, and were very happy. On that night I and my daughter retired at eleven o'clock, but Joseph said he would sit up and see the New Year in. He — he was found under the cliff in the early morning — with his neck broken."

"There were no marks of violence on his body?"

"None. The doctor stated that all his injuries could be accounted for by his fall."

"You have no idea why he left the house?"

"Oh no."

"Did you see Naga at all round about that time?"

"No, but a few days after the — the tragedy I received a post card from London. It merely said 'With compliments — Naga,' and was written in Japanese."

McLean was interested. Conrad was undoubtedly sincere, but how much was due to hallucination it was difficult to say. That he was in a state of cringing fear was self-evident. Periodically he mopped his brow, and put his hand inside his collar as if it were choking him.

"I want your help," he said. "Unless something is done I — I am doomed."

"I don't think there is much to worry about," said McLean. "In the first place this is a civilised country. In the second place English houses are rather well built. There is nothing to prevent you from locking yourself in your bedroom, and keeping a pistol under your pillow. Alternatively you can spend the last night of the Old Year in a big hotel — "

"You don't know Naga."

"You think such precautions would be of no avail?"

"I doubt it. I can't take any risks."

"What do you propose?"

"I want someone near me — a man of courage and intelligence. I have servants, but they — Are you prepared to come down to Palling Manor and stay for a period?"

"That is impossible. I have other work on hand. And Christmas I intend to spend in Scotland."

"But what am I do to? You don't realise how serious this is to me. I know few people in this country. I am utterly at Naga's mercy. He is cunning — cunning as a fox. Will you — will you come for that night only? It is the night he has chosen. I am convinced he will try to carry out his threat. For God's sake help me — "

"Steady!" admonished McLean. "You must not let this business get on your nerves."

"Will you come?"

McLean reflected for a few minutes and then inclined his head. Conrad breathed a sigh of immense relief. He was prepared to pay any reasonable fee. All he begged was that McLean would come as a friend and not divulge the object of his visit to his daughter. This McLean agreed to do, and Conrad went away much more content in mind.

Before leaving for Scotland McLean dug up details of the Conrad accident and read them in the train. So far as he could gather there was nothing unusual in the affair. The house in Sussex had access to the sea on its southern side, and a portion of the grounds was unfenced. This danger spot was a favourite walk of the dead man's, and the night in question was cold and fine, with a full moon. Joseph had undoubtedly had several drinks, and might naturally have experienced a desire to go to his favourite haunt for a breath of fresh air before retiring.

He appeared to have slipped and fallen clean over the cliff on to the rocks below.

The straightforward evidence rather damped McLean's interest. He had not the slightest desire for the company of Cornelius in normal circumstances, and rather wished he had not given his promise. In due course he returned to London and then went down to Sussex. The house was a modern one and built on palatial lines. It was handsomely appointed and great wealth was in evidence everywhere. When McLean saw Conrad he was startled. His host's face was as pallid as a sheet of paper, and his eyes were crowded with fear. He grabbed McLean's hand.

"Thank God you have come. I've seen him."

"You mean Naga?"

"Yes. It was yesterday — along the cliff. We came face to face and he — "

He gulped and placed a hand over his heart.

"He spoke to you?"

"Yes. He said 'To-night is New Year's Eve, Mr. Conrad.' Then he went away." He broke into an hysterical outburst, but McLean stopped him and led him into the library, where he forced him to sit down.

"You must control yourself," be admonished. "What can he hope to achieve here? He dare not force an entry into your house. I am quite sure it is sheer bluff and — "

The door opened and a pretty girl entered. Conrad made a praiseworthy attempt to appear calm. He stood up and smiled, and presented his daughter to McLean.

"This is my old friend, Mr. McLean, Ethel," he said. "He has come to see the New Year in with us."

Ethel smiled and extended her hand. It

137

was very warm and soft, and it seemed to linger for a moment in McLean's.

"I am so glad," she said. "Daddy is far too much of a hermit. Do you think the frost will continue? I am anxious to try my luck at skating."

"There is every chance. Have you a pond close at hand?"

"There is one in the park. I should like to show it you later, and you can tell me if you think the ice is thick enough."

After lunch he and Ethel went for a walk together. She showed him the pond, and he gave it his opinion that the ice would not bear for at least another day. Incidentally, he wrung some information from her about her life in Japan. She knew that both her father and uncle had made their fortunes out of a big business deal, in which the Naga family was involved, and it seemed to him that she rather suspected some sharp practice on the part of her relatives.

"I was always sorry for the Nagas," she admitted. "Of course, daddy says it was their own fault. They didn't understand modern business methods, and tried to fight the combine. In the end they were obliged to sell out for a song. There was a terrible sequel. Mr. Naga's brother committed suicide, after killing his wife and daughter."

It was obvious that she knew nothing about the alleged threat to her father and to herself, nor presumably about her father's allegations in connection with his brother's death. McLean found her charming, and sympathised with her rather uneventful life.

"Daddy is very worried about something," she said. "I suppose it is business. He can't leave it alone — even now when he is rich. I wish he would cease to interest himself in stocks and shares and go in for more exercise — hunting or motoring even. For the past week he has looked dreadfully ill. I wanted him to see a doctor, but he refused."

"I shouldn't worry," said McLean.

* * *

The day passed and the trio had dinner together. Afterwards they repaired to the lounge, and Ethel entertained them at the piano. She was an excellent pianist and

McLean enjoyed the music. Towards ten o'clock the girl appeared to be tired, and Conrad suggested she should retire.

"But daddy — Mr. McLean is our guest and he — "

"I should never forgive myself if I thought I was the means of your losing your beauty sleep," put in McLean. "As a matter of fact, your father and I have a small matter of business to discuss."

"Oh, business!" she pouted.

"Nothing to do with stocks and shares."

"Well, in that case — "

She kissed her father affectionately and shook hands with McLean. As she left Conrad's gaze went after her, and he sighed when the door closed.

"To think that anyone should threaten her!"

"It isn't worth thinking about. You have to rid your mind of this unhealthy obsession. There is absolutely nothing in it."

But Conrad would not be consoled. He moved uneasily in his chair and kept filling his glass with port. Every few minutes he would shudder and gaze about him furtively. Suddenly the telephone bell rang. It was the instrument on the sideboard, and the butler informed Conrad that a gentleman wished to speak to him on the telephone.

"Who is he?" asked Conrad irritably.

"Wouldn't give a name, sir."

"Oh — all right. Put him through."

There was a pause. Then Conrad said "Yes, I am Mr. Conrad." Two seconds later the telephone receiver dropped from Conrad's palsied fingers, and he collapsed sideways. McLean ran to him and supported him.

"What is the matter? Who was that speaking?"

Conrad rolled his eyes.

"It was — Naga. He told me — he told me — "

"What?"

"It is to be to-night — at midnight."

McLean laughed derisively. He managed to get Conrad back into an easy chair, and then he drew a pistol from his pocket and laid it on the corner of the table.

"I don't often bet, Mr. Conrad," he said. "But I am willing to wager any reasonable sum that Mr. Naga does not enter this house to-night."

"You don't know him as I do."

"He is trying to scare you."

"No — he means to get me. The window — !"

The large casement windows possessed shutters and these were firmly closed and bolted on the inside.

"There is no way in except through the front door," said McLean. "But have no fear. He will not come."

The clock on the mantelpiece struck the hour — eleven. Conrad commenced to drink a very large glass of port, but McLean stopped him.

"I should go lightly with that stuff," he advised. "Why not go to bed?"

"Bed! My God — I couldn't sleep. I would rather stay here — with you."

"Very well — we will give him until midnight — just to prove his bluff."

The minutes passed with dreadful slowness. Despite McLean's advice Conrad drank heavily, and towards twelve o'clock he was in a state of absolute terror. McLean did all he could to induce courage but failed. It was ten minutes to twelve when the telephone bell rang again. The butler had gone to bed, but he left the line through to the extension. McLean himself answered the call. A curious voice said, "I am coming for you."

Conrad uttered a cry that was like a howl — for he had overheard the message in the great stillness. His eyes bulged as they stared at McLean.

"I told you so. The pistol is useless. My time is coming — I know it — I feel it."

"Rubbish! If he tries to enter I shall most certainly hold him — shoot if necessary."

Conrad's hand went to the decanter, but it was caught by McLean.

"No more!"

Five minutes passed.

Conrad made to stand up, but McLean pushed him back into his chair. There was a noise outside — merely the wind in an old cypress tree, but Conrad read it differently. He snatched up the pistol.

McLean took it from him and laid it on the table. The business was getting on his nerves, and he regretted having wasted his evening with this maniac.

"One minute to go," he said. Conrad was listening intently, McLean heard nothing but a bit of wind and the ticking of the clock, but Conrad's eyes seemed to be bulging from his head. Suddenly the clock struck once. Conrad sprang to his feet and faced the window. At the next stroke of the clock he staggered and fell heavily. McLean ran to him, turned him over and gazed into his face. He was dead!

★ ★ ★

Almost a year had passed since the death of Cornelius Conrad and the big house was now run by his heiress, with the assistance of her aunt — a Mrs. Crowther. The girl had felt her father's death keenly, but remained in total ignorance of the real cause. McLean himself had been surprised at the strange outcome of his visit to Sussex. When Conrad had dropped dead the truth burst upon him. Naga had succeeded as Conrad vowed he would, and by a scheme as clever as any that McLean had ever heard of. No doubt he knew all there was to know about his intended victim. Unlike his brother, Cornelius was a moral and physical coward, suffering from an affection of the heart. It was only necessary for Naga to play upon Conrad's nerves — set him into a state of panic, and craven fear would do the rest.

He had taken his revenge without lifting a finger, and so far as McLean could see the law was powerless to act. There was no written threat — nothing but Conrad's allegations. It could not even be proved that it was Naga who spoke on the telephone with such telling effect. Truly the whole business was cleverly thought out and most ingeniously perpetrated. McLean gave his evidence, and wisely held his tongue.

Later he was successful in finding Naga in a small curiosity shop in the West End of London. He was small and wizened — a typical Japanese of the intelligent type. He moved about his shop with the silence and stealth of a cat, and gave one the impression of being thorough in everything.

Now with the approaching New Year McLean was recalling the tragedy, and also Conrad's allegation. Naga had threatened three lives. Two had been taken. Would he attempt the third? It was a gruesome thought and yet all the arguments that McLean could bring forward gave weight to such a possibility. A year had passed between the deaths of Joseph and Cornelius. Naga had not forgotten then, why should he forget now? But in Ethel Conrad's case there was no question of illness nor cowardice. She was abundantly healthy, and full of high spirits now that the first great shock of her father's sudden death had worn off. McLean had seen her during the summer, and she had given him a warm welcome, believing him to be an old friend of her father.

Shortly before Christmas came an invitation from Scotland for McLean to spend a week or two with his sister. He wanted to go but at the last moment he wrote tendering his apologies with regrets. It was no use — he could not rid his mind of the sinister figure of the curio dealer. That bright-eyed girl by the sea was living in complete ignorance of the danger that threatened her. To go on holiday was impossible in the circumstances. He decided to keep Naga under the strictest observation for the next few days.

McLean's Christmas was thus completely spoiled — save for the little excitement he derived from his shadowing of the Japanese. Nothing suspicious happened until the 29th of December. At half-past six on that evening, Naga left his house and wandered down Oxford Street. He halted in front of a large confectioner's shop and gazed in the window for a few minutes. Ultimately he entered the place, and bought a medium-sized box of chocolates. McLean saw the girl go to another part of the shop with a view to wrapping the box. He went across immediately and pretended to interest himself in some sweetmeats. The girl laid Naga's box on the counter and dived for a sheet of wrapping paper. Swiftly McLean pencilled a minute shorthand note on the side of the box. The girl looked up and saw him.

"I want a pound of sugared almonds," he said, pointing to the sweets in question. Then in an undertone, "I am a police officer. Take a look at that mark — also try to remember the gentleman who has purchased this box. Don't look in his direction — now, please."

The girl was quickwitted and carried out her instructions. She completed her packing and handed the parcel to Naga, who was lingering close by. He departed immediately and McLean went after him. All that evening was spent watching Naga's house from a safe distance. But he did not reappear. McLean was on duty again at seven o'clock the next morning. He waited three hours before the Jap appeared, and on this occasion he carried a small parcel, bearing a label.

McLean, wearing a tiny moustache and horn-rimmed spectacles, was successful in tracking him to a post office. Here the parcel was handed in. It was addressed to Miss Ethel Conrad at her address in Sussex!

Naga paid the amount required for postage and went out. McLean had a few words with the attendant, and then went out and bought a box of candied fruits which he dispatched at once to Ethel Conrad with his best wishes for a happy New Year. An hour later he was talking to her on the telephone.

"Mr. McLean speaking. You remember me? Good! I fear I have made a silly mistake. I have sent you two little presents instead of one. The larger box in blue wrapping paper is the right one. Could I trouble you to return the flat box in light brown paper, with the red cross on the side? It contains something that is urgently wanted elsewhere."

She thanked him for his kind thought and promised to do as he requested immediately the parcel reached her. Two days later, back came the box of chocolates. McLean took it straight to Scotland Yard. His old *bête noire* Inspector Datchett greeted him somewhat cynically.

"Needing our help, Mac?"

"Not really. Only the use of one of your jails. I want to see the Chief."

"Engaged."

"Then I'll wait."

"What's on now, anyway?"

"Nothing much. Just a little incident which may go to prove that Cornelius Conrad wasn't quite so demented as you

149

appeared to believe."

"Conrad? Oh, I get you — the man who died from heart failure, and who came here with some wonderful story about wholesale revenge on the part of a chink or Jap. Nothing doing there."

"Ah — we shall see."

★ ★ ★

Twenty-four hours later it was established that the innocent looking chocolates had all been tampered with. In each one was a fatal amount of very elusive poison. The box carried McLean's pencilled note — 'sold to Mr. Naga on Dec. 29' — and inside was a printed New Year's card, signed Norma. McLean found out that Miss Conrad really had a girl friend of that name.

"Cute," he said. "Mr. Naga remembers everything. Here I have a specimen of his handwriting. The girl at the chocolate shop and the post office assistant will be able to identify him. Are the facts sufficient?"

Late that night Naga was arrested, and on his premises was found a phial of poison identical with that found in the chocolates. In due course he was tried and sentenced. It was necessary for Ethel Conrad to give evidence. Afterwards she came to McLean — her eyes eloquent with gratitude.

"I never knew," she said. "How can I ever thank you?"

"I have had my reward. Naga was a genius. One does not meet many such men. It is regrettable that we can only get him on this charge, but you can rest assured you will never be troubled by him again."

McLean carried away with him the memory of her deep, trustful eyes, and he rather suspected that a bachelor's life wasn't quite so as it might be. But there was her open invitation to him to spend a week or two fishing in the season. That rather appealed to him. He even went so far as to make a note of it.

7

OCCASIONALLY McLean dropped in to lunch at the little pub not far from the scene of his old activities. It was patronised largely by men from the 'Yard' and one could be sure of meeting three or four sleuthhounds of the law there almost any day between twelve and two o'clock.

On more than one occasion he had worked hand in glove with the force which had intimated that it had no further use of his services, and it would not have been difficult to find a dozen men steeled in the fire of hard experience who would swear unequivocally that the loss was more the Yard's than McLean's.

The bitter dregs of humiliation having been swallowed and digested long since, McLean found it possible to face his old colleagues with comparative calm. The great majority of them had never failed to believe in his integrity and loyalty. Only one or two, actuated by spite, due to a deep-seated envy of finer intelligence, were prone to curl a contumelious lip.

On this day McLean found Darke, Rattenly and Wilberforce enjoying a grill in the far corner of the grill-room. All were young officers of the better class type. Darke had worked his way up from a provincial constable, and Rattenly and Wilberforce boasted public school education. McLean had termed them 'the three musketeers' and this rather hit off their close companionship. They were a hardy trio, and were in splendid fettle at the moment to judge by their spirits.

"Here comes Scotland," said Rattenly. "Get out of that comfortable chair, Will, and tell the waiter to stick that last fillet on the fire. Great heavens, where did you get that hat, Mac?"

McLean hung up his new purchase, and took the arm-chair which Rattenly had most condescendingly vacated. He gazed at three different bottles of wine in the centre of the table — all very much depleted of their contents.

"Somebody's birthday?"

"Somebody's funeral," corrected Darke.

"Whose?" asked McLean.

"Spike Melford's. You remember Spike?"

"I do — but I thought he was in Broadmoor."

"He was until ten days ago. We lugged him last night."

McLean was interested. Melford had figured in several crimes during the last ten years. He was known as a dangerous criminal — a man who would stick at nothing to gain his ends, but so far he had escaped any serious charge. Of his antecedents the police knew nothing, but it was obvious that he had the advantages of a good education.

"What is the present charge?" asked McLean.

"The Apsley murder."

McLean had not read the details of this crime. All he knew was that the body of a young woman had been found near the village of Apsley in Hampshire, and that so far she had not been identified.

"Quick work," he remarked.

"Not so bad. We were wise in keeping Melford under observation when he left quod. We traced him as far as

154

Stoneleigh — the next village to Apsley. He hung about there until the day of the murder — when we lost track of him. We knew that he had bought a cheap second-hand car, and subsequently we found a witness who stated that he saw this same car near the spot where the body was found — on the evening of the murder. Well, we found Melford and also the car. Under the seat of it was a blood-stained jack-handle, and in Melford's possession was a gold wrist-watch and a ring. The corpse had a finger injury which in the opinion of the doctor was caused by the forcible removal of a ring."

"Why wasn't the woman identified?"

"In the first place the body was only half clad, and secondly, she suffered from severe facial injury."

"Not much to get a conviction on."

"Enough, in our opinion, taking Melford's record into consideration. He can't explain how he came in possession of the ring and the watch, nor the bloodstains on the jack-handle. Of course identification of the exhibits would make the case more certain. But he'll swing all right."

It afforded McLean ample food for reflection. Melford was notoriously a 'big job' man. Why should he commit so serious a crime with the prospects of so scant a reward? There was of course always the possibility of spoil at present unknown to the police. But it didn't sound quite like Spike Melford.

"Was the ring of any great value?" asked McLean.

"Fifty shillings."

"And the watch?"

"Ten pounds, at the outside."

"You think Melford would risk his neck for a few pounds?"

"Well, there may be other factors. But the medical evidence supports our view. The iron jack-handle was square, and fits exactly the fatal head wounds. He did it all right."

On reaching home McLean turned up the newspaper reports of the case, and he became more and more interested. It was revealed that the victim was found dressed in nothing but her underclothing. Even her shoes had been removed, and there were signs on an undergarment which led the police to believe that a laundry mark had been deliberately removed. In McLean's opinion the ring and watch had been removed — like the laundry mark — to render identification difficult and not from motives of gain. Also the shoes. In which case there was much more in the case than appeared on the surface. After making notes of every detail of importance, McLean saw Darke again.

"Any developments in the Apsley case?"

"None. Melford was committed for trial yesterday."

"You are satisfied he waylaid and murdered that girl, with no other motive than gain?"

"Oh, no. She may have been an old flame. He was always getting mixed up with women. You may remember that Annie Young figured in his last exploit, and went to prison at the same time as he did. But Annie is still alive and kicking. She came out of quod six months ago and went to America."

"Aren't you inclined to underrate Melford's intelligence?"

"How?"

"He doesn't play for small stakes. There is a bigger motive than you suspect."

Darke shrugged his shoulders a trifle uneasily.

"You're a devil for theories, Mac," he said. "If you've got a new one here, why not have a shot at proving it?"

"That is exactly what I intend doing. Can you spare time to show me the scene of the crime?"

"I could run you down to Apsley this afternoon — but I can't stay there for any length of time."

"There is no need. I merely want to see the exact spot where the body was found. I am capable of carrying on alone after that."

Three hours later the pair were speeding into Hampshire.

★ ★ ★

Apsley was a sleepy little village some ten miles from Winchester. The main line passed quite close to it, and there was a modest station called Apsley Junction. The district was at a considerable

158

elevation, and was mostly moorland, thickly covered with gorse and bracken. Darke stopped the car on the moorland road — about two miles from the village — and pointed to his left, where McLean could discern the workings of a large gravel pit. Close to the car was a narrow cutting through the steeply rising bank.

"This is the place. We will get out here."

The two men passed through the cutting and finally reached the disused pit. Digging had ceased long since for the gravel had depreciated in quality since the first opening of the pit, and was now not worth the carting.

"Here is the exact spot," said Darke, indicating a large and damaged gorse bush. "The body was lying in the centre of it. A rustic found it early in the morning — twelve hours or so after death in the doctor's opinion."

"The underclothing was of fair quality?"

"Oh, yes. Nothing unusual — but certainly better than one would expect to find on the average working-class girl. Do you propose to stay on here for a bit?"

"Yes."

"Then I advise you to put up at 'The Crown.' There are two inns in the village, but the other one is none too clean. I am sorry I must get back to town immediately."

"Don't tarry. I am all right now."

Darke drove away a few minutes later, and McLean wandered round the deep pit for some time. Ultimately he left it and climbed to the top of the working. The vertical distance was about fifty feet. From the road to the top of the pit was about fifty yards — up a very steep bank practically covered with gorse. McLean took the line of least resistance and found a fairly well defined path between the big bushes. He was of the opinion that the girl had been done to death on the road, and her body carried up the path. He sought a reason for this, for the obvious thing for the murderer to do was to use the cutting into the pit instead of laboriously scrambling up the steep path, and flinging the body into the disfiguring bush. The only reason he could ascribe was that the murderer was intent upon ridding the body of all means of identification, and he feared a possible intruder while he carried out this grim task. From the vantage point of the pit top he could see in every direction.

For hours McLean lingered near the pit, searching the ground systematically. When darkness fell he had not nearly finished, and he resolved to continue on the following day. On applying at 'The Crown' he secured a comfortable room and, after taking a bath and a meal, he wandered into the bar-parlour with a view to listening to local gossip which was always interesting. The recent tragedy was the reigning topic, and while he sat there listening to the landlord's wild theories, a man entered with an evening newspaper. He nodded to the landlord and to McLean, and called for a glass of beer.

"Terrible business — that murder," he said. "But it looks as if the police have got the right man. Anyhow, he's been committed for trial."

"I wonder who the poor girl was," mused the landlord. "Anyway, she didn't come from anywhere around here. Why, they know every young woman for miles."

"The poor creature was all disfigured."

The landlord nodded his head sympathetically.

"Shocking affair. The worst ever since I bin living in Apsley, and that's nigh on forty year."

"Horrible, I call it, to kill a pretty young woman for the sake of a bit of jewellery. Well, you never know what kind of jackals there be within reach."

He sighed and turned over the newspaper noisily. Two or three more villagers came in, and all had something to say about the local scandal. The man with the newspaper changed the subject abruptly.

"Squire Dennison's making no progress," he remarked. "Says here, condition unchanged. That means he's worse. He'll be a loss to Apsley if he dies."

"He won't die," put in the landlord. "Hard as nails is the squire. He's been ill before and has always pulled through."

"Maybe, but this time it's touch and go. My brother George is chauffeur up at the Manor. A week or so ago they had to wire for a night nurse, and George says the family is prepared for the worst."

"Well, I'll wager the squire pulls through," said the landlord loyally. "He always was a fighter. I knew him when he was a boy — him and his brother Henry. No pride about them. They used to play in the village cricket team. When the war came both of 'em joined up at once, though the squire had no need to go. Henry never came home — and no one knows why. But there was a rumour that Henry married the woman his brother loved. Ran off with her, they say. Well, it seems to have turned out badly. She died and he went to the dogs — drank himself to death in Africa. But maybe it ain't true. Folks are such liars."

The subject changed every few minutes, and at last McLean went to bed. The following morning he was up betimes and busy on the scene of the crime. He continued where he had left off on the preceding evening, and at last he made a discovery. It was the broken half of a large bone button!

He resumed his search with more eagerness now — but found nothing more. The button interested him. It had undoubtedly come from a feminine garment, for he could not imagine a man wearing buttons of so large a size, and the state of the broken edge convinced him that it had not lain for any length of time in the spot where he had found it. He was too well used to disappointments to permit this possible clue to raise any undue optimism, but it shed a ray of hope and started a theory which developed apace.

Returning to the inn he raised a few inquiries about the neighbouring residents. The landlord knew them all from the local M.P. to the Squire himself. McLean was not interested in the M.P., but he was in the Squire — who lived at Apsley Manor.

"Where is the Manor?" he inquired.

"Three miles across the moor. It's the only big house in that direction. You take the main road — past the sand-pit where that poor woman's body was found. You can see the house from the next rise in the road."

McLean thanked him and decided to pay a visit to the Manor. He found the fine Elizabethan house without difficulty, and went in search of George — the chauffeur. George lived over the garage with his wife and child, and turned out to be a quite intelligent type of man. McLean did not hesitate to tell him a white lie.

"I am a police officer," he said. "We are still seeking for further evidence in the local murder case. I think you may be able to help me in one respect."

"Only too pleased, sir."

"You remember the night of the murder — that is to say, the evening before the body was found?"

"Quite well. I was on the road the same evening."

"You went to the station to meet someone?"

"Yes, the nurse who was to look after the master during the nights. I was told to meet the 6.42 train."

"Did you see any suspicious person near the old sand-pit?"

"No. The police have already asked me that question."

"You met the nurse?"

"As a matter of fact, I didn't. I got a puncture about a mile after leaving the garage, and had to change a wheel. Then

I got a second one, and that meant going back to the garage for a second spare wheel. In all I wasted about half an hour. When I reached the junction the train had come in and gone. I thought Nurse Parsons couldn't have travelled by it, otherwise I should have met her on the road. So I waited for the 8.30 train. She didn't come by that and I decided to go home. When I reached the house I heard that nurse had arrived. It appears she found no vehicle waiting for her and started to walk, but she took the old road instead of the new and that is how I passed her."

"I see. And have the local police questioned her as to her seeing any person or persons loitering near the sand-pit?"

"Oh, yes, but as she took the old road she did not pass the pit at all. She said she met no one on the other road."

"Hm! I think I should like to see Nurse Parsons."

"She's asleep now — doesn't come on duty until 10 p.m."

"I will come back later."

"Shall I tell them in the house?"

"I had rather you did not."

McLean was building up his theory every minute, but there were one or two blanks in it, and much had yet to be proven. He had no intention of giving Nurse Parsons some five hours' grace, but he was anxious to settle a small point in connection with the puncturing of the car tyres. He walked along the road for about three-quarters of a mile and then commenced to examine the surface carefully. A hundred yards farther on he picked up a long, flat-headed nail, then another and another. In less than a quarter of a mile he collected over a score of these things — all exactly alike. Most of them were now in the gutters, and he had no doubt that there had been a lot of tyre-changing during the past week or so!

That point settled, he returned to the house, and as he entered the drive he saw the blinds lowered. A frown crossed his face, and he hurried forward. Near the house he ran into the chauffeur who was about to enter by the side door. The man's face was sad.

"Bad news," he said. "The master has just passed away. Went off suddenly just now. Hadn't you better — ?"

"I wish to see Nurse Parsons at once. If you are going inside you can inform the butler or the housekeeper."

The chauffeur nodded and entered the silent house.

★ ★ ★

The housekeeper came to McLean, with her eyes full of tears. She had been told of his business, and she suggested that in the circumstances he would defer it until a more convenient time. But McLean was adamant.

"I am sorry, but the matter is more urgent than you imagine. I should like to see Nurse Parsons immediately."

"Very well. I will send her down to you. Please come inside."

She showed him into a small room on the left of the hall, and then went to rouse the night-nurse. As soon as she was out of the room McLean was across the hall making investigations in a cloak-room which he had noted previously. It contained a number of coats, and among them was a blue mackintosh. At the bottom of this was half a bone-button of large size. He drew in his breath with a little hiss, and then compared the half-button which he had found with that remaining on the garment. The two halves fitted exactly. He was satisfied!

He returned to the waiting-room just in time to receive the housekeeper. She told him that Nurse Parsons would be down in a few minutes, but that she had already been questioned by the police and had nothing further to communicate. McLean merely nodded and waited.

Ultimately came Nurse Parsons herself. She was round about thirty-five, dark and keen-eyed. Her features were hard, and her chin stubborn. She smiled when she met McLean's glance, but immediately the smile vanished, and her cheeks went pallid.

"Good evening, Annie!" said McLean grimly.

"I — I don't know what you mean. My name is — "

"Your name is Annie Young. Don't try to bluff. You know me well enough. I saw you just before you were sent to jail — after that little job with Spike Melford. Until quite recently I overlooked the fact that in your innocent youth you had a hospital training. But Spike evidently remembered it. You'll be wanted for murder."

"Murder!"

"Oh, not the sand-pit murder. That was Spike's job, but murder nearer home. Squire Dennison has just died. Isn't that significant with you here in a nurse's garb? Explain that, if you can."

She became very agitated, was silent for a few moments, and then faced him.

"I can explain it, and I'm going to. Spike got me into this hole — but I'm innocent. I didn't know all the facts when he suggested the job to me. He came to me when I was broke and desperate. He had a great idea, he said. It was to do with this house and the Squire. He had intercepted a telegram to the hospital in Winchester, asking for a night-nurse to be sent at once. All I had to do was impersonate the nurse. He could supply the proper uniform, and I was to meet him at a certain place not far from here. I was to go as Nurse Parsons — "

"How did he know that — at that juncture?"

"He didn't. It was later when he told me the name. I didn't realise what that signified exactly at the time. I was to go to the house and see — see that the Squire did not recover."

"He supplied you with dope?"

"Yes, but I never used it. I had no intention of using it. I thought there was a good chance of the Squire dying anyway, and of my getting hold of five hundred pounds. I wondered how he managed to get the uniform and the suit-case, but I didn't guess the truth until I heard he was arrested. Then I wanted to run away, but I feared it would look suspicious — also the doctor had told me confidentially that the Squire couldn't last another week. I can show you the bottle which Spike gave me to use. The seal is still unbroken. I may be a crook but I've never had a finger in murder. All I wanted was some easy money. I'm telling you the truth. Can't you see I am?"

McLean was inclined to believe her. She agreed to accompany him to the police station and wait the arrival of Inspector Darke to whom she undertook to make a full statement.

"How was Melford going to benefit by the Squire's death?" asked McLean.

"I don't know, but he swore he had a plan which couldn't fail. I had to trust him."

McLean left it at that, but after lodging her with the local inspector of police he made another journey to the Manor. There he had a few words with the two sisters of the dead man, and incidentally possessed himself of the suit-case which had been taken from the real Nurse Parsons. In it was a bottle of poison, but as Annie Young had averred, the seal was unbroken. Upon taking the doctor into his confidence he was assured that the Squire had died a perfectly natural death. He was leaving when he noticed a portrait in the hall. That induced him to tarry a little longer, and before he ultimately departed he had filled up all the blanks in the mystery.

Inspector Darke had reached the police station in record time, and had taken a full statement from Annie Young before McLean arrived. Darke looked at him with unconcealed admiration.

"Smart work that, Mac. We're in your debt again. She has made a long statement, — and a true one, in my opinion. What a swine that fellow is! But even now I haven't got his motive."

"I have. Take a look at that photograph."

Darke gazed at the rather faded print.

"Good God! Why, it's Melford!"

"More than that — it is Henry Dennison — brother of Squire Dennison, who was believed to be dead. The two quarrelled years ago. The Squire never knew that his brother had taken to crime as a profession. But Henry knew that under his brother's will the big estate was to be equally divided between the surviving members of the family. That was where Henry would barge in — and benefit to the extent of fifty thousand pounds."

"Well I'm blessed! And had he merely

waited he could have got it — and enjoyed it."

"One of life's little ironies — that. He was beaten by his own cleverness. I suppose he wrote to the matron at the hospital in Nurse Parson's name, and allayed all suspicion there."

"That is so. I have just rung her up. She will be able to identify the watch and ring, as the watch was a gift to Nurse Parsons from some members of the staff. That spells 'gallows' for Spike."

"Yes — I think so."

"I still can't think why the nurse was not met at the station."

"Spike saw to that. He planned everything rather well. How he came to see the first telegram I don't know, but having seen it he was quick to get to business. He guessed there would be a reply, and doubtless waited on the messenger near the Manor. There he pretended he was the butler or someone in authority, and intercepted the reply. It is comparatively easy to open a telegraphic envelope. After reading it he delivered it by slipping it in the letter-box and ringing. Then he took steps to impersonate Nurse Parsons. Annie was brought post haste, and he littered the road with nails to prevent the chauffeur from reaching the station in time. It was he himself who met Nurse Parsons, and having disposed of her he picked up Annie, and coolly handed her the uniform and suit-case. He drove her to the Manor by the old road — and left her in complete ignorance of what he had done. She must have changed in the car."

In due course Spike Melford got what he richly deserved, and Annie Young received a minor sentence. McLean got nothing out of it but the satisfaction of having ridded the earth of a soulless scoundrel. But he and the 'three musketeers' had another little celebration when the curtain rang down on the Apsley crime. Darke gave the chief toast.

"To your speedy return to Scotland Yard, Mac."

McLean smiled but made no response. Before that could happen much water was to flow under London Bridge.

8

MCLEAN sat in his reception-room turning over the card which Tiny had presented. It bore the name of Miss Gladys Hartner — and no address of any kind.

"What is the lady like, Tiny?" he inquired.

"Young, sir, and jolly pretty. Seems a bit worried, too."

"I shouldn't wonder. This is an asylum for worried persons. I suppose I had better see her. Show her up."

"Certainly, sir."

Tiny vanished in a flash, and a few minutes later the door opened to admit the charming Miss Hartner. Tiny had not exaggerated in the least. She was all he averred, young, pretty and obviously distressed. McLean offered her a chair and she sat down, facing him.

"You are Mr. McLean himself?"

"Yes."

"I must apologise for not writing and

fixing an appointment, but there was no time. Last night something happened — I rang up a friend this morning and he advised me to come and see you."

"What happened last night?"

"My house was entered again — the third time in two years. But I must tell you everything. The story dates back nearly sixteen years, to the time when I was a small child. Perhaps you have heard of my father, Julius Hartner?"

"Not the explorer?"

"Yes. He was killed in Peru in 1912. I was with him at the time — a child of five years of age. My poor mother had died two months before from a strange kind of fever, and my father was unwilling to turn back. He took me along with him, and his native bearers."

McLean nodded. He recalled the strange case of Hartner, and the dramatic end of it. The explorer had come into possession of an old inscription which related a story about some buried jewels among some ruins in the heart of Peru. He had started off with his wife and child in order to see what truth lay in the story. Simultaneously a second party set up in competition, having heard rumours from another source. According to reports, the two parties had come into conflict and Hartner had been shot — by natives, it was alleged.

"You — you were the little girl who was ultimately found and sent to England?" he asked.

"Yes."

"You were present when your father was killed?"

"Yes, but I can't remember much. There was some shooting, and ultimately our natives ran away. All I know is that my father was successful in his quest."

"You mean — he found the jewels?"

"Yes. He showed them to me. I didn't quite understand then, but I do now. And I can remember that after the fighting was over some men came to our camp and turned out everything. They were rough men, and asked me many questions. What they wanted were the jewels, but they never found them, though they dug up the ground round about the camp."

"But you knew where they were?"

She shook her head.

"After my father was wounded he continued to keep the other party at bay. He had time to bury them, and I am sure he did that. To cut a long story short I was found and taken to England. My father had already made a will, and trustees were appointed. Last year I came into his small estate. Among the things that had been deposited was a box containing all kinds of souvenirs of travel, and in this box was a flat piece of sandstone bearing queer signs. I have brought it with me now."

She produced the object in question. It was about three inches long by two inches wide, and was evidently only a portion of the original slab. The signs were entirely new to McLean, but he concluded they were in the ancient language of some vanished South American tribe.

"This is all you have?" he asked.

"Yes. I have searched everywhere for the missing piece but cannot find it."

"Have you tried to get this translated?"

"No. It only occurred to me last night that this might contain a message from my father to me."

"You think he scratched the signs on the stone before he died in order to tell you where he hid the jewels?"

"Yes. I told you that on three occasions my house had been broken into, and things turned upside down. On the first two occasions the stone was not in my possession. Last night I heard noises downstairs. I crept down and found they came from the lumber-room where the box was. I raised an alarm and the chauffeur came over. The burglars got away, but I found that they had been busy on the lock of the box in which this slab was contained."

"It looks as if they suspected its existence."

"I am sure of it. I need your help — not to get the jewels for myself, but to prevent those men from benefiting from my father's sufferings and endeavours. Will you take care of it for me?"

"Certainly. But you would like to know what these signs stand for?"

"Yes, if that is possible."

"I will consult an authority. Have you communicated with the police?"

"No. My friend told me I should

do better to leave the matter in your hands."

"I will do what I can. Where shall I communicate with you?"

"At 'The Towers,' Dipley, Surrey."

McLean made a note of it, and after answering a few more questions his fascinating client took her departure. McLean possessed a splendid reference library. He amused himself that evening by attempting to translate the writing, but had to abandon the task ultimately. Only an expert could hope to succeed.

On the following morning he rang up an authority, and an hour later was closeted with him. The professor displayed great interest in the signs, but signified that it would take him several hours to translate them with any certainty of correctness. He undertook to send the translation and the slab to McLean some time during the afternoon.

McLean spent the rest of the morning at the Old Bailey where an interesting case was being tried. When he emerged at the luncheon interval it was drenching with rain, and he decided to have lunch at the Savoy Hotel. The downpour continued without abatement, and after lunch McLean decided to take a taxi home. He saw one with the flag up, and jumped aboard after shouting his destination at the driver. But as he entered it a dark woman opened the opposite door.

"I beg your pardon," he said. "Yours, I believe?"

"Oh, don't bother. I'll — "

She looked at the pelting rain and hesitated.

"I am only going as far as Piccadilly Circus. If you are — "

"I pass by there," he said. "Please stay."

She smiled rather sadly.

"Thank you so much. Every taxi seems engaged at this moment."

In the Strand the traffic was dense. Every minute the taxi was held up. Drivers looked savage and out of temper. McLean's temporary travelling companion also looked anxious.

"Is that the right time?" she gasped as she saw a clock.

"Yes — within a minute. Two-twenty-five."

"Oh, I must get to Piccadilly by half-past two. It is a matter almost of life and death."

"I am afraid we are helpless. Ah — we are moving at last!"

"Thank heavens!"

Her agitation was tremendous. She sat twisting her fingers — displaying every sign of both anxiety and fear. Near Piccadilly there was another hold-up, but now the rain had ceased. The woman peered across the street.

"That's where I want to go — No. 18 — over the hairdresser's. I — I think I can get out here."

"Better wait," warned McLean. "There is a maze of traffic."

"No. I — I must."

She opened the door and wedged herself between two vehicles. Taxi-men swore at her, and McLean realised that she was in some danger of getting injured if the traffic suddenly started. He went after her, and gave the taxi-driver half a crown as he alighted.

"Let me escort you," he said.

"Thank you."

They dived through the traffic,

and ultimately reached the pavement immediately outside No. 18. The woman looked up and appeared to shudder.

"Are you quite well?" inquired McLean.

"Yes — but — " She gulped and then spoke impulsively. "Would you help me to avoid great trouble? I have no right to ask — and yet, if — "

"What is wrong?"

"I am going upstairs — on the third floor. If everything is all right I shall be down again within ten minutes. This little box contains a token. I want my brother to get it if — if I am not down here within ten minutes. His address is No. 7, Cranbourne Gardens — near Baker Street — on the first floor. Is that asking too much?"

"Not a bit. — But have you any fear that you may not come down here again?"

"I — I don't know."

"Then permit me to accompany you."

"No — no. That would spoil everything. It is quite possible that everything will be all right, and there will be no need for you to take — But perhaps you would rather not — "

"I will do as you request."

"Thank you. Take — take the box, in case — "

She put a kind of pill-box into McLean's hand and immediately ran up the stairs. McLean was more than interested. The box bore the name — Arthur Withers — on the lid, and was amazingly heavy for its size. He slipped it into his pocket, and scanned the names of the occupants of the overhead offices, which were painted on the wall inside the main entrance. There was a solicitor, a branch office of a touring agency, a philatelist, and a civil engineer. The third floor housed the solicitor, but there was a blank space as if an apartment on that floor was now vacated.

He stood and watched the hands of a clock on the opposite side of the road, trying to work out the odds on the woman's safe return. Her behaviour had been such as to lead him to suspect that she herself was doubtful of the outcome, but why there should be any kind of danger in a busy London street it was difficult to imagine. Five minutes passed, six-seven-eight — and then ten.

185

He pursed his lips and looked up the stairs. Save for the tapping of a typewriter he heard nothing. He decided to give her another ten minutes, and continued to wait. But during that period no one entered and no one emerged from the building.

An unoccupied taxi came close to the kerb. He hailed it and instructed the driver to go to the address given him by the vanished woman. Very soon he was in Cranbourne Gardens. It contained about a dozen large houses, all built in exactly the same style. No. 7 was by far the dingiest, and was divided up into flats. Under the bell on the first floor was a card bearing the name of Arthur Withers, F.R.C.O. McLean pushed the bell, a few seconds later the door was opened, and a pallid face was seen. It was difficult to say whether it belonged to a man or a woman, for the body was totally hidden. McLean was about to put a question when something seemed to snap in his brain. The whole world was immediately blotted out.

★ ★ ★

It was almost dark when McLean opened his eyes and blinked. He was lying on his back on an uncarpeted floor, and his head was aching maddeningly, in addition there was a pungent smell all about him. He gasped as the truth burst upon his consciousness. It was chloroform, and he had been both bludgeoned and doped! His fingers found the painful wound on the back of his head. His hair was matted with congealed blood, and near him was his felt hat in a shapeless condition.

He staggered to his feet and made for the window. Upon opening it a gust of fresh air entered and helped to revive him. He commenced to blame himself for getting into this mess, for it was not often he was caught napping. The woman had played her part with consummate artistry, and all the circumstances were such as to disabuse his mind as to the real object of her cunning. It had to do with the Hartner affair — of that he was already convinced. He ran to the door. It was open. He was free to go — now. Obviously the idea was to render him helpless for a few hours — to enable certain persons a free field for investigation elsewhere. And where else but his own house?

He remembered the sandstone tablet. Here was the key. They knew that Miss Hartner had brought that souvenir to him. They wanted him out of the way in order to ransack his premises. But the tablet was not there. The professor — He drew in his breath as he recalled the professor's promise to deliver the tablet and the translation that afternoon. There was Tiny, of course, but what could the diminutive page-boy do in the face of an invasion on the part of, perhaps, several determined men?

Jamming his hat on his head he blundered out and ran down the stairs. There he found a woman — evidently the housekeeper — who looked at him in amazement. He asked her who lived in the flat above, but she swore it was empty. A gentleman had called that morning to look over it, but had told her it was too small.

"Have you a telephone here?"

"Yes, sir — in the hall."

McLean rang up his house, but was told that there was no answer. He wasted no more time, but drove as fast as he could to the Sign of The Owl. Upon opening the door he called for Tiny, and heard a queer cry from the kitchen. There he found Tiny with a scarf bound round his mouth, and his arms secured behind him. The excited boy blew out his cheeks when he was freed.

"Someone called, eh?" snapped McLean.

"Yus, sir — two crooks they were, but dressed like gents. One of 'em asked to see you. I told him you were out. He said he would wait, and I was showing them into the waiting-room when the tall one caught me and shoved me in here — like you found me. They were here quite a long time. Lumme, have they pinched anything?"

"We shall soon know. Did any parcel come for me?"

"Yus, sir — a small parcel — very heavy. There was a letter with it, and I had to sign for it."

"Where did you put it?"

"On your table."

McLean ran into his sanctum sanctorum. The place was littered with papers and articles. Evidently the intruders had not found the tablet at first and had turned out every drawer and cupboard. But it was clear that ultimately they had examined the parcel on the table, and got away with it. Tiny came in with his face all twisted from excitement.

"They — they got the parcel, sir?"

"I am afraid so."

Tiny looked as dejected as a dog with the mange.

"I couldn't do anything. It was two to one sir — and the housekeeper had her afternoon off. I did try to lay hands on the poker, but — "

"All right, Tiny. It is just a bit of bad luck. Now go and make yourself presentable while I do the same."

Half an hour later McLean was wearing a strip of plaster on his shaven scalp, but a strong brandy and soda had revived him considerably and he felt ready to its problematical finale. His first step was to ring up the professor, to whom he had to confess the loss of the tablet and translation. Upon inquiring if a copy of the translation existed he was gratified to learn that it did. It was dictated to him over the telephone:

. . . have taken the only means to ensure that the jewels shall be safe from my enemies. They lie in my body and are for you, my dear child, should you ever need them. If not, then disturb not my poor bones. I have left a note begging that whoever finds my body shall have it interred with that of your dear mother, the cost of such to be reimbursed from my estate.

Your loving Father.

McLean blinked at this. No wonder the marauders had failed to find the jewels! The dying man had actually swallowed them! It looked as if the tablet had been broken after the fight. One half must have been recovered by the party who eventually found the child and the dead man. Probably the other portion was found by the gang who now apparently had possession of the whole. It meant that they knew that the tablet contained definite information — and were able to translate it!

The need to see Miss Hartner was pressing. First of all he had the humiliating task of confessing his loss, secondly it was necessary to discover if the unknown personages who had gone to so much trouble to get possession of the complete message, knew where the explorer and his wife were buried. He sent a telegram to Dipley and then hired a fast car and took the road into Surrey.

Upon reaching the Hartner house, he was informed that Miss Hartner had gone for a walk before dinner. The telegram had been received half an hour before, and so far Miss Hartner had not seen it. McLean said he would take a walk up the lane and return in a quarter of an hour. The chauffeur he left smoking a cigarette at the driving wheel.

It was a balmy night and the lane was full of perfume. A flying beetle smashed into McLean's face but flew off again with a low burring. A few seconds later the thing happened again, but on this occasion the beetle came to earth at McLean's feet. He stooped and examined the thing under the light of a pocket torch. It proved to be rather a rare specimen, and he was about to pick it up when a car came round the bend at a great speed. The electric horn shrieked and the vehicle swerved to avoid him. McLean dived for the bank, and as the car slowed appreciably he caught sight of two men in the interior. They were sitting well back, and between them was the rigid form of a pretty girl. In a second he recognised Miss Hartner. The car gathered speed and sped onward, but McLean had already observed the number on the rear plate!

★ ★ ★

Two days later three men sat before a table in the room of a house in the southern suburbs of London. Two of them were Spaniards, but the third was an Englishman. Before them were two pieces of sandstone fitted together, and close by a sheet of paper. The eldest man scowled as he took up one of the pieces of sandstone, and perused for the hundredth time the strange characters engraved on it.

"We can do nothing without her help," he growled. "What a fool I was not to guess at the time. Diaz, the porter, saw the diamonds. He said there were eight of them — as large as hazel nuts."

"Would a man swallow stones that size?"

"Yes — if he knew he was dying. He had plenty of time. There is only one thing to do — make that girl tell the truth."

"But we have tried. She swears she does not know the place where her mother was buried."

"Rubbish! She may not have known at the time — but afterwards she would make inquiries."

"Can't we find out that for ourselves?" asked the Englishman.

"No. It happened over fifteen years ago. When I got on to Hartner's trail he had already buried his wife. The girl knows. She went to Peru five years ago. She must have gone to look at her parents' grave. It is no use wasting time. She is going to tell us what we want to know — and at once. Bring her up, Beale."

The Englishman nodded and then hesitated.

"I warn you you will find her stubborn, Alvarez," he said.

Alvarez's dark eyes flashed.

"She will find me stubborn, too. By the Holy Mother I will not be beaten by a slip of a girl — after fifteen years of hunting."

Beale went off, and a few minutes later returned with Gladys Hartner. The girl's face was lined with suffering. For two days she had been imprisoned in a damp cellar, and during that time no food nor water had passed her lips. When she stood before Alvarez she made a brave attempt to defy him, but she was swaying all the time from faintness.

"Now," said Alvarez. "I hope you will be reasonable. All this suffering has been brought on by your foolish stubbornness. For the last time, will you tell us where your father was buried?"

"I — I don't know."

"You lie. Five years ago you went to Peru. On his body was found a note begging that he might be interred with his wife. You know where that grave is situated."

"So it was you who — who murdered him," she retorted.

"You are wrong."

195

"If you read that note you must — "

"It was told to me. But I have no time to argue. Will you tell us what we want to know?"

"Never! Do you imagine I would permit a human ghoul to open my father's grave for the sake — "

"Ah! Then you do know."

"Yes — but I will never tell you — you monster."

"We shall see."

He stood up and approached her. In a second he had pinioned both her arms.

"That cord — from the blind!"

His Spanish confederate broke off the short length of cord indicated, and handed it to Alvarez. A few seconds later it was slip-knotted and encircled the girl's throat. Alvarez grinned fiendishly and gave it a tug. The strong cord bit into the white, soft flesh.

"Now will you speak?"

She could not had she tried, but he was waiting for her pain-stricken eyes to give answer. They closed in agony, but opened again and gave no sign.

"Damn you!" he snarled, and gave another tug on the cord. Beale made a forward movement.

"Steady, Alvarez!" he said. "I can't stand — "

"Stand back, you dog!" roared the Spaniard. "Don't you interfere or — "

Beale was cowed by the furious eyes. He muttered something and turned his head away. Alvarez was now almost demented. The cord almost disappeared into the crimson flesh. He tugged and tugged until he realised that his victim was unconscious. With a savage curse he loosened the cord, and she dropped inert at his feet.

"I told you so," blurted Beale.

"You think I am beaten, eh? She will recover in a minute. Then we will try again. Elipso, bring some brandy!"

The brandy was administered and the girl soon opened her eyes. Alvarez grinned down at her.

"Perhaps you are a little more sensible now?" he sneered.

All she did was to grasp her throat and groan. He produced the cord and advanced on her.

"You want more, eh?"

"You — you may kill me," she

said hoarsely, "but it will make no difference."

"Then by G — I will!"

The noose was actually over her head when the casement window broke inwards with a tremendous crash. The light shone full on a tense face before which was an outstretched arm — and a steady pistol.

"Sapristé! McLean!" gasped Alvarez.

"Glad to meet you," said McLean. "I advise you to stay exactly as you are — "

Alvarez considered the advice not worth taking, and made a lightning leap at McLean. The pistol cracked and the big Spaniard clapped his left hand to his right shoulder.

"It is never too late to learn prudence," said McLean grimly. "Ah, my friends have arrived in the nick of time."

From his rear appeared two forms — one in plain clothes and the other in the uniform of a police sergeant. They took in the situation at a glance.

"Better take them all," said McLean. "You brought the car?"

The plain clothes man nodded, and proceeded to handcuff the prisoners while

McLean kept them covered. Alvarez spilled his blood all over the carpet as he staggered away. Before he vanished he turned round and treated McLean to a torrent of invective in his best Spanish.

But McLean did not hear. He was busy helping Gladys Hartner into a chair. Despite the pain she suffered she smiled at him, and McLean smiled back, somewhat self-reproachfully.

"It was partly my fault," he said. "They played a clever trick on me, and got hold of the other portion of the tablet. I presume they asked you certain questions?"

"Yes. They wanted to know where my father was buried. It was only then that I realised where the jewels were hid. I refused to tell them and — "

McLean winced as he gazed at her injured neck.

"I am sorry," he said.

"Sorry! Why, I am more than grateful to you. Had you not come I think he would have killed me in his rage. But how did you find me?"

"The car nearly ran me down in the lane. But I was fortunate enough to get the number. It belonged to the woman who was used to lure me into a place of security while her accomplices robbed my house. Well, we got the woman, and from letters found in her flat I was able to locate you, after trying various rendezvous. That gang is well known both here and elsewhere. I believe it was Alvarez who shot your father, but we shall never be able to prove that. Notwithstanding, he is never likely to enjoy freedom again. Are you feeling well enough to be motored to your home?"

"Yes — but I am starving."

"Shall I bring you some food?"

"No — just a glass of water. I — I want to get home."

Later she reclined in the back-seat of the car, with McLean by her side, relieved to know that she would suffer no further molestation.

"And the jewels?" queried McLean. "I presume they stay where they are?"

"Of course. My father earned his quiet rest. I shall never disturb him. Thank God I have not even the need to do so."

"Then that is all over."

"Yes — thanks to you."

McLean dined with her later. She wore a most becoming necklet round her injured throat, and save for a slight swelling none would have guessed she had endured the most painful torture. She raised a glass of sparkling champagne.

"My toast to you," she said. "Many — many successes, Mr. McLean!"

McLean went home feeling that he had settled accounts, after starting with a rather heavy debit balance.

9

"**B**EFORE the second news bulletin is read, here is an SOS. Will anyone knowing the whereabouts of Mrs. Gertrude Cartwright, of The Yews, Fargate, who has been missing from her home since yesterday morning, kindly communicate either with Mr. Charles Cartwright, at the address mentioned, or any police station. Mrs. Cartwright is believed to be wearing a green cloche hat, blue tailored costume, and brown shoes. She is five feet six inches in height, aged 35 years, fresh complexion, fair hair."

McLean lay back on the settee, and then listened to the news, nine-tenths of which he had already read in the evening paper. Followed the announcement that Mrs. Gupper would now read a selection from her own poems, at which McLean promptly switched off the set, and pulled a book out of the bookcase at his elbow. It was a treatise on instinct in insect life, and it held him like a charm until the bell rang and notified him that he had a late visitor. Tiny entered the room a few seconds later, and presented a card.

"I thought I told you I was out to everyone, Tiny."

"You did, sir — but the gentleman was so insistent. He said he knew you were in, because the blind was partly up and he could see you from the other side of the street."

"Very observant of him."

He scanned the card and read the name — Charles Cartwright. Immediately he remembered the wireless announcement, and concluded it was the husband of the missing woman.

"I may as well see him," he said.

"Yes, sir."

Charles Cartwright was shown in. He was a robust man of about forty-five, well dressed, but at the moment decidedly depressed.

"Mr. McLean?"

"Yes. Please be seated. I understand your wife is missing?"

"How did — ? Ah, I see — the wireless. I didn't know the police had arranged that. I want your help — I want everyone's help. It is the most mysterious occurrence. On Wednesday she was perfectly well and happy, but yesterday morning she walked out of the house and I have not seen her since."

"You saw her go?"

"No. I was in bed — later than usual. She called up to tell me that for some reason or other the newsboy had not left the morning newspapers, and that she was going into the High Street to buy them."

"How far is that?"

"About half a mile."

"Why should she take all that trouble?"

"It was her way. She knew I should miss the papers. I told her not to worry, but she only laughed and added that she knew I should die if I didn't get my silly old papers. I got up at once, had my bath, dressed and went downstairs. Breakfast was all ready, but I waited for her return before I started. She — she never came back."

"You have a maid?"

"We had one until three days ago. She left because we refused to give her extra

204

time off. The new girl is due to start to-morrow."

"Normally your wife enjoyed good health?"

"Perfect. That's what the police asked me. They thought it might be a lost memory case, but I can't believe it. My wife has never suffered in that way."

"You know of no other reason which might cause her to go off like that — on a mere excuse?"

"None. Why should she? She thought the world of her home. My chief complaint is that she did not go about enough. She was always busy making and mending things. But of course I wired to her various relations. None of them knew anything about it. They were all amazed."

"Have you made inquiries at the various newsagents in the town?"

"Of course. She is known to most of the shopkeepers, and not one of them saw her that morning."

"She had money with her?"

"I think she took her purse, for I cannot find it anywhere. There could not have been much money in it, for on the previous evening she ran out of cash and asked me for some. All I had in change was a ten-shilling note. I gave her that."

"How long have you been married?"

"Eleven years."

"Children?"

"None, unfortunately."

"What made you come to me?"

"I came to town to see my sister-in-law, and she had heard of you. She suggested that we should have two strings to our bow, and I decided to call despite the late hour. I am sorry to disturb you, but I am worried out of my life. Will you — will you help us if you possibly can?"

"Yes. I will come down to Fargate to-morrow morning — if you will be there."

"Thank you. I intend to catch the last train to-night. The wireless announcement may have good results. I am greatly obliged, Mr. McLean. The house lies off the north end of the common — not far from the old church."

McLean made a few notes on his pad, and promised to be at the house by ten-thirty. Cartwright sighed heavily, and was shown out. McLean went on reading about the queer ways of the Sphex wasp and clean forgot about Mr. Charles Cartwright until early the following morning.

Fargate was an hour's run from London, and McLean reached his destination at the appointed time. Cartwright's house was about half a mile from the railway station, and an equal distance from Fargate Common. It was old and in a bad state of repair. The garden which enclosed it was large and choked with vegetation. The general impression was one of deadly gloom. Cartwright himself opened the door.

"There is someone here," he said. "An officer from Scotland Yard. Would you rather not meet him?"

"What name?"

"Inspector Daniels."

"That is all right. Daniels and I are quite old friends. He will have no objection."

Two minutes later McLean met Daniels. He was sitting at a table hunting through some old correspondence, and his face relapsed into a smile as he saw his old colleague.

"So you're in this, Mac?"

"I was requested to take a hand."

"Good!"

"Is there anything I can do at the moment, Mr. McLean?" asked Cartwright.

"Nothing, thanks. I should like a word with you later on."

Cartwright vanished, and McLean gazed round the rather untidy sitting-room. It smelt musty so he flung open one of the windows and let in a draught of good, fresh air.

"Any progress?" he inquired of Daniels.

"A little. I have an idea Cartwright is to be disillusioned."

"In what direction?"

"He swears that his wife was beyond reproach — happy and contented with her lot, which includes her husband."

"You suggest she wasn't?"

"Well, I'll let you in on the first clue. Have a look at those bits of paper."

He handed McLean a large envelope, and inside it were many charred pieces of paper. All of them contained typewriting, and by piecing one or two of them

208

together McLean was able to get an idea of text. There were many endearments — mention of the future — of a secret, but no date or name in any case.

"Where did you find these?" inquired McLean.

"In the dustbin — under some old flowers. The dust is collected twice weekly here. I deduce that Mrs. Cartwright burnt some incriminating correspondence before she left the house that morning."

"A man, you think?"

"The phraseology is bold, and gives that impression. I have been hoping to get a complete letter, but she seems to have made a clean sweep."

"You haven't told Cartwright?"

"Not yet."

"What is he by profession?"

"Nothing. Lives on a small annuity left him by a fond aunt many years ago."

"The wife had means of her own?"

"None. Her wardrobe is in a shocking state. Remaining virtuous after eleven years of wretched impecuniosity may be easy for an angel, but — "

McLean laughed shortly, and went on examining the room and its contents.

Finally he slipped through the casement window into the garden. He wandered across the over-grown lawn and ultimately reached the kitchen garden which backed on to the domestic part of the house. There was a good deal of litter, including the dustbin which Daniels had been through. McLean trusted Daniels not to have overlooked anything there, and strolled into the coal shed. He was emerging from this when he noticed a small ball of buff paper on the ground. He picked it up, and found it to be a telegram and envelope rolled up together. The envelope bore the name of Gertrude Cartwright, and the message ran as follows:

Station end of Common to-morrow morning ten o'clock. — Ted.

The corner of the telegram containing the post office stamp was missing. McLean spent the best part of half an hour searching for it, and finally he had to give it up. Daniels, having finished his job, came round the end of the house.

"I wondered where you had vanished to," he said. "Hallo, what have you got there?"

"A small thing you overlooked. One good turn deserves another. Have a glance at it."

Daniels did so and whistled.

"As I expected — a rendezvous! Who the devil is Ted, and where was this sent from?"

"Cartwright may be able to throw some light on that."

"But he swore — !"

"I should ask him all the same. I'll come with you."

They re-entered the house and Cartwright was called. He entered the sitting-room with a glum expression on his face.

"Do you know a man whose Christian name is Ted?" asked Daniels.

Cartwright seemed to wince, but he shook his head.

"Are you aware that your wife received a telegram either on the night before her disappearance, or on the actual morning?"

"No. But I — "

"Go on."

"I heard the bell ring rather late in the evening, and my wife went to the door. When she returned she said it was a motorist inquiring the way. Was it — was it a telegram?"

"You are prepared for a slight shock?" asked Daniels.

"What — what do you mean?"

"Read this!"

The telegram was passed to Cartwright. His mouth opened slowly, and then closed displaying his clenched teeth.

"I — never guessed," he said hoarsely. "No — no, it's all wrong. She couldn't do a thing like that. I should have known. I should have guessed."

Then he collapsed in the chair and buried his head in his hands. McLean smiled to himself.

★ ★ ★

That same evening McLean interviewed a girl named Amy Floyd, who hailed from a village some three miles distant. She was a robust girl, good-looking and intelligent; and was evidently surprised at

212

being visited in this manner.

"You were employed by Mrs. Cartwright until just recently?"

"Yes, sir. I left only a few days ago."

"Why did you leave?"

"It was Mr. Cartwright — I couldn't stand him. He found fault with my cooking, and told me that if I couldn't do better I would have to clear out. He said it so rudely that I told him I would go right away — and would make him a present of the wages that were due to me."

"What did Mrs. Cartwright say?"

"She tried to get me to stay on, but I had made up my mind. I left that evening."

"How long were you with the Cartwrights?"

"Six months."

"Did you ever overhear them quarrelling?"

"No. They seemed to be quite happy together."

"Did they use the sitting-room much?"

"Oh, yes. When Mr. Cartwright was home he used to sit there and read quite a lot. Mrs. Cartwright used to do needlework and darning there."

"You remember that room well?"

"Why, of course."

"I have here a photograph taken this morning. Examine it well and tell me if the room is very much the same as when you saw it last."

She took the print, which had been hastily made, and was still damp. It was a highly successful snapshot, and showed the room looking towards the fire-place.

"It's just the same," she said. " I don't believe a single thing has been touched."

"I think you are wrong."

"No."

"Look at the carpet."

"The carpet is all right. The end used — Oh, I see now — there is something missing. The hearthrug has gone."

"So I concluded. I believe it was oval in shape, and about five feet in length. The stain is badly worn all round it, but comparatively good underneath. Describe that rug."

"It was oval, as you said — and hand-made, in blue wool. Mrs. Cartwright was always making things to save expense. It was there when I left. I saw it."

"Before I took the photograph I removed a square piece of carpet from before the fireplace. It was red and black and had a stain in one corner."

"That must have been brought down from the bedroom. It was always used there."

"Thank you. That is all I want to know — at present."

He tipped her and went again to the house on the common. Cartwright was apparently out, so he filled up time by examining the garden again. For over an hour he probed everywhere, and then Daniels came back.

"I'm just going off," he said. "The whole thing seems to be pretty clear. She just went off with her lover, and left her husband guessing. The excuse about the newspaper boy not arriving was quite genuine. He was ill that morning. Cute sort of woman, I should imagine. Well, I dare say we shall find her, and leave the matter for Cartwright to deal with."

"I don't think you will find her," replied McLean.

Daniels eyed him narrowly.

"What are you hiding, Mac?"

"Not much. At the moment I am concerned about an oval home-made hearthrug in blue wool. I shouldn't go back yet, if I were you. If we fail to find that hearthrug, you may take it from me that all we are ever likely to find of Mrs. Cartwright is her dead body."

"But — !"

"S-sh! Here comes Cartwright. Say nothing about the hearthrug. We will look over the house together."

Cartwright expressed his surprise at seeing them both back again. He said he had been thinking over matters, and had been obliged to change his mind about his wife. Could it be kept out of the newspapers? The village was a terrible place for gossip. His life would be made unbearable once the truth leaked out.

"I'll see what can be done," promised Daniels. "But we should like to look over the house again."

"Certainly, but there is no doubt now — "

They were shown upstairs first of all, and McLean noticed that the front double bedroom was devoid of a hearthrug. While they were still on the upper floor Daniels expressed a desire to be alone with McLean. Cartwright nodded and went downstairs.

"The hearthrug is not up here," he said. "What is the idea?"

"Until a day or two ago that oval hearthrug was before the fire-place in the sitting-room. Now it is replaced by another brought from up here. People do not pawn hearth-rugs, nor sell them when there are other things to be sold first. Why should a man destroy a hearthrug?"

"I get you there. Bloodstains. But the motive — I can't find it. His wife had no money. He would not benefit by her death. Moreover he called you in when there was positively no need to do that. The police is another matter. Obviously he must do something to express a desire to have the mystery solved. And the telegram and fragments of those love letters?"

"Daniels, there is one point I am amazed you should have overlooked. Nowhere among those fragments was there either a date or a signature. The telegram, too, had a very important corner missing. That is stretching coincidence too far. I am convinced that Cartwright himself sent that telegram, and found among his wife's papers some old love-letters of his own, fortunately typewritten. Though professing to believe absolutely in his wife, he meant us to discover her apparent infidelity, and after due reflection he accepts the inevitable like a broken-hearted and completely disillusioned husband. All very well staged — so far."

"I see. He tore the corner off the telegram in order to make it difficult for us to find the office of origin."

"Yes, but he has failed."

"How?"

"That telegram would have to arrive after his wife's death. We know that she was alive and well on the previous evening. If Cartwright murdered her that night he would not have time to go far to get that telegram off. We will give him a radius of twenty miles. Some post office within that perimeter has the original message. First we will find that."

"There is something else to be found," said Daniels grimly.

"The corpse — yes. I have been

218

looking for that, but it is cunningly hidden. We will continue our search for the hearthrug, but I fear it will be vain."

They went over every remaining part of the house, and the oval hearthrug remained missing.

★ ★ ★

Within twenty-four hours it was proved that the telegram had been handed in at a post office some eight miles from Fargate. The wording on the original form was in capital letters, and the name of the sender was given as Edward Hammond, at an address which turned out to be false. It was received between ten and eleven o'clock on the morning when Mrs. Cartwright was alleged to have disappeared, but the unobservant clerk stated that he could not remember the person who gave him the form, as he was very busy at the time.

"By Jove, you were right," said Daniels. "The telegram was sent after Cartwright swore his wife left the house. That means that he himself must have received the telegram, and left it about as a red herring across the trail."

The boy who delivered the telegram was found. He stated that he found no one at the house, and slipped it into the letter-box. The time as near as possible was eleven-thirty.

"Long before that Mrs. Cartwright was dead," said McLean. "Two things remain to be recovered — the motive and the body. We will have Mr. Cartwright watched, and visit the house while he is off the premises."

Daniels was agreeable, and for the next day or two Cartwright was kept under close observation. One afternoon he packed a suitcase and went off in the direction of the railway station. Half an hour later McLean and Daniels were inside the house. They attacked floorboards, old cisterns, every possible place that might conceal a corpse, but found nothing.

"It must be in the garden," said McLean. "He disposed of the body quickly — we know that, and he has no car. I very much doubt if he is the kind of man to engage in any dismembering. That requires a quite different temperament."

They repaired to the overgrown garden, Daniels working along the north side of it, and McLean the south. Both men looked especially for newly turned up soil, but there was no trace of such. At last they met, and Daniels mopped his brow.

"Beaten," he muttered.

He pulled out a cigarette case, extracted a cigarette and struck a match on the body of a large Cupid which was poised on a substantial pedestal. The Cupid moved a little, and McLean put his hand to it. To his surprise it was quite light — a mere plaster imitation of marble. A lift and the figure came clean off the pedestal. Swiftly McLean's gaze went to the large circular base. It did not quite fit into the depression in the long rank grass. It had been moved!

"Lend me a hand," he said.

But there was scarcely any need, for the top of the pedestal was separate from the bottom, making the whole thing easily movable. At last the bottom was shifted. Beneath it were damp boards covering a circular hole.

"An old well!"

"Yes. I think we are getting pretty warm now. Up with those boards!"

They were removed and McLean leaned over the deep hole and peered down.

"Can you see — anything?"

"Yes — it's there. There is something half covering the face. The oval rug, I imagine. We shall need a rope."

This was brought from an outbuilding, and Daniels volunteered to go down. Some time later the dead form of Mrs. Cartwright was brought to light. The well proved to be dry, and the crimson stain was still on the blue rug. Across the woman's temple was a long, deep gash. They carried the body into the house.

★ ★ ★

Very late that night Cartwright returned home. As soon as he opened the front door the light went up and he saw Daniels and McLean standing in the hall.

"This — this is unexpected!" he gasped.

"Excuse our breaking in," said Daniels

222

calmly. "But we have something interesting to show you — in the sitting-room."

Cartwright's eyes moved nervously as he passed by the two men and entered his sitting-room. They went in after him, and suddenly switched on the light. Lying on the couch was the still form of his late wife. Cartwright let loose a cry of horror, put his hands to his eyes and tried to blunder out, but he came up against McLean, who pushed him back. Then he took his hands away and saw Daniels dangling a pair of handcuffs.

"I am going to arrest you for the murder of your — "

"Wait — wait!" he almost screamed. "It is all wrong. I — I didn't do it — not what you think. It wasn't murder. It was an accident."

"You can tell that to the — "

"Let him speak, Daniels, if he wants to," begged McLean. "He is telling the truth. Cartwright, what happened on that night? You quarrelled with your wife about something. What was it?"

Cartwright moistened his lips several times before he could speak.

"It — it was a letter. My wife opened it

by mistake. This — this is it. Read it."

He produced a letter bearing an address up country. McLean took it and read it for Daniels' benefit:

My Darling,

For God's sake come and see me again. G. has to go to Glasgow for the week end. I shall be all alone. Wire me and tell me that you will come —

There was much more, all couched in very intimate vein, and the thing was sun-clear. Daniels winced.

"What happened then?" he asked.

"She was in a towering rage — quite hysterical. I never thought she would take it like that. I lied to her — tried to explain, but she ran for her hat and coat and swore she would leave me at once. I caught her and brought her back here, struggling. She was mad — quite mad with jealous rage. She picked up a table knife, and struck me — here." He turned up his sleeve and exposed a wound. "I — I pushed her savagely and she fell with a crash. She — she didn't get up, and when I stooped down to look at her I realised that she had hit her head on the left dog-iron as she fell. It was bleeding on to the blue rug. I was going to call the police, but I feared the result of investigation. I remembered the old well that was filled in ten years ago, and I carried her there — also the rug. After that — "

"We know what happened after that," interrupted Daniels. "Now you must come along."

Cartwright was ultimately tried and sentenced. The judge was comparatively gentle with him, and Inspector Daniels was complimented upon his excellent work. It was just another of those fairly numerous cases out of which McLean got nothing but self-satisfaction.

10

SIR RANDOLPHE CUNLIFFE entered the lounge of his palatial house to find McLean gazing out into the garden, which at this time of the year was a riot of colour. It was scarcely an hour since he had telephoned, and his surprise at the prompt response was clearly marked on his aristocratic face.

"I scarcely expected you so soon," he said. "But the sooner the better. I am gravely disturbed."

"About your son?"

"Yes. That is he — painted two years ago."

He indicated a full-length portrait in oils of a fine-looking young man. McLean had already seen it and taken in every detail.

"Looks fit enough," he mused.

"He was, until — It is the old story — too much leisure and the wrong set of friends."

"Last night things came to a climax.

I sent him packing."

"I am sorry to hear that. You had a definite reason, of course?"

"A dozen reasons. The boy is making a hash of his life. At Cambridge he got mixed up with an indolent fast set of men. He gambles, refuses to work, and generally behaves as if life were nothing but a kind of joke. Among his degraded acquaintances is a man named de Wynter."

McLean's eyes narrowed a trifle. Here was de Wynter cropping up again like the bad penny. Sir Randolphe did not miss the slight start and the grim expression.

"You know that man?" he asked.

"Very well indeed. But please continue. Am I to understand that you have cut off your son's allowance?"

"Yes — so far as my personal estate is concerned. But his mother, who spoilt him with the very best of motives, left him a large sum of money in his own right. In a month or two he will come of age, so my drastic action doesn't worry him much."

"What do you wish me to do?"

"Watch him on my behalf. I like Cecil.

He has many fine traits, but I will never tolerate drunkenness in my house. He is heading for the rocks, as fast as he can go. My chief concern is to save him from his so-called friends. I know that this de Wynter person is an unscrupulous adventurer — and I believe there is a woman in it too. Cecil is headstrong — impetuous. He thinks he knows the world, and these people flatter him, and pluck him at the same time. Unless some strong action is taken I fear he will go to the dogs completely."

"Where can I find him?"

"I don't know, but it is not unlikely he has gone to stay at his club — the Grosvenor. At any rate they will know where he can be found. For obvious reasons I don't want him to suspect that I am taking this step. I can trust you to be discreet?"

"Discretion is certainly necessary where de Wynter is concerned. I rather welcome the chance of putting a spoke in his wheel. I will keep you posted up as to developments."

McLean congratulated himself on the journey home. Nothing pleased him more than a case in which de Wynter was involved. That cunning master of crime was a worthy antagonist. Well educated, well travelled, possessed of an alert brain, he could always be depended upon to put up a fight. For months McLean had heard nothing of him, and he imagined he was abroad on some dishonest venture. But his interest in the heir of the wealthy shipbuilder made it certain that he would keep in close touch with his intended victim. Cecil Cunliffe was therefore the link between McLean and the man who shattered his police career.

No time was lost in getting on to the trail of young Cunliffe. McLean spent an hour in his bedroom changing his appearance. With his naturally abundant bristly hair plastered down on his head, and parted in the centre with geometrical precision, a tooth-brush sandy moustache, and a monocle attached to a broad black ribbon, he looked like the latest product of a Bond Street beauty parlour. He had already rung up the Grosvenor Club and been told that Cecil Cunliffe was staying there. He now resolved to go along and introduce himself. The card he presented bore the name of Lord Tiverton — a fairly safe impersonation, as Lord Tiverton was at that moment many thousands of miles away — and likely to stay away.

"I am sorry, your lordship," said the commissionaire. "But Mr. Cunliffe is not in the club."

"You have no idea where he is dining?"

"Yes. I telephoned a short time ago booking a table for him at the Zig-Zag Club. I think he is entertaining some friends there."

"It is possible I may meet him. In any case please give him my card when he returns, and inform him that I may look back later in the evening."

The Zig-Zag Club was a new venture in the West End, and was already exceedingly popular. It catered chiefly for the indolent rich — especially for the younger generation. One had to be a member to gain admission, but McLean soon got over that difficulty. He went to the club and waited until a member arrived with a party of guests. By hanging on to the man's tail he conveyed the impression that he belonged to the party.

The big main room was already packed, and exceedingly noisy. A negro band was playing the latest jazz tunes, and a half-nude woman was giving a display of the crudest kind of dance in a small space set apart. McLean had some difficulty in finding a seat that suited him, for the simple reason that he was searching for Cecil Cunliffe. At last he detected the boy seated at a table with three other persons. He chose a vacant seat as near them as possible. Now he could scrutinise the boy at leisure. There was a noticeable difference between his present appearance and the portrait in Sir Randolphe's lounge. Upon the handsome face was stamped the indelible signs of immoderate living, and the hands played nervously with things on the table.

The boy's companions were all older than he. They were two women and a man. The man was dark and sinister, with oily eyes set close to a large nose, and repulsive lips. The woman on his right had no looks to recommend her, and was in no respect attractive. But the other woman was a beauty. She was scantily attired, displaying as much of her fine figure as decency would permit. Her shoulders were beautifully formed, and her features classic. She too was dark, but with a strange romantic beauty. Between courses she smoked, and her eyes always went to the boy, who was already flushed with champagne. The situation was perfectly clear to McLean. Here was the decoy — the incomparable siren. Next her was the poor victim. The other man and woman were simply stage 'props' — and the manager of the show was not on view — de Wynter.

As the evening advanced the party grew exceedingly merry. Corks were constantly popping, and the table became littered with cigarette ends. The big-nosed man danced with his partner, and the boy danced with the siren. By ten o'clock the boy was mildly intoxicated, but he still drank between dances, and McLean's face grew hard as he realised how far gone the boy was.

At eleven o'clock the party prepared to leave, the big-nosed man lending the boy an arm to keep him steady on his feet. McLean guessed that in the circumstances Cunliffe would go straight to his club, so he contrived to get there first. He was sitting in the vestibule when Cunliffe arrived. The commissionaire handed him McLean's card.

"Lord Tiverton," hiccoughed Cunliffe. "Name seems a bit familiar. Where is he?"

The commissionaire indicated McLean, and Cunliffe made his way across. McLean stood up and tendered his apologies.

"Sorry to call so late. As a matter of fact my young brother — John Curry — was at Cambridge with you. He asked me to look you up when I was in town."

Cunliffe looked pleased, and wrung McLean's hand.

"Now I've got you," he said. "I knew I'd heard your name mentioned. So you're John's brother who went abroad? Jolly glad to meet you. Splendid — hic — splendid fellow, John. Got our rowing blues together. Rotten luck him having to go to Canada. I should hate it. Give me jolly old London Town. Are you staying long?"

"A week or two."

"Good! What about a bit of dinner to-morrow — and a show? I can show you all the bright spots."

McLean was agreeable. It was all he hoped to accomplish that evening. On the following day he met Cunliffe, and found him completely sober — and contrite.

"Afraid I had one over the eight last night. Met some friends and went the pace a bit. Fact is I had a fearful row with the guv'nor the night before, and felt desperate."

"Nothing serious, I hope?"

"Yes — damned serious. The pater loves to treat me as if I were a child in petticoats. He doesn't seem to realise that this is the twentieth century. Doesn't approve of my way of living, my friends. Well, it had to come. Thank God, I'll be of age in a few weeks. I'm sick of being hard up."

"But if your father — "

"Oh, I'm not expecting a bean from him. He made that pretty clear. I've some money of my own coming along. Useful little packet — about fifty thousand pounds, and when I get it — In the meantime I have to depend upon friends for loans. Not a nice state of affairs, but thank heavens it is nearly over."

During the next week McLean made it his business to see a good deal of Cunliffe. There was much that he admired in him. He was generous, clean in speech and thought, humorous at times. But his worst enemy was his impetuosity. He would suddenly get an idea, and start to put it into practice without a moment's consideration. On one occasion he mentioned de Wynter.

"Jolly good sort. He knows the old man and his old-fashioned ways, and has been a friend all along. With my allowance cut off, I had to get money on the strength of my legacy. Winnie wouldn't let me go to a money-lender. He lends me what I need and won't hear a word about interest, but of course I shall insist upon paying it."

McLean smiled. The idea of de Wynter playing the part of benevolent friend was too funny. It was clear that the scoundrel had completely won the boy's confidence and trust, and was playing a cunning game of his own. When the time was ripe, he would swoop down like a vulture and make mince-meat of his trumpeter.

★ ★ ★

At last McLean achieved the first part of his programme. He was now hail-fellow-well-met with Cunliffe, who called him 'Tivvy' and eagerly sought his company. He was particularly keen for 'Tivvy' to meet some bosom pals of his.

"Mr. de Wynter?" asked McLean.

"Not at the moment. He is in Paris. Some other people. I have told them I am bringing you along to their flat to-night, for a bit of food. Now, no excuses! You'll like them immensely. Do you play bridge?"

"A little."

"Good! There will be five of us, but we can cut in. Shall I call for you, or will you pick me up at the club?"

It was agreed that McLean should call at the Grosvenor. This he did, and Cunliffe took him along to a well-appointed flat in Kensington. Cunliffe's friends turned out to be the same clique that McLean had seen at the Zig-Zag

Club. The big-nosed man was introduced as Walter Livingstone, and the plain woman as his sister — Kate. The dark eyed beauty carried a Russian name — Nalda Kishnov, and she spoke with a rather captivating lisp.

"Now we all know each other," said Cunliffe. "Walter, I warn you that 'Tivvy' had been most carefully brought up, and I don't want his morals ruined by any un-drawing-room-like remarks. Besides, we ought to set an example before the peerage."

They all laughed and ultimately sat down to a most amazing meal. Its richness and variety would have put most hotels to shame, and the quantity of drink in the centre of the table was sufficient to have stocked a small bar. Nalda sat next to Cunliffe, and was constantly touching him — almost caressing him. Throughout the meal the bottles were kept very busy, and the quartet became very lively. McLean played the part of a simpleton, and pretended to be mildly intoxicated.

"Lord, you are going it, Tivvy," said Cunliffe. "You've actually blossomed. Well, what about a rubber at bridge?"

McLean excused himself with the plea that he felt slightly dazed, so the other four cut for partners, and left McLean lounging on a settee close to the table. It was a wonderful game that he watched through half-closed eyes. Livingstone was undoubtedly a professional card-sharp, and the two women possessed a code. Cunliffe seemed to hold good cards, but he scarcely ever won a hand.

The score against him — at one pound a hundred — rose and rose. But he took his bad luck sportingly.

"No use," he said at last. "My luck is right out. How much do I owe altogether?"

"Twenty-seven pounds, ten shillings."

"We'll call it thirty, and I'll give you an IOU. Will that be satisfactory?"

"Absolutely."

"Here you are, then. Good lord! There's Tivvy fast asleep!"

Nalda threw a cushion at the recumbent form, and McLean opened his eyes and blinked. Then he found his monocle, and was about to expostulate when the bell rang in a curious way. Cunliffe looked at Livingstone and grinned.

"It's de Wynter! He's back from Paris, Tivvy. I'm keen for you to meet de Wynter. He's a regular sport."

Half a minute later Arnaud de Wynter entered. He was as immaculate as ever, calm and collected in the face of a vociferous greeting. Kate vacated the most comfortable chair for him, and Cunliffe slapped him on the back.

"Just in time for a peg. Oh — this is a friend of mine — Lord Tiverton."

McLean came forward and bowed. He saw de Wynter's eyes focused intently on him — and he saw in a second that his disguise was useless on this occasion. But de Wynter contented himself with bowing.

"Charmed to meet his lordship," he said.

Followed some drinking, and more card-playing, at which Cunliffe lost as before. Ultimately McLean intimated that he desired to seek his bed. De Wynter was sitting out that rubber.

"I'll see his lordship to the door," he said. "You four carry on."

Out in the passage the two men faced each other — McLean calm and de

Wynter burning with ill-concealed hate.

"What do you want here, McLean?"

"I am interested in certain spheres of social life, as you should know."

"You are playing a dangerous game."

"Not more dangerous than yours. I see you have another lamb ready for shearing. I am rather hoping it won't materialise."

"So you haven't yet learned to mind your own business?"

"On the contrary, I am minding it now."

"Do you think he will listen to any lies from you?"

"I am quite sure he will not even listen to the truth. He is far too dazzled to make use of his natural intelligence. Only when his nice little legacy is inside your pockets will he listen to plain sense. But that hasn't happened yet."

De Wynter laughed scathingly.

"May I remind you that you no longer have the police force behind you? We are man to man now, and I warn you that people who make it a habit to threaten me usually meet with most unsatisfactory ends."

McLean put on his hat and twirled his cane within an inch of de Wynter's nose.

"We will leave it at that," he said. "By the way, your friend Livingstone is still as dexterous as ever with his hands. He has a veritable ace-factory up his sleeve. In the words of your native country — *au revoir!*"

★ ★ ★

With the sword now unsheathed, McLean went into battle. He strove to see Cunliffe again, and was not greatly surprised when he received a haughty note from the boy:

I have just learned that Lord Tiverton is in Africa. Please do not attempt to speak to me again.

Here again was the hand of de Wynter, but it had not the slightest effect upon McLean. It was essential now to tell the boy the truth, and he sought every opportunity to do so. But some time passed before he succeeded in cornering

Cunliffe. It happened in the American bar of a Piccadilly hotel, when only Cunliffe and himself were present. Cunliffe's eyes flashed resentfully when he saw McLean at his elbow.

"I should like a word with you," said McLean.

"I have nothing to say to you."

"Please sit down."

"I tell you — "

McLean literally pushed him into a chair, and sat opposite him, in such a position that it was impossible for him to pass without physical force.

"Young man," said McLean. "You are in the hands of an unscrupulous gang who will pluck you — ruin you — and fling you aside. De Wynter — "

"De Wynter is a gentleman, and you are nothing but an impostor. I can see your game. You accuse him of doing what you tried vainly to do yourself."

"Thank you! Now listen to me. Unless you cut yourself adrift from that crowd you are doomed. That was my sole object in an assumed name — to see to what length you had gone."

Cunliffe suddenly got an inspiration.

"Now I understand. You are a hireling of my father's. He is at the bottom of all this. Well, you can go back to him and tell him that I object to be spied upon, and that I intend to lead my own life in my own way. De Wynter has been my best friend, and I am not going to forsake him just because my father has old-fashioned prudish ideas. You can tell him, too, that in a very short time I shall be married."

McLean knew what that meant. The boy had not slept at his club for the past two nights. De Wynter had furthered his scheme — everything had gone as he had planned it. Doubtless the boy had compromised himself with Nalda, and had done the only decent thing, from his way of thinking — offered her marriage. Within three weeks he would come into his legacy. How long would that last with Nalda as his wife, and de Wynter pulling the purse strings all the time?

It was necessary to report the state of affairs to Sir Randolphe. The fine old man was deeply affected. His worst fears were practically realised.

"Poor boy! Perhaps I ought to have

been more patient. But I will save him yet. You must buy that woman off. I can't have my son's whole life ruined. Will you see that scoundrel, and the girl, and come to terms with them?"

"Not yet. There may be other means. Their terms to you would be harsh. De Wynter has been playing for this situation. Either he takes toll from you — or from your son later through the wife he means to provide. But there is many a slip . . . You must trust me to act for the best. I intend to pay our friend de Wynter a visit — a rather informal call."

Followed some good work on McLean's part. One night de Wynter's flat was entered, without its owner knowing the slightest thing about it. Drawers were turned out, and things replaced as they were found. Ultimately McLean took away with him a document which he believed was the key to the whole situation. On the following morning he was called to the telephone, and to his surprise he recognised young Cunliffe's voice.

"Is that Mr. McLean? I was told that

is your real name. I must see you at once. Will you — will you come down and see me?"

There was entreaty in the voice — genuine emotion. McLean decided to go to the Grosvenor at once, and within a quarter of an hour he was closeted with Cunliffe. The boy's face was flushed — his expression one of remorse and humiliation.

"I owe you an apology," he mumbled. "You — you were right about de Wynter. I must have been blind. The wedding is fixed for to-morrow. I was twenty-one years of age yesterday. For some days I have been wondering what to give Nalda for a present. De Wynter suggested a pearl necklace and told me he could get one at a reduced price. Last night he bought it. I had no money — not until I see my solicitor to-morrow. De Wynter said it didn't matter. An IOU would suit him just as well. I gave him one for six thousand pounds — "

"Six thousand?"

"He said the necklace was valued at ten thousand. Later in the evening I happened to show the necklace to a club member who is an expert. He told me it wasn't worth five pounds."

"Ah, so at last you are disillusioned! And this marriage — don't you realise it is all a plant? Either your father pays now — or you do later. Nalda is his tool. She will bleed you like a vampire."

Cunliffe bit his lip and hung his head dejectedly.

"I — I have committed myself," he confessed. "I don't know how it all came about. I went to de Wynter's house, and drank a lot. Nalda was there, and I stayed the night. There seemed to be only one thing to do — afterwards."

"There is a limit to scruples of conscience. You must call the wedding off."

"If I did that she would get me for breach. What a hash I have made of things! I see it all now — "

"You don't. There will be no marriage and no damages. Now you must do exactly as I advise. Get on to de Wynter and give him to understand that you wish to redeem the IOU's — early to-morrow morning. Tell him to come here, and to bring Nalda with him."

"But — !"

"Fix the time for ten o'clock. I will arrange to be here before that."

Cunliffe carried out these instructions, and at ten o'clock the next morning he and McLean were waiting for de Wynter and Nalda in a private room at the Grosvenor. Punctually on the stroke of ten came the two confederates. De Wynter entered the room jauntily, and then scowled as he saw McLean.

"What the devil — !"

"Sit down," said McLean sweetly. "You too, Miss Kishnov. Mr. Cunliffe has appointed me his legal adviser, and I have advised him not to get married."

Nalda smiled, and de Wynter laughed amusedly.

"Rather a sudden change of mind," he said. "But of course, if he feels like that, it cannot be helped. It is simply a question of damages. We should prefer to discuss that with a proper solicitor."

"It never occurred to me," said McLean. "The easiest way is for Miss Kishnov to write a letter freeing Mr. Cunliffe. There is a pen — and paper."

"Shall we talk sense for a change,"

sneered de Wynter. "Is there to be a wedding or not?"

"Most decidedly not."

"In that case we will not stay."

"Wait! I want that letter — now — "

"You must be mad."

"Not a bit." McLean produced a thin, black book. "I have here an interesting passport. It is made out to Mr. de Wynter and wife, and was last stamped at Dover — "

"You thief!" roared de Wynter.

"The wife bears such a striking resemblance to Miss Kishnov that I fancy any person would swear she — "

De Wynter struck the table with his fist.

"You don't get me that way," he snarled. "Lydia was never my wife. She is as free to marry as any woman."

"Then you evidently made a false statement," cut in McLean. "And, in the circumstances, I rather think the authorities would take a serious view of it. The penalty exacted might be a trifle hard on you, de Wynter. Hadn't we better do a swop — the letter for the passport?"

De Wynter saw the corner he had been pushed into. He bit his lip in silent rage and hesitated. Nalda, however, took the situation coolly.

"What am I to do?" she asked.

"Nothing," snarled de Wynter.

"Very good," said McLean. "The choice is entirely with you. I will retain the passport."

He was putting it into his pocket when de Wynter changed his mind.

"Tell her what you want her to write," he snapped.

McLean dictated the wording and Nalda wrote the letter. McLean took it and nodded.

"One more little thing," he said. "You have a particular IOU against Mr. Cunliffe for six thousand pounds. I have here a beautiful necklace worth — er — ten thousand. We will do another swop. Mr. Cunliffe will liquidate the other little notes — later on."

De Wynter scowled, and then produced the required note. He swept up the imitation pearls and thrust them into his pocket.

"That is all I think," said McLean.

At the door de Wynter turned his head and glared at McLean.

"We have our ups and downs," he said. "To-day — you are up — a little bit, but to-morrow — "

He slammed the door noisily, and McLean sighed.

"A million thanks," said Cunliffe, gripping his hand. "What a conceited ignorant ass I have been!"

"You have."

"What am I to do now?"

"I would suggest you go to your father, and repeat the last remark."

"By Jove — I will. I'm through with this kind of life. It's time I got a job."

McLean walked home later, feeling quite pleased with himself. It was not every day one could win hands down against de Wynter, and even now that cunning scoundrel had a long lead. But McLean could afford to wait. Give the devil enough rope and he would hang himself!

11

SHE had given her name as Agnes Dillington, and now sat before McLean moving her beautiful hands nervously and generally displaying all the symptoms of one who has much to conceal. McLean had begged her to make clear her business, but a long time passed before she could control her voice sufficiently for her to begin.

"It was three years ago when it happened," she said. "I was barely twenty then, and left to my own resources, on account of my father's sudden death — following my mother's. I imagined he was well off, but discovered afterwards that the house was mortgaged and that he had saved nothing from his army pension. It was necessary for me to find work, and I searched everywhere. Ultimately I saw an advertisement for a girl clerk in a solicitor's office, and I went for a personal interview. The advertisement did not state that experience was necessary, but I was told that that was so, and although they were very kind they were not willing to risk my inexperience. After disappointment upon disappointment this was the last straw, and I broke down as I was leaving the office. A well-dressed man in the waiting-room saw me, and thought I was ill. He came to my aid, but I explained that I — I was quite all right.

"I went to my lodgings — absolutely hopeless and penniless. The solicitors had taken my address in case they should hear of an opening which would suit me, but I concluded that was merely a — a sympathetic gesture. To my astonishment I received a letter from them the following morning, asking me to call on them again. Hopeful once more, I kept the appointment. The senior partner explained to me that he had no permanent post to offer me, but if I were willing to earn ten pounds he could put me in the way of doing it.

"I asked him to explain, and he told me that a client of his was unhappy with his wife. Both he and his wife wanted a divorce and neither had any real grounds. The wife loved another man and wanted to marry him, and the husband was willing to make the way easy for her. He had seen me on the last occasion — as I left the office, and the present interview was arranged at his behest. All I had to do was to go with Mr. St. Just to a certain hotel. He would book a double room and sign as 'Mr. and Mrs. St. Just.' There was to be a bath-room adjoining, and Mr. St. Just would sleep there. In the morning he would come in, and we should have early morning tea together. That was all. Nothing more would be asked of me. My name would never be mentioned."

"You did not take kindly to that idea?" asked McLean.

"No. I was horrified, but the solicitor said it was done every day to circumvent the ridiculous law. I said I would have nothing to do with it, and went home in anger. But when I reached my lodgings my door was fastened with a padlock, and the landlady told me I could not occupy my rooms, nor move my belongings until she received the arrears of rent. I went into the street. It was raining and miserable. I felt like suicide, and even went as far as the Embankment with that terrible idea in my mind. But as I walked the solicitor's suggestion was ringing in my brain. Why should I starve when money could be gained so easily? I could not see that anyone would suffer, since both Mr. St. Just and his wife desired to be free. Half an hour later I was in the solicitor's office agreeing to do what was necessary."

"Ah. You saw the man?"

"Later. He was telephoned for, and he met me in the office. I had a few words with him, and found him exceedingly kind and sympathetic. He assured me that there was nothing to worry about. All I had to do was to wear a wedding ring, and if I spoke to him to call him Arthur. He telephoned there and then for a bedroom at the hotel, and we drove out to it that night. Things went exactly as he had said. I soon realised that he was a charming man, and my fears vanished. On the following morning we parted and I was paid not ten pounds but twenty, at Mr. St. Just's request."

"You saw no more of him?"

"No, but some time later I saw in the newspapers the notice of an undefended action for divorce — 'misconduct with a woman unknown.' That caused me qualms of conscience until I remembered his kindness, and the motive. Well, the twenty pounds gave me a new start in life. I learned to typewrite and to do shorthand, and in due course I got a good job. I worked very hard, and was appreciated by my employer. I became his confidential secretary and all my troubles vanished. A year ago I met a young man named Lanbury, and — and fell in love with him. We became engaged two months ago and the wedding is fixed for June 23rd."

"Six weeks' time?"

"Yes, but quite recently I suffered a terrible blow. A man called at the office and asked to see me. He knew my name, and all about me, but I did not recall him until — until he asked me if I remembered his bringing early morning tea to me at the Riversdale Hotel, three years ago. I was dumbfounded, and then remembered clearly. I — I admitted it and asked him what he wanted. He said he had fallen on bad times, and needed a loan of five pounds. Could I oblige him?"

"And you did?"

"Yes."

"That was foolish."

"I know, but I wanted to be rid of him."

"That is the certain way not to be rid of him."

"That is obvious now. He came again within a week, and told me that he had the chance of taking up a post in Canada. If I would lend him twenty pounds he would undertake to repay it in monthly instalments. He wanted to cable at once, and to catch the next boat."

"And you parted again with your money?"

"I thought it was worth twenty pounds to be rid of him. He swore I should never see him again."

"He would. And when did he come again?"

"Last night. He had seen the announcement of my forthcoming marriage. He had been drinking and was less subtle. He asked me how much it was worth for him to keep silent. I tried to appear defiant, and said I would deny that I was ever at the Riversdale, but he told me that he had been clever enough to take a snapshot of me with Mr. St. Just as we were leaving the hotel. He threatened to post it to my fiancé with full details unless — unless I paid two hundred pounds."

"Ah! And the upshot?"

"I told him I wanted time to consider the matter, and he gave me two days."

"You know his name?"

"No."

"Address?"

She shook her head.

"Well, describe him as best you can."

She did so and McLean made rapid notes. Having taken her address he promised to call on her on the following evening, after he had made inquiries elsewhere. That afternoon he paid a visit to the Riversdale Hotel and learned that the blackmailer was named Thomas Pycraft. He had been a waiter there for six months, but had been dismissed because he was strongly suspected of theft. A man still in the employ of the hotel volunteered the information that Pycraft had lodged at a boarding house at an address near Paddington Station until fairly recently, but he did not know where he was at the moment.

McLean found the boarding house, and was successful enough to obtain Pycraft's present address. It was another boarding house less than half a mile away. He called there, and waited over two hours for Pycraft's return. He proved to be a man of about thirty — a shifty-eyed individual whose every action revealed the habitual crook.

"A friend of mine asked me to see you," said McLean. "A Miss Dillington."

"How did she know my address?"

"She didn't. I discovered that myself."

"Very clever. Anyway, what do you want?"

"In the first place I want to tell you that blackmail is a very dangerous occupation."

"Mind what you are saying. I know the law as well as you. I've got a photograph to sell. There's nothing illegal in that. If she won't buy it I know someone who will."

"Mr. Lanbury presumably — her

258

prospective husband?"

"Well — perhaps."

"You place a high value on it?"

"It's worth two hundred pounds — to her. I won't part with it for a penny less."

"I don't believe any such photograph exists."

"Would you like to see it?"

"Yes."

Pycraft went to a drawer and extracted a print. It was of uncommon size, and was exceedingly clear as regards detail. He held it a yard from McLean's nose, and at that distance McLean could recognise his very attractive client.

"How am I to know that you have not other copies of this?" he asked.

"You got to take my word for it. But I've got the negative, and I'll hand that over with the print. Here it is."

He displayed the negative. It was a flat film — obviously from a film pack. McLean measured it carefully with his eye.

"Be reasonable," he said. "Make it twenty pounds and I will advise her to pay up."

Pycraft laughed scornfully.

"I'm not a silly fool. She is going to make a fortunate marriage. Mr. Lanbury is the son of Lanbury, the Bond Street jeweller. She'll have tons of money after the wedding. If there's any delay I'll deal with Lanbury."

He put the print and negative away, locked the drawer and made it clear that he had no more to say. McLean sized him up fairly well. He was not new to this infamous game, and would prove a hard nut to crack. To entice him into a room elsewhere and attempt to record incriminating conversation would be useless. Pycraft knew his profession too well. Not one word would be dragged out of him anywhere where there might possibly be concealed a witness — human or otherwise.

"I'll see you to-morrow," said McLean. "I am not sure that Miss Dillington can raise the money."

"She had better," was Pycraft's parting shot.

★ ★ ★

McLean saw his fair client and related what had transpired. The girl bit her lip in her anxiety.

"Hadn't I better pay?"

"Most certainly not. One more display of weakness and you will have him battening on you for the rest of your life."

"But if he informs my fiancé it will ruin everything. Don't you see — ?"

"Please leave matters in my hands for the time being."

Again McLean went to the hotel, and there he made a discovery that caused him to nod with satisfaction. It solved one part of the problem, but not the other. In order to do that he decided to see the man in the case —

Mr. St. Just, and found him in a very comfortable flat in Bayswater. St. Just was a well-built, amiable man about town, with charming manners and a pleasant smile.

"My business is of rather an unpleasant nature," warned McLean.

"Well?"

"Do you remember a girl named Agnes Dillington?"

St. Just started, and then inclined his head.

"You once engaged her on a delicate matter of business?"

"That is so — and I rather wish I hadn't. I acted on impulse. She was down and out, and at the time I thought I was doing her a good turn. But afterwards — I don't know how to explain my feelings. I realised that she was not the type of girl one should employ — in such a manner. I can recall her clearly — a dark, wistful figure. She — she made a great impression upon me. But please continue."

"She is now being cruelly victimised by the man who came into the bedroom with morning tea. He is an unmitigated scoundrel and threatened to ruin the girl's future happiness by informing her prospective husband."

"Blackmail!"

"Yes — and quite cleverly done. He has a snapshot taken of you and her, as you left the hotel. He must have been concealed in the bushes along the drive. It is the photograph he wishes to sell for two hundred pounds."

St. Just was greatly perturbed. He walked up and down the room a few times and then stopped and came to a resolution.

"Look here, I got her into this mess, and it's my duty to get her out of it. I'll pay the ruffian, and — "

"Oh, no. I do not intend that anyone shall pay him a penny. In a few days I have every hope of clapping him into jail, but out of spite he may still inform the girl's fiancé."

"Then what is to be done?"

"It is up to you to swear that Miss Dillington is not the girl who went with you to that hotel."

"But the photograph?"

"There will be no photograph. The police will require it for other purposes. It so happens that Mr. Pycraft has cooked his own goose. The print he showed me was of unusual size. There are only two cameras that make that size of negative. Our blackmailing friend was suspected of theft at the hotel — chiefly of articles left in the care of the hotel by a guest who was called away. Among the missing articles was a German camera, loaded with a film pack. I saw Pycraft's negative, and believe it was taken with the missing camera. If the police find that camera Pycraft will go to prison, and his precious negative and print will be used as exhibits. But Mr. Lanbury will never know."

"Lanbury! Not Henry Lanbury — John Lanbury's son?"

"Yes. You know him?"

"Slightly. So that is the man she is going to marry?"

He seemed very perturbed.

"I will do anything to help her," he added. "I'll lie if need be, for the whole fault is mine. Can I see her? I should like to express my very deep regret."

"That is for her to say, but here is her address. Now I intend to visit a certain friend at Scotland Yard. I will get into touch with you again later."

Agnes Dillington, while waiting for further news from McLean, was surprised by a visit from St. Just. He looked exactly the same as when she had seen him three years before, save that his eyes were brighter — happier.

"I couldn't resist the temptation," he

said. "I have thought of you a thousand times. I wanted to come and tell you in person how dreadfully sorry I am for what I did."

"But you have no need to be sorry. You acted generously all through — and it enabled me to find my feet. You — you got your divorce?"

"My wife did."

"You are happy now?"

"Well — happier than I was. My wife was a most excellent woman, but we never succeeded in understanding each other. Perhaps it was my fault."

She felt that it couldn't have been, and liked him all the more for defending his late wife. Then he asked about her own future. Was she happy — thrilled at the thought of her approaching marriage?

"You know that, then?"

"McLean told me. He told me — everything."

"I see — that is how you found me. I wish I knew what to do. I feel like accepting that man's terms, but Mr. McLean — "

"McLean is right. You must not traffic with that scoundrel. There is every chance

265

of his going to prison."

"But that won't save me if, out of spite, Pycraft informs my fiancé."

"You can plead innocence. Refer him to me — and I will swear I have never seen you in all my life."

"Thank you," she said. "But I couldn't lie to him."

St. Just spent quite a long time with her, and his lip curled when he left her, and he reflected upon her faith in young Lanbury. He happened to know the prospective husband, and wondered that such a jewel of a girl could ever fall in love with such a man. Lanbury had had love affairs by the score, and among men he was looked upon as the worst kind of bounder, who would lie and deceive at the smallest provocation.

Meanwhile McLean had gone to Scotland Yard and interested some old friends in Pycraft. As a result a lot of secret investigations were set afoot. To delay matters McLean got into touch with Pycraft and haggled about terms. His friend — Miss Dillington — could not possibly afford to pay more than a hundred pounds. She had a relative who might help her, but it would take some days to get a reply. In the end Pycraft agreed to hold his hand for a week, but asserted emphatically that that was his limit.

"I'll get her to send a cable at once," promised McLean.

He went away chuckling, for the real object of his visit had been achieved. He had spotted another of the missing articles — a gold cigarette case.

A few days later he saw Sergeant Brook at the 'Yard,' and Brook produced several photographs. They were all of Pycraft in different guises and at different ages. In addition there were finger-prints and a terrible record.

"Five previous convictions," said Brook. "About that camera — if the negative is from a film pack, and exactly agrees as to size, I think we can get him, whether we find the camera or not."

"You won't need the camera now. In the drawer where he keeps the print and negative there is a cigarette case, marked with the initials T.B. I induced him to show me the negative again, and I saw the case . . . Presumably he hasn't risked pawning it with those initials to assist identification."

"Splendid! Then we've got him."

"Yes. But I don't want those other exhibits hawked round too openly — I mean the print and the negative."

"There will be no need, provided we can land the cigarette case. You can leave that to me."

That night Pycraft was visited by the police, and certain incriminating articles were found in his possession. He was promptly arrested. Brook rang up McLean later.

"All right," he said. "That print and negative have ceased to exist. Pycraft will get it in the neck."

★ ★ ★

Two days later Pycraft expressed a desire to see McLean, and was permitted to do so. He twisted his ugly mouth as McLean entered his cell.

"You worked this — I know. I had forgotten your name until just before they pulled me. You've been damned clever, but not clever enough. I may get a stretch, but your pretty little friend isn't going to get away with it. I had a letter written in case anything went wrong, and by this time Lanbury has got it. That settles you and her."

"Why waste my time bringing me here to tell me an obvious thing like that? It is precisely what I knew you would do. You have done her a great service — without knowing it. Well, a pleasant journey to — wherever you are going."

When McLean reached home he found St. Just there, waiting eagerly to know what had transpired.

"The letter has gone," said McLean. "He brought me there to tell me that."

"That means — "

"What?"

"Lanbury will interpret it wrongly. I know the little whelp. He hasn't a decent thought in his mind. McLean, I'm going to see him."

"To deny — everything?"

"Yes. It's the only way."

"You go too fast. At the moment you are not supposed to know that he has received such a letter."

"Agnes" — he blushed at his own

boldness — "I mean Miss Dillington is bound to hear from him soon. Have you spoken to her yet?"

"No."

"Then get her on the telephone."

This was done, and they learned that Miss Dillington had just received a letter from Lanbury, asking her to meet him that afternoon, as he had received an extraordinary communication which needed verifying.

"Yes, it is Pycraft taking his revenge," said McLean. "Will you come here and see me first?"

She agreed to do this, and St. Just intimated that he wished to stay. Half an hour later Agnes Dillington called. Her face was pale, but she seemed very composed.

"Already he judges me harshly," she said. "His letter is cold and domineering."

"You must deny everything," put in St. Just. "Later I will call and tell him it is all an infamous lie, and that if necessary I will produce the woman who went with me — "

She cut him short by shaking her head vigorously.

"No. I shall tell him the truth. Isn't that best, Mr. McLean?"

To St. Just's astonishment McLean was in entire agreement. When Miss Dillington had gone, St. Just turned on McLean.

"Why did you encourage her to risk her whole future? You don't know Lanbury."

"Don't I? I am accustomed to finding out things about people connected with cases in which I am interested. She will tell him the truth and he won't believe her. Even if he did, his proper pride would be so shocked he would ask her to return his ring."

"But that means — ?"

"Freedom for her."

"Good God! Is that what you are planning?"

"Yes."

"Why?"

"Well, she is rather too nice a girl for Mr. Henry Lanbury. I have noticed that she is not so thrilled with the prospects of her marriage with him as a girl deeply in love might expect to be. And this has been even more obvious since — since she met you again."

St. Just started. He glared at McLean, but McLean remained quite unruffled.

"Is that a startling proposition?" he asked.

"Don't you think she is rather — charming?"

St. Just stared through the window for a few seconds and then faced McLean.

"You're right," he said. "I love her."

"Then why waste time? She has gone to Lanbury's house. You know his address."

St. Just grabbed his hat and stick, and then McLean by the hand.

"You're a subtle devil to have brought this situation about. I've been lonely, but now — Lord, I hope he acts up to his rotten reputation."

"He will. Good-day — and good luck!"

★ ★ ★

An hour later Agnes Dillington emerged from Lanbury's house. She found a big car waiting outside, and standing by it was St. Just.

"Forgive me," he said. "I simply had to come — to know — "

"It is all over," she said with a wan smile.

"He flew into a rage and started to ask me questions — horrible questions. I — I knew then that he mistrusted me, and somehow — somehow I realised it had all been a dreadful mistake. I gave him back his ring."

A smile of immense joy passed over St. Just's face. He opened the door of the car, and she stepped in, seating herself beside the steering wheel.

"I scarcely thought that Mr. McLean would fail," she mused.

"Fail!" He laughed merrily. "Are you sure he failed? His chief idea was to make you happy. If that isn't yet a fact, I believe it is going to be."

It was only later that she discovered exactly what he meant to imply, and three months later McLean attended a quiet little wedding at which Agnes Dillington became Mrs. St. Just.

12

IT was towards the end of a miserable November day that McLean came home to be told that a Mr. John Bancroft had been waiting to see him for over half an hour. He scanned the card which Tiny gave him, and saw that it bore an address — Mingate Manor.

"I had no appointment, Tiny."

"No, sir. The gentleman rang up twice, and said he had been advised to see you. I told him I expected you home about seven o'clock and he said he would call and take his chance."

"You can show him in."

John Bancroft was accordingly shown into McLean's reception-room. He was a big, hard-jawed man of about fifty years of age, and as soon as he spoke it was evident that he hailed from America. But apart from a slight nasal drawl his speech was excellent, and he somehow conveyed the impression of wealth and position.

"I'm sorry to call without an appointment,

Mr. McLean," he said. "But I was advised to come to you by a friend at whose house I have just passed the night. I need your help."

"In what connection?"

"I had better introduce myself. My home is in Boston, where I am fairly well known. In fact my family has lived there ever since my ancestor landed there over three hundred years ago, on the *Mayflower*. It was my ancestor who built Mingate Manor — Joshua Bancroft. It has always been my wife's desire to see the home of the founder of our family, and recently an opportunity came whereby I was enabled to rent the Manor for a year — during the absence of the Earl of Mingate. I brought my family from Boston, and they are now enjoying themselves — up to a point. But our peace of mind is disturbed by strange occurrences. The Manor is reputed to be haunted."

"Most old English houses are."

"But this is more than a rumour. There are most certainly other persons in the house than my family and our servants. I was sceptical myself until a few days ago, when I actually saw strange figures in one of the corridors. My wife knows nothing of this, but I believe my son knows."

"You saw — what did you see?"

"Two forms clad in a sort of black monkish gown. They were at the far end of a corridor, and vanished before I could reach them. I am not a nervous man, and not subject to hallucinations. These figures were real, and I am baffled to know what it means."

"You have not missed any property?"

"No."

"You have not advised the police?"

"No. I am anxious not to unnerve my wife. That is my object in begging your help. I should like to get a helper who would come in the capacity of guest. It is impossible to sit quiet while these visitations are going on."

"How long has the estate been in the Mingate family?"

"Ever since old Joshua Bancroft was exiled. He got into trouble and was forced to flee the country. We have found an old diary of his which makes it clear that he fought a duel with a favourite at the Court. He killed his man, but received a bullet in his intestines at the same time. When he recovered he sold his house to the first Earl of Mingate and joined the Pilgrims at Plymouth. In New England he prospered and laid the foundations of a considerable fortune. We know little of his life prior to his sailing — apart from what the diary reveals. In Boston we have a fairly complete set of portraits of all the Bancrofts — except Joshua. It is my wife's ambition to find one on this side. I must tell you that the local superstition is that old Joshua does not rest quietly in his grave in Boston, but walks the old Manor House at nights. That of course leaves me cold. All the same I am puzzled by what is taking place at Mingate."

"Are the servants aware of these visitations?"

"Well, they know the local story, and many of them say they have heard unaccountable noises about the place, but I fancy I am the only person who has actually seen human forms."

McLean was interested. There was always a fascination about alleged haunted houses, and more so when a level-headed man, such as Bancroft appeared to be, vouched for queer phenomena.

"Mingate is in Devon, I believe?" asked McLean.

"Yes, on the edge of Dartmoor. It is a magnificent specimen of Elizabethan architecture, amid wonderful scenery. The village is three miles distant, and the nearest railway station is Okehampton."

"You would like me to come down?"

"That is my hope. For the sake of my wife's peace of mind. I could introduce you as a business friend. She is not likely to have heard your name. Are you willing to assist me in unravelling this mystery?"

McLean looked up his diary. It was impossible to leave London for three days, but he intimated that he was prepared to go down to Mingate on the following Wednesday. Bancroft showed his considerable relief, and promised to have a car at the station. As soon as McLean's business in town was completed, he packed a suit-case and caught the westward-bound train. At Okehampton he found a sumptuous car awaiting him, and was soon being whirled between browning hedgerows.

Mingate was reached in half an hour, and from there the narrow undulating road wound between the hills until a broad valley disclosed the magnificent park of Mingate Manor.

The historic house lay well back in the timber, and in the dusk of evening presented a striking appearance. It was in a marvellous state of preservation, and it transported McLean back three centuries in time. The lodge gates were open and the car moved up the avenue of immense chestnut trees, now stark and bare. The sun was now below the horizon, and tinging the heavy cloud masses with deepening purple light.

McLean was welcomed by Bancroft himself, and then shown to his room by the butler. After a bath and change of clothing he came downstairs and was introduced to the family, who were in the big lounge hall awaiting the dinner gong. Mrs. Bancroft was magnificently attired. In a few seconds it was made clear to McLean that she was really the head of the family. She had an air of authority about her and very soon advertised the fact that she was the incurable snob.

"Quite exciting, Mr. McLean," she said. "Living with the ghosts of one's ancestors. We are used to running a big house, but nothing quite so large as this. Claude tells me there are over eighty rooms here — not to mention cellars and secret passages."

Claude, the good-looking heir to Bancroft's millions, concurred.

"I've been trying to make a plan of the house," he said. "It is a regular maze. Katherine has now discovered a grotto in the old Dutch garden. It is full of toads and vile smells."

Katherine, the daughter, was two years younger than her brother. Like him she was quite unspoiled, and seemed quite ignorant of the fact that she was superbly beautiful. McLean wrote them down as clean-living, healthy specimens who took more after their father than their mother. Mrs. Bancroft could never forget her husband's lineage. She was always on her dignity, and treated the servants with the air of one who considers herself immensely superior. She complained about their lack of breeding.

"I find them awfully interesting," put

in Claude. "Old Timmer, the head gardener, told me his people had lived in the village for over four hundred years. He has an old Bible with all the family names in it since lord knows when. Why, that beats anything we can dig up in Boston."

"You shouldn't encourage such confidences," remonstrated his mother. "Timmer is apt to forget his position. He needs keeping in his place."

Bancroft winked an eye at Katherine, who managed to conceal her amusement. Before dinner was over McLean had the family all very carefully sized up. He liked them all, including the proud Mrs. Bancroft, for her worst fault was that she never ceased to forget that she had married a great name — not to mention a greater fortune.

"I hope you aren't superstitious, Mr. McLean," said Claude suddenly.

"I don't think I am. Why?"

"Because you have been put into the haunted room."

"Claude!" remonstrated his mother.

"Well, I chose it myself," said McLean. "So I can't very well complain. It isn't often one gets a chance to sleep in an alleged haunted room. But what form does the haunting take?"

"Strange and inexplicable noises, among which is a dry sort of cough. Timmer says — "

"We don't wish to hear what Timmer says," interrupted Mrs. Bancroft. "The fact is all these local people are eaten up with superstition. Two maids left last week because they heard a tapping in the middle of the night. Old houses are bound to harbour rats."

"Rats with coughs are not very common," complained Claude. "Anyway forewarned is forearmed."

"Thanks!" said McLean. "But somehow, I don't think I shall be disturbed."

"If you are, you can call me," said Katherine. "I have a patent formula for banishing ghosts. You lift two fingers of your right hand and — "

"Katherine, do be serious," begged her mother.

The conversation changed to healthier topics, and later McLean was shown the diary of Joshua Bancroft, which Mrs. Bancroft prized greatly.

"It ends suddenly on the date immediately prior to his departure for Plymouth," said Mrs. Bancroft. "It is in Latin, but Claude has translated most of it for us. I intend to ask the Earl if he will sell the book to me. It cannot be of much value to him, intrinsic or sentimental."

McLean examined the volume. It was in splendid condition, and bound in thick leather. The writing was small and flowing, and the phraseology quaint. McLean had not forgotten his Latin, and read the entries with comparative ease. At Bancroft's invitation he took the volume to bed with him, and lay awake for some time reading it. He was about to turn out the light when a strange sound caused him to start and turn his head. It seemed to come from the corridor, and was undoubtedly a dry human cough!

★ ★ ★

McLean slipped out of bed and opened the door which led on to the corridor. The place was in darkness, but the light from the room enabled him to see with some difficulty. He thought

283

he detected a tall form disappearing round a bend. Re-entering the room he slipped on a dressing-gown and put an automatic pistol in the pocket of it. Then he emerged and moved forward in the darkness. Again he heard a noise — a curious tapping. It was difficult to locate it, and a few seconds later it ceased. For some time he moved about in the darkness, straining his ears and eyes. But nothing further was heard, and he was obliged to give up the quest for that night.

The next day was spent in getting an idea of the lay-out of the big house, but it was difficult to memorise its scores of rooms and passages. There were all kinds of unexpected niches and dead-ends, and he suspected there were secret passages. Bancroft found him in the garden, and inquired if he had heard anything. McLean nodded grimly.

"Your son was not drawing on his imagination. The ghost is suffering from asthma."

"That was it! What do you make of it?"

"Some intruder."

"More than one. I personally have seen two forms. But what can be their object? I swear they are not common burglars."

"We may discover — when we catch them."

"I hope we shall, but please do not let my wife suspect that this thing is taking place. I think she rather credits the ghost story, but she is not greatly alarmed at that possibility — probably because she thinks we have nothing to fear from my great ancestor. I believe she would be quite pleased to meet him — even in the spirit — failing the acquisition of his portrait, which she still hopes to get."

Some days passed, and McLean made good use of his time. He now had a fair idea of the lay-out of the place, and he had made a discovery of some importance. It was the stump of a special kind of cigarette by some persons suffering from asthma. It was lying on a path in the Dutch garden when he found it. So the cough was human!

It was during the week-end that Mrs. Bancroft made a discovery on her own account. A neighbour had paid a social visit, and he turned out to be Sir George

Henson, whose lineage was as long as the Bancrofts. He had in his possession a fine, full-length painting of the first Bancroft, and would be delighted if Mrs. Bancroft would come up to the Hall and see it. Mrs. Bancroft was there within two hours, and within twenty-four she had induced Sir George to part with the portrait for a sum greatly in excess of its real value. John Bancroft wrote the cheque and sighed.

"Now she is happy," he confided. "Well — well, she gets great enjoyment out of her picture gallery. Personally I can't see that it matters much what my dead and gone ancestors looked like."

The picture was brought to the Manor. It had evidently been in the great hall of the Manor itself, for it showed old Joshua standing on the broad stairs. To Bancroft's surprise the figure was immensely tall, as could be seen by the position of the balustrade against its side.

"I had an idea he was a short man," he said. "Well, I can't see any family likeness."

"Why, John dear — he is exactly like

286

you," said his wife. "It will look splendid beside the portrait of his son Benjamin, when we take it to Boston."

Pride and joy shone in her eyes. She sent for the chauffeur and instructed him to see that her new acquisition was safely hung on the stairs. He was to go to the village and get a reliable man to plug the wall, and so forth.

McLean in the meanwhile was puzzling over several small points. The diary was one of them. Why had Joshua Bancroft left his precious diary in the library when starting off for a new life? How did the asthmatical man and his companion gain entry to the house — and for what purpose? He was assured that all the doors and windows were bolted and barred at nights, and that there was no sign of any of them being forced. He was wandering in the Dutch garden when he noticed the entrance to the grotto. He cut across a lawn and entered the place. At some distant date the roof had caved in, and masses of concrete barred his progress, but in one place there was a circular orifice between the broken blocks — big enough for a man to squeeze himself through. McLean tried it, and subsequently found himself in a well-bricked, low passage. He lighted a match, and saw that it extended for some distance. The floor was damp, and on it were distinct footmarks. McLean bent down and examined them. He was able to identify two distinct sets of footprints.

"Two men!" he mused.

He proceeded along the passage, which became drier farther on. After taking a hundred and twenty-one steps it ended in an iron-studded door. This was locked, but close investigation proved that a key had been used fairly recently. Going back to the house he displayed a desire to look into the vaults. Half an hour's hunt along passages brought him at last to the door he had seen from the other side. It formed the back part of a wine-bin, and the portion was hinged to swing with the door. No ordinary visitor to the cellar would have noticed it — but the nocturnal visitors knew, and had the key to it!

With so much achieved it was only a question of watchful waiting. Each night McLean concealed himself in the vault, and after a lapse of three days the expected thing happened. At close upon midnight there was a noise from the direction of the wine-bin. McLean held his breath. A few seconds later a ray of light appeared — a torch held in a hand. Behind it was a form clad in a long gown with a hood over the head. The door closed quietly, and the man advanced.

"Hands up!"

McLean's powerful torch fell full on the hooded head, and his automatic pistol was levelled at the fellow's chest. The intruder gasped and came to a halt.

"Off with that hood — quick!"

The hood was flung back, and a long, thin face came to view. It was that of a middle-aged man.

"Now," said McLean. "Perhaps you will enlighten me as to your object in paying periodical visits to this house. What is your name and where do you come from?"

"I prefer to say nothing."

"In that case you will go to prison. The inference is fairly obvious. It may mean three months or three years, according to your past history. Hadn't you better talk up?"

"I have nothing to say. You'd better call the police."

"Thanks for the advice. But the owner of the house may be glad to have a look at you first."

"The owner is abroad."

"You are certainly well primed. I should have said 'tenant.' Walk ahead of me, and don't try to get away, or something serious may happen."

McLean drove his prisoner up the stairs, and finally into the library. From there he used the house telephone which communicated Bancroft's bedroom, and two minutes later Bancroft appeared clad in a dressing-gown.

"A midnight visitor," said McLean. "But he comes alone this time. I am wondering whether you are acquainted with him."

Bancroft stared hard at the long, lean face, and hesitated.

"Where have I seen you before?" he demanded.

"You've never seen me before."

"I have. I never forget faces. Now where the devil — It was in America — somewhere. Anyway, what are you doing in this house?"

The prisoner shook his head stubbornly.

"Our friend prefers a stretch of imprisonment for housebreaking to a plain confession of his object," said McLean. "People have curious tastes. Shall I ring up the police?"

"Yes."

He picked up the telephone, but here the prisoner changed his mind.

"If I tell you the truth will you let me go?" he asked. "I swear I haven't taken a single thing from this house, nor done any damage."

"Let us have the truth," said Bancroft. "I will then consider what action I shall take."

"Well, I know very little. It is true you have seen me in America — in Boston, in fact. I used to run a second-hand book-shop, but it failed some months ago. I was hunting through some useless stock when I happened to open an old Bible. It bore the name of Colonel Dinton — "

"Dinton was a great friend of Joshua

Bancroft," said Bancroft. "Why, Dinton was with him when he died."

The prisoner nodded.

"I know that much," he said. "Well, inside the Bible was a letter — or rather a piece of manuscript. It was written so badly and in such queer language that I could not make head or tail of it. The writing was almost invisible, too. I showed this to a man named — never mind his name. He became very interested in it, and said there was a pile of money to be made out of it. We struck a bargain. I was to come to England with him, and we were to share up the proceeds — two-thirds to him, one-third to me."

"What proceeds?" asked McLean.

"I don't know — exactly. All I know is that something is concealed in this house. Laramy said — "

"So that is the name of your asthmatical friend?" put in McLean swiftly.

"It slipped out. Well, it can't be helped now. Laramy knew about the grotto passage. We found the key still in the lock. But the secret door to the hidden room could not be found. The manuscript didn't make it clear where it was. We have been searching for months past. When we started the house was empty, but then Mr. Bancroft and his family took possession and made our work difficult. To-night I came alone, because Laramy had another bad attack of asthma. He insisted I should come."

"And you do not know what this secret room contains?" asked Bancroft incredulously.

"No. Laramy is cunning. He would not let me see the manuscript again. I was trained to be an architect, and that is why I was useful to Laramy. I have been trying to find a secret door in the old oak panelling and so far I have failed. That's all I know."

Bancroft looked at McLean. Strange as the story was, the narrator seemed to be sincere. McLean, too, looked as if he did not treat the whole thing as a mere ruse.

"Where is Laramy living?" he asked.

"I won't tell you that. You can't expect me to squeal on him. Are you going to let me go? I undertake to have no more to do with the business."

"That needs thinking over," said McLean.

"For to-night, at least, you stay here."

The prisoner protested, but ultimately he was lodged in a secure place, and the key turned on him. Bancroft looked at McLean questioningly.

"We can't afford to let him warn his confederate," explained McLean. "It is quite likely that Laramy will come himself when he fails to hear from his crony. In the meantime we will take up the search ourselves."

"You believe in this secret room?"

"I do, and I rather fancy we shall find something there that will surprise you. It is a theory I would rather not discuss at the moment. There is nothing more to be done to-night."

★ ★ ★

For two days the prisoner languished in the great house, and still Mr. Laramy failed to put in an appearance. McLean had tried to run him to earth, but failed to do so, and he concluded that wherever he was, Laramy was not using that name.

In the meantime every suspicious bit of panelling had been tested, and the secret room remained as far off as ever.

Late one evening McLean was sitting in the library, toasting his feet before the dying fire, when his attention was taken by a section of the bookcase which seemed to fit rather badly. A narrow vertical piece close to the fireplace was boxed in, and the carved front panelling was loose. McLean rapped it with his fist and the whole board swivelled a trifle. He put more weight on to it, and it swivelled completely, exposing a dusty interior in which was an iron lever. He pressed the lever down, and then uttered a little cry of triumph, for the near section of the bookcase opened with a grating sound and brought to view an arched doorway. McLean went down two stone steps, turning a corner, and found himself in a small chamber. He flashed his pocket torch and found the secret of Mingate manor. Lying in the corner close to an iron box was a complete skeleton. The third and fourth ribs were fractured, and the thing as a whole was immensely big. McLean kneeled before it and examined the floor beneath it. The bright light revealed a large round object. It was a leaden bullet, slightly misshapen!

McLean retrieved the bullet and then examined the iron box. It was empty. Later he returned to the library and closed the secret entrance behind him. He had no sooner done this than he heard a dry cough, apparently from the passage immediately outside the library door. He switched off the light and concealed himself behind the door, on the hinged side of it. There came a fumbling at the handle and then it opened. A figure entered armed with a hand-torch. The lights went up suddenly and McLean put his back to the closed door. The intruder was garbed similarly to his imprisoned confederate, but the hood of his gown was down, and his sinister face was visible. He winced at the levelled pistol.

"Good evening, Mr. Laramy!" said McLean. "I was hoping you would pay us another visit."

Laramy scowled and his left hand moved swiftly towards a pocket in the gown, but McLean anticipated him.

"Put up your hands or I shall shoot," he threatened.

Laramy obeyed with a muttered curse.

"Ah, that's better! Keep them up there!"

McLean's groping fingers found a small revolver, then a few useful tools. In an inner pocket was a long envelope. McLean took possession of it, and opened it while still seeing Laramy covered. It contained what he hoped to find — four pages of old manuscript signed "Amos Satterly."

"I think we are now replete," he said. "I will conduct you to your confederate. He will be delighted to have your company."

Laramy was driven to the room where the prisoner was enclosed, and locked in with him. Then Bancroft was again brought from his bed.

"Something has happened?" he inquired.

"Yes. I have the second man. The two are together. Also I have discovered the secret of this house."

"What is it?"

"Can you bear a shock? I warn you it may not be pleasant information."

"I don't understand you — but I want to know the truth."

McLean nodded and went to the secret panel. One pull and the hidden chamber was brought to view. Bancroft blinked as McLean bade him enter. A few seconds later he stood staring down at the white skeleton.

"Great heavens! What is this?"

"All that remains of — Joshua Bancroft."

"What!"

"He was murdered in this room by his valet — Amos Satterly. See the fractured ribs referred to in the diary! Here is the bullet also mentioned. That box contained papers and money — probably the money received by the sale of the house. Joshua Bancroft never reached Plymouth. It was his valet who went on the *Mayflower* in his master's name. You will remember that Joshua states in his diary that he had not yet met the pilgrim leaders. He carried with him letters of introduction to Myles Standish. The valet evidently knew that. I wondered why he had sailed without his intimate diary."

Bancroft mopped his brow.

"Then I — my children are — "

"Why dig up the past?"

"You are right, but it is a blow. Even now I don't understand the motives of those men."

"Here is the last link," said McLean, producing the document. "The man who was known as Joshua Bancroft to the Pilgrims died away from his home, and in the arms of his friend Colonel Dinton. It is evident that his crime troubled him, and that he wrote this confession and gave it to his old friend. Dinton, out of regard for the surviving children, kept the confession. He placed it in his Bible, and after his death the book must have passed into other people's possession. It is fairly certain it was never read, but after three hundred years it came into the possession of Laramy's confederate. Laramy saw a way to make money, provided he could find this skeleton."

"How?"

"By blackmail."

"But I wouldn't pay a penny — "

"There is Mrs. Bancroft. She is immensely proud of her name. Laramy knew that and meant to trade upon that human weakness. The document by itself was not conclusive enough but backed up by this skeleton and the bullet — "

Bancroft saw it all now. A man of character himself, the disillusion did not trouble him greatly. But he realised that his wife would never survive such a bitter truth.

"What am I to do?" he asked. "I dare not charge those men. The truth would come out."

"I suggest you let them go," said McLean. "Without the actual document they are powerless to harm you. No one would believe anything they might say without evidence to back it up. We will dispose of the remains of Joshua Bancroft without delay — also the document. Let the past keep its secrets."

Early the following morning the two dejected prisoners were set free, and in a secluded part of the garden new earth had been turned up. When Mrs. Bancroft came down to breakfast she stopped on the stairs to admire the Portrait of old Joshua. She started to realise that McLean was just behind her.

"Splendid old man," she said. "It makes one feel proud to be a Bancroft."

"It should," said McLean dryly. "By the way, I have decided to return to London to-day."

"What a pity! I hope you are not scared by our ghost?"

"Not a bit. That bedroom of mine is the pleasantest in the world. I suppose you will take the portrait back to Boston when you go?"

"Why, of course. I would rather leave my soul behind than it. How amazingly fortunate I have been!"

McLean smiled to himself.

13

OCCASIONALLY McLean interested himself in cases, the solution of which promised no pecuniary reward, from motives of pure sympathy. The Willard case was in this category. One morning he received a letter signed Alice Willard, and the contents were the soul of brevity:

Sir,

I am in great trouble. For pity's sake give me an interview to-morrow morning. I will call shortly after nine o'clock. I must warn you that I am practically destitute.

He had scarcely finished reading the note when Tiny announced the writer of it.

"I will see her at once, Tiny."

Alice Willard was shown in. She was a beautiful woman of about thirty years of age, and her assertion that she was in great trouble was endorsed by her expression. The dark eyes were very sad, and the fine mouth quivered. Her dress was simple but becoming, and she seemed listless and tired.

"You — you are Mr. McLean?"

"Yes. Please sit down."

"I — it was good of you to see me. I went to the police last night, but I cannot hope for much help there, because time is of the utmost importance, and I have no influence to accelerate matters."

"What is your trouble?"

"My — my child was stolen last night. Perhaps I had better tell you my story, then you will understand better. It will not take long. Four years ago I was employed in a large London emporium. I was an orphan but comparatively happy, for I had a good post, and one or two staunch friends. In the spring I became interested in a man who used to call and purchase things in my department. He was a foreigner, but very handsome, and spoke English perfectly. He always insisted on my attending to him, and I discovered that his name was Count Leo Feber, and that he was reputed to be extremely wealthy. Time passed and he induced me to accompany him to various places of amusement. I was dazzled — flattered. In due course he proposed marriage, and I accepted.

"We were married in Paris within two months, and I went to live at his château at Clalons. For a year I was happy, and then — then he met another woman. My child was born, but even that did not hold him. I endured insults, humiliations for the sake of my child, but at last could stand it no longer. I sued for a divorce and got it, with custody of the child. He was to contribute five hundred pounds a year in monthly instalments, but after two months he wrote asking me to meet him. I saw him, and he offered me a large sum for the surrender of my boy. This I refused, but he threatened to stop the allowance unless I did as he wished. I stood firm and he carried out his threat. I sought legal advice, but was told that nothing could be done as the Count had sold up all his property in France and his address was unknown. My little bit of capital vanished. I had to seek a job. I found one — at starvation pay. My baby then became ill and I had to give up the job in order to nurse him. Then came a letter from the Count, bearing no address. He offered me money as before, if I would surrender the child to him. I was to send a reply poste restante to a town in Spain. I did not reply. I got into another job, and ever since have been fighting to make both ends meet. Last night I came home from work and dismissed the girl who looks after my little boy during the day. I bathed him and put him to bed. At nine o'clock I went into the bedroom and then — then I found his cot empty. He had been stolen."

Her emotion was strongly marked on her fine but rather care-worn face.

"You heard nothing alarming?" asked McLean.

"No. There was no sound, no cry. We live in a very tiny wooden bungalow, and the two bedrooms are at the back looking out on to a garden. There is no door on that side of the bungalow, but I had left the window slightly open."

"You live at Barnet?"

"Yes — just outside."

"I will come along and see the place."

"Thank you a million times."

In due course they reached the bungalow. It was a poor building, but had the advantage of being in open country. The heart-broken woman showed him the bedroom where she and her child used to sleep. The window was a casement one, and opened on to a garden about fifty yards long by ten wide. This was surrounded by a quite low fence, which was broken in places.

The interior of the bungalow was humble enough, but it was spotlessly clean. The floors were bare, but stained with oak varnish, and in two of the rooms this had been recently applied. The baby's cot was exactly as the mother had found it when she came in to find her baby gone.

"Have the police been here?" inquired McLean.

"No. They thought there was no need. They merely asked me for details. I told them that I suspected the father of the child, but I was unable to tell them where he was. They did not appear to be very hopeful."

"Police officers have their shortcomings. I can say that, having been one myself. They might at least have come to look at the room. It is rather — interesting."

She looked at him sharply, and saw him examining the floor between the bed and the window. Then he raised his head and sniffed once or twice.

"Filthy habit — snuff," he mused. "Entirely kills one natural sense. When did you stain this floor?"

"Yesterday morning."

"That chair has not been moved?"

"Not since I did the staining."

"Have you ever known a man with a wooden leg — and addicted to taking snuff?"

She gave a start and then nodded her head several times.

"Yes, there was Matioli — the lodge-keeper at the château. The Count had an interest in shipping, and he once told me that Matioli met with an accident on one of his boats, and had to have his leg off. He gave him the job of lodge-keeper when he took the château."

"What kind of shipping business was the Count interested in?"

"Coastal traffic, I believe. But his ships used to go as far as Belfast and London, with cargoes from Marseilles — chiefly wine. He owned three ships in all."

"Can you recall their names?"

"One was the *Côte d'Or* and another the *Hélene*. I don't think I ever heard the name of the third."

McLean nodded with satisfaction. It was now fairly certain that the man with the wooden leg — who had left the small circular marks on the new stain — was one of the Count's hirelings, and that being so, it was more than likely that the Count was utilising one of his recently owned boats for the purpose of conveying the child to its destination.

"Time is of the utmost value," he said. "I may be too late to achieve much. I shall be in a better position to tell you what chance you stand of getting your baby back, within a few hours. I will wire you later."

"Thank you. Is there nothing I can do?"

"I fear not. Unless I can make contact with our snuff-spilling, wooden-legged friend at once, the trail will be obliterated for ever. The Count is evidently determined to have the boy, and may be living anywhere between Berlin and Madrid. You must be both patient and hopeful."

"I will — I will. If I lose my boy, life will not be worth living. He is all I have."

"Has the child any identification marks?"

"Not on his body. But there is a small ironing-mark on his vest. They say — they say he is like me — young as he is."

McLean did not tarry longer. He drove as hard as he could to Lloyd's, and there interrogated a friend who was a walking encyclopædia in regard to world shipping.

"Leo Feber," he mused. "Oh yes, we know him. He used to run three old tubs, but he sold them a year or two ago to a syndicate calling itself the Syndicate Maritime du Sud, or some such name. They had the boats reconditioned and are still running them."

"Is Feber still interested financially?"

"I rather fancy he is — under a pseudonym. I heard he was obliged to perpetrate a financial wangle owing to some business connected with his divorce — wily sort of a devil."

"Where does he trade?"

"Chiefly between Marseilles and London. As a matter of fact, one of the boats is lying in St. Katherine's dock at this moment. They call her *Neptune* — and like *Neptune* she ought to be at the bottom of the sea."

"Is she taking a cargo back?"

"If she can find one — which is doubtful. She may have some luck at Cherbourg or elsewhere. I believe she is sailing this afternoon."

McLean thanked him, and made his way to St. Katherine's dock. There he saw the *Neptune*, and was able to appreciate his friend's remarks. She was a small ship, and filthy dirty. She looked as if she had been saturated with her own cargo — and smelt like it. From the position of her water-line it was evident that she was minus cargo at the moment, and steam was rising from her grimy smoke-stack. McLean did not venture too near her, but made a casual inquiry of a stevedore on the other side of the dock.

"She'll be going out with the tide," said his informant. "That'll be about seven o'clock. If you want the skipper you'll find him in Doggett's, along East Street."

McLean had a desire to visit Doggett's, but this was out of the question in his present attire. He made a swift decision, and hurried through some back streets until he found a cheap second-hand clothes shop. The owner rubbed his long hands together and gazed with some astonishment at his well-dressed visitor.

"I'll do a deal with you," said McLean. "I'll swop this suit, boots and hat, for something less conspicuous. I rather like the look of that jerkin and coat — yes, and those boots. Hurry up. I'm in a hurry."

The dealer became electrified, and in a very short time a ten-guinea outfit passed into his hands in exchange for a rig-out he would have been pleased to sell in the ordinary way for thirty shillings. In a side street McLean dirtied his hands in a pile of sawdust and other refuse, and rendered his face a trifle less becoming. Then he sought Doggett's, and found it to be a fairly large dockside restaurant, and frequented almost entirely by men whose work lay in the neighbourhood. He ordered some tea and toast, and kept his eyes and ears wide open.

The man he hoped to see was not there, but after lingering for half an hour success favoured him. A dark, short man entered in company with two others — and his gait at once advertised the wooden leg, without McLean troubling to lower his gaze. Here was Matioli — and a short distance away was the *Neptune*. It seemed a favourable moment to institute a search for the missing baby, and he at once left the place and made towards the dock.

* * *

When McLean reached the dock-side, in close proximity to the *Neptune*, the upper deck of the vessel was deserted. Presumably most of the crew, with the exception of the engine-room staff, was busy feeding its inner man prior to going to sea. McLean hesitated for a moment, and then stepped swiftly across the gangway. But he had scarcely reached the deck when a man emerged from below. McLean moved behind a ventilator, and a game of hide-and-seek took place. Unfortunately, while seeking to avoid being detected, his foot caught a bucket and raised a din. He heard the seaman ejaculate something in French, and realised that he was coming to investigate the noise. The big smoke-stack lay between McLean and the seaman, and farther back a partly uncovered hold. McLean swung himself into the hold — just in time. From below he heard the seaman muttering something about the cook's cat. Then there was a hail from another quarter. Apparently it was the mate who wanted to know why the what-not the hatches weren't fastened. A name was called, and McLean retreated into the darkness just as two forms appeared above him and commenced to put the big hatch into position. There was a clanking of metal following almost complete darkness — and then silence, save for the sound of hissing steam.

McLean was quick to realise the position he was in. Unless he could attract the attention of the seamen above him, he would be destined to make an uncomfortable voyage down the river and along the French coast. On the other hand, if he did succeed in bringing them, he would be put ashore immediately, and the ship would sail without his having achieved anything worth mentioning. The baby might be landed in some nearby French port, and the Count's scheme brought to fruition. He pondered the matter for ten minutes, and then decided to take a risk, and wait until the ship was well at sea before making known his presence.

In a short time his eyes grew more accustomed to the darkness, and he discovered that there was a small amount of cargo in the end of the hold. It consisted of wooden crates, many of which were labelled 'Preserved fruit.' They were consigned to Cherbourg. The thing that troubled him at the moment was the possibility of the child not being on board at all, but the only sensible thing to do was to act on the supposition that it was.

Time passed, and then he heard

the sound of a bell and immediately afterwards the throb of the ship's engine. A slight heaving motion told him that the ship was moving. He climbed on to a packing-case and gazed through a dirty port-hole. In the semi-darkness he saw moving lights. The adventure had begun!

He endeavoured to make himself comfortable for the night, and was fortunate in finding a couple of sacks which would serve as a pillow. But it was hours later before he dropped into a light sleep — and thereafter he dozed at intervals, until the morning light roused him up. Again he had recourse to the porthole, and he found himself well out to sea — and out of sight of land. It was now time to announce himself. With a length of timber he banged on the hatch — and continued to bang until at last there were sounds which indicated that his summons had been heard. The hatch was removed, and two faces looked down at him.

"A stowaway!"

The words were spoken in French, and two minutes later McLean was hauled out to face a dozen dusky seamen. The captain came along post-haste and interrogated him in French, but McLean feigned ignorance of that language.

"I wanted to get to France," he said in English. "I am willing to work."

"I t'ink I do better to give you a rope end," retorted the irate captain. " Maybe you are a t'ief, hey?"

"No. I wanted to get abroad, and hadn't any money," lied McLean. "I'll earn my food if you'll let me."

The captain hesitated and then agreed. He called the mate and told him to put the stowaway to a job, and ultimately to have him put ashore at Cherbourg. McLean was subsequently provided with a bucket and mop, cleaning up the cook's galley. By noon he had spotted Matioli, who was evidently travelling in the capacity of super-cargo. The cook was a negro, and McLean was soon pumping him.

"He come fetch his piccaninny from London," said Sambo. "Wife die, he say."

"Is he landing at Cherbourg?"

"No — Marseilles."

That evening it was abundantly clear that the child was aboard. McLean heard a wailing from the forward part of the ship. He crept along the deck and heard a convulsive voice crying for 'mummy.' Matioli, who had been lounging near the bridge, entered a deck cabin, and soon the sobbing ceased. He subsequently emerged with a fine baby boy in his arms, and placed him on the deck with a pile of cardboard boxes to play with. McLean was able to examine the child at leisure. He was plump and dark, and very much like his mother. Presumably Matioli had bought some clothing, for the boy now sported a diminutive sailor suit and cap. His eyes were red from his recent sobbing, but the cardboard boxes were now commanding his attention.

A few minutes later the mate came to McLean and ordered him aft. Sambo was told to keep him employed, and for two solid hours McLean peeled potatoes. He learned that the *Neptune* would reach Cherbourg the following evening, but it was a little difficult to know how to act in the circumstances. To get ashore with a plump baby of some two years was almost an impossibility. It needed some careful thought. Ultimately he decided not to risk failure by such a hopeless act.

On the following day he overheard a conversation between Matioli and the captain which made it certain that the Italian and the child were bound for Marseilles. That simplified matters a great deal, for while the ship was rounding the coast he would be afforded abundant time to complete his own plans. At Cherbourg he was put ashore and he managed to evade the passport officials. A change of clothing was now necessary, for the greasy garb he wore offended his sensitive nose. That night he took train to Paris, and then to Marseilles.

★ ★ ★

At Marseilles McLean became exceedingly busy. In the first place he secured a passport made out to Robert McLean and child. The child he christened Robert Hope, and gave its age as one year and eight months. Then he visited three different institutions devoted to orphans and destitute children. In due course he found a dark-eyed, wistful child, whose mother had abandoned it six months before. The child was French, but his vocabulary was limited to the one word 'momma.' He appealed to McLean. The infant certainly deserved a chance in life.

"What is his name?" asked McLean.

The matron shook her head.

"We do not know, m'sieur. We call him 'Chic,' here, and we should be sorry to lose him."

"I can guarantee him a good home, with every attention. But it is necessary to secure complete surrender."

"M'sieur would furnish credentials?"

"Naturally. I am acting for a gentleman whose name I may not divulge, but you have my assurance that he will be treated as if he were that gentleman's own child. There will be no lack of money and attention."

Within two days the business was transacted, and McLean was advised that he could take the child away when he was ready. He went to the port, and discovered that the *Neptune* was due to arrive on the following evening.

Incidentally he learned that Count Leo Feber was in harbour on board his own yacht. Later he saw a dark, sinister man in yachting garb leave the quay in company with a neatly uniformed nurse, on the tender to the yacht. Several parcels were put aboard. Evidently the nurse had been shopping in the interest of her pending charge.

On the following morning McLean hired a boat and went fishing outside the harbour. He managed to hook a few fish, but they were not his real object. As evening came down he saw a steamer beating into harbour, and soon he recognised the *Neptune*. Immediately he pulled in his line and got to work on the floor boards of his small craft. He rowed back into the harbour, and when he was under the white bows of the Count's palatial yacht his boat foundered under him. A member of the yacht's crew witnessed the incident, and promptly threw out a life-buoy. McLean gave a fine exhibition of drowning, but at last managed to grip the life-buoy. He was hauled aboard in a — presumably — semi-conscious state. The Count was nothing if not hospitable. McLean was given a bunk and time to recover. While lying there he saw the *Neptune* anchor. A little later a boat was put off. It contained the child wrapped in a shawl, and apparently fast asleep. Matioli came aboard, and did some business with his employer. Then the boat went back with only Matioli and the rowers aboard. The child had been safely delivered.

The Count came into McLean's cabin later, and inquired how he was feeling. McLean assured him he was now recovering, and if the Count would be good enough to allow him to remain aboard for a few hours he would be fit enough to go ashore.

"Certainly," said the Count. "I do not sail until noon to-morrow. If you need anything, ring the bell."

He rubbed his hands together, and smiled to himself.

"I am sorry to have left you alone," he added. "But I happened to have a little pleasant business to attend to. As a matter of fact, my son has been delivered to me — after an absence of nearly two years. His mother — " He frowned evilly. "His mother — is dead. I can't pretend that I am exceedingly grieved: I think you will understand?"

"I think I can," said McLean dryly. "You are exceedingly kind. I will go ashore early in the morning."

The hours passed, and at last the yacht was sunk in silence. McLean's clothing had in the meantime been dried and brought into the cabin. He dressed himself and ventured out. There was no 'watch,' and everyone on the vessel seemed to be asleep. Upon Matioli's arrival with the child he had heard the Count's penetrating voice say, "Take him to No. 8" — and he concluded that No. 8 was the cabin reserved for the nurse and the child. He approached the door of No. 8 and found it latched but not locked. Upon opening the door slightly, a light from off-shore revealed the recumbent form of the nurse in one bunk and the child in another. McLean closed the door and crept out on deck. A few minutes later he was swimming towards the quay.

A quick change at the hotel, and he was ready for the more delicate business.

Asleep in a cot opposite his own bed was his recent human acquisition, and in the next room a hired nurse. He awakened the nurse to her great surprise.

"Mademoiselle, I wish to show the boy to a friend of mine who leaves France to-morrow. Will you bring him along? I will go and get a taxi."

"Shall I dress him, m'sieur?"

"Oh, no. Wrap him in a blanket — and try to keep him asleep. We shall not be long."

A little perplexed she did as she was bid, and within a quarter of an hour McLean was at the harbour. There were no boatmen available, but plenty of boats swinging at their moorings.

"I will take him now," said McLean. "You wait here in the taxi. I shall be back within twenty minutes."

He carried the boy to a boat and laid him gently on the floor. Then he took the oars and made for the yacht. No. 8 was still sunk in sleep when he arrived. He entered it, and after laying the boy at the foot of the other child's bunk, he passed a slightly doctored handkerchief under the sleeping nurse's nose. A minute later he ruled her out as a possible obstacle. The stolen child whimpered as McLean swopped over the nightgowns, but the child from the orphanage slept like a log. The exchange was made and the waiting nurse dispatched to the hotel.

"We leave for Paris in the morning," said McLean. " I shall be back later. Look after the boy."

Again he rowed to the yacht, and on reaching it he shoved the boat as far away from it as possible, and then sought his cabin again.

The Count was up and about very early in the morning. He found McLean dressed and pacing the deck.

"Good morning, Mr. McLean!" he said cheerily. "So you have quite recovered?"

"Quite."

"I hope that youngster of mine did not disturb your slumbers. I heard him cry out once."

"Not in the least. I spent a most enjoyable night."

"Good! You will stay to breakfast?"

"No, thank you. I regret I must go ashore at once."

"As you wish."

At that moment the nurse emerged with the freshly washed and garbed infant in her arms.

"Ah, here he is!" said the Count. "It is the first time I have seen him clearly. Fine looking boy. Not too much like his mother — thank God!"

"Lucky boy," said McLean. "With such a rosy future before him."

The Count nodded.

"I shall devote the rest of my life to him. Ah, Mr. McLean — here is the tender. I wish you *bon voyage*."

McLean thanked him again, and stepped into the motor-boat. On shore he found the man from whom he had hired the first boat. More good money had to be found to satisfy the rapacious old scoundrel. There was another boatman, too — wondering how one of his craft had slipped her mooring!

The Paris bound express left to the minute, and young Robert Hope McLean — otherwise Henri Feber — was told that very soon he would see his 'mummy,' who had been wired to meet the boat at Dover. His young face was so radiant with joy that McLean did not begrudge the money and time expended on a case for which he could not hope to be reimbursed. And when ultimately the boy's mother clutched him in her arms, and wept tears of joy over his pleased face, McLean considered it all very well worth while. The next client would have to pay a little more — that was all!

14

ON a few rare occasions McLean was precipitated into tragedy, and the Sandygate mystery was one of these. It was mid-August, and McLean found himself pining for a whiff of moorland air. Tiny had been given a holiday in order that he could go camping with his Scout patrol, and generally things were slack. Why Sandygate should persist in looming up in McLean's mind he did not know, for his only experience of the place lay in the fact that he had spent ten days there in the spring at the behest of a client who had been in receipt of certain anonymous letters demanding money. McLean had cleared up the business and had made a half-promise to spend a week with his grateful client when business permitted. He now decided to accept that outstanding invitation, and wrote to Templeton to that effect.

Hugh Templeton was a clever barrister at the Scottish Bar, and was at this period at the summit of his career. He had built a house at Sandygate, chiefly because it was within half a mile of the famous golf links, and less than half an hour's motor ride to Edinburgh. At his favourite game he had a handicap of plus one, and for two consecutive seasons had captained his team. McLean, who played an indifferent game of golf, brought his clubs only because Templeton insisted, and expected to be thoroughly trounced despite the gift of ten strokes per round.

Templeton met him at the station, and smiled when his keen eyes observed the golf clubs. They drove to the big house on the fringe of the links, and McLean was given a room which pleased him immensely, after the heat and smells of London. It commanded a splendid view of the verdant moorland, some two hundred acres of which had been turned into a first-class course. The fairways and greens were like rich carpets — emerald green in a purple setting, and the salt-laden breeze filled the house.

Within twenty four hours he and Templeton were engaged in a ding-dong battle, but on this occasion the barrister did not do himself justice. He was not on his game, and played many shots that even McLean would be ashamed of.

"The result of too much work," he said. "Can't concentrate. I've been up to my ears in briefs for the past six months. It will take me a week to forget them. If I go on like this in the competition, the Lord help me."

McLean was surprised at his own game. He played steadily the whole time — keeping straight down the fairway, and putting like a machine. After an admirable dinner he succumbed to Templeton's inducements to enter for the open Bogey competition, which was to take place two days later.

"With your handicap you ought to pull the thing off," said Templeton. "I shall be satisfied if I return a card at all."

The day of the competition arrived, and McLean was drawn with a player of his own calibre — a rather finnicky elderly man to whom golf was more like a religion than a game. They had played about six holes when an incident occurred which had the effect of cancelling the whole thing. McLean saw several pairs of players hurrying across to the thirteenth tee. It was obvious that something was wrong, for a crowd emerged from the distant club-house and commenced to make for the tee, around which a fair group of people was already gathered.

"An accident," said McLean's partner. "Looks like it."

"That's Doctor Rathbury hurrying — "

They joined the excited crowd and soon reached the tee, which lay in a wooded hollow. On it was stretched a still form, and there was blood —

"Templeton," said a voice.

McLean started and pushed forward. He caught a glimpse of his host's face. It was as white as a sheet, and the eyes were closed. The doctor then obscured the view. He turned the long body over and revealed a terrible head wound.

"Is he — ?"

"Dead. Someone must have driven into him with tremendous force. I should say he died instantly. You were playing with him, sir?"

Templeton's partner gulped and nodded. He had no clear idea of what had happened. Templeton had been about to drive off when there was a crack — and he fell to the ground. The twelfth green was a blind one, and he could only conclude that the oncoming players had sliced a ball badly to the thirteenth tee.

Templeton's body was removed, but there was no more golf for that day. The cause of the injury was clear enough. Twenty yards away a blood-marked golf ball was found. It had struck Templeton behind the left ear and shattered the base of his skull. McLean was badly shaken. It was a gruesome experience, gazing at the dead body of his late charming host — reflecting upon their recent conversation. Moreover, it seemed as if Templeton had received some divination of his pending death. For the past two days his attitude had been just a trifle strange. His nerves were all to pieces, and McLean had seen him gazing into space with a grim expression on his intelligent face. Yes, it was all very uncanny!

The players held a conference, to ascertain exactly how the accident had occurred. The players immediately behind Templeton and his partner were Conington and Westall, and presumably the death-dealing ball had been played by Conington, for Westall's was found quite near the green.

"It was my second," he said. " I drove short and played a full brassie shot for the green."

"You couldn't see the flag?" asked McLean.

"Oh, no — only the direction post on the high bank. I certainly did slice a bit."

"Where was the caddie?"

"Neglecting his job. He should have been on the bank, but he was yarning to the other caddie. In the ordinary way I should have driven the green all right, but just as I was about to make my shot there was a noise from the house behind the orchard."

"You had the wind with you?"

"No; the wind was slightly against me."

"There is no doubt that this is your ball?"

McLean took up the fatal golf ball. It was a Dunlop and marked P.C.C. The cover of it was slightly split, and on one side there was a fairly deep cut. Conington nodded.

"No doubt at all," he said. "Of course, it was all a complete accident, and it only goes to prove that the thirteenth tee should be moved away from that blind green. On other occasions players have been hit."

All the members sympathised with him. But McLean was not at all satisfied that matters were as simple as they appeared to be on the surface. Later he got Conington by himself.

"I want to try an experiment," he said. "The wind is about the same as it was this morning. Will you try another brassie shot to the twelfth green, from the same spot as you played the other one?"

"But I can't see — "

"I want to settle a small point."

"Very well."

They went out together and Conington found the exact place from which he had played the fatal shot. He identified it by a small triangular hole into which his ball had almost fallen from the drive.

"It was here," he said. "You see,

the flag is quite invisible — also the thirteenth tee."

"Place the ball how you like and play the longest shot you can. I'll go to the bank."

He did this and Conington carried out his instructions. In all he drove four balls, three of them went past the green, but they all pitched well short of the thirteenth tee. McLean was more or less satisfied.

"Could you do better than your third shot?" he asked.

"I don't think I could. I put all I knew into it."

"Ah; that is rather interesting."

"Why?"

"I don't believe it is possible for you to hit a brassie shot from that spot which would reach the head of a man standing on the thirteenth tee."

"But it did reach him!"

"There I disagree."

Conington stared at McLean — slightly puzzled.

"I don't understand you," he said.

"You did not search for your ball after you had played the shot?"

"No. I told you that the caddies were not at the bank. By the time they reached it poor Templeton was lying on his back. Of course we all went straight to him. But the ball was found not twenty-five yards away."

"Yes; a ball, but not the ball you hit. We will look for that now."

Conington appeared to be in doubt, but he helped McLean in his search. Ten minutes elapsed and then McLean stooped and picked up something from the long heather.

"Got it!" he ejaculated.

"My — my ball?"

"I think so — a Dunlop. Here are your initials — P.C.C."

Conington took the ball and examined it closely.

"By Jove; I believe you are right. But I couldn't swear to it. Both balls are similar."

"No — the first one has a cut, made by a topped shot. Did you top a ball during the morning?"

"No. I started with a new ball. It was in perfect condition when I played it from the twelfth tee. You're right. I never played that cut ball. What does it mean?"

"It means," said McLean grimly, "it means that poor Templeton was not the victim of a mere accident. I suspect a plot on his life, but in the meanwhile I think it would be better if you and I kept our own counsel. Are you agreeable?"

"Yes; if it will help."

"I rather think it will."

"But the police!"

"I will communicate with the police when I have something tangible for them to work upon."

★ ★ ★

McLean stayed on at the house of his dead host to await the arrival of his brother — Henry Templeton. He arrived late in the evening, much distressed at the sad news. McLean introduced himself.

"My brother has often mentioned you," said Templeton. "Ever since you nailed that infamous blackmailer. This is a very sad business. The golf club must feel it acutely. Such accidents do not often happen."

"The club is not to blame in any way. I should like you to tell me more about your brother. Normally, I believe he was a cheerful man?"

"Most. Hugh never allowed things to worry him much. I have seen him smiling after a most gruelling time in the court — when everything went against him."

"Has he been the same of late?"

"Well — no. But it wasn't worry — merely an overdose of work. I advised him to take a holiday, and he did so — though he refused to go away. His idea of a holiday was a round of golf every day."

"He had no enemies?"

"Crowds — that is to say, people who suffered directly or indirectly from his triumphs at the Bar. No eminent barrister could hope to be entirely free from that sort of enmity."

"Can you recall any occasion when he has been threatened?"

"No."

"He has figured in certain murder cases — cases where the culprit has been severely dealt with?"

"Yes. There was one quite recently — last

February, in fact. It was a case of manslaughter. Hugh was complimented from the highest quarters on the way he conducted the prosecution. Perhaps you remember the Rowden tragedy?"

"Only vaguely."

"It was an old man done to death by one of the Rowdens. That family is of criminal tendencies, from father to son. Their history is appalling. Hugh got Searle Rowden sent to penal servitude for life."

"Who are the Rowdens?"

"Farming stock — good at their business, too. The old man, who died two years ago, made a fair fortune out of sheep, and invested it wisely. Two sons are living in Scotland — Searle, who is in prison, and Angus in Aberdeen. There were other children, but heaven knows what became of them. They were always quarrelling among themselves."

McLean was interested in these details. On the following morning he suggested that Templeton should examine his brother's innumerable documents. Templeton gazed at him keenly.

"I don't quite understand the drift of

this," he said. "Isn't this a plain case of simple accident? My brother was hit in a vital spot by a golf ball. What can his private papers have to do with that?"

"They may have a great deal to do with it. I believe your brother possessed an astute and cunning enemy, who plotted against his life and finally achieved his end."

Templeton was obviously amazed.

"But the ball which struck my brother was driven by his old friend Conington. Do you suggest that Conington — ?"

"Conington never drove that ball."

"What!"

"He thought he did — until quite recently. There is a man in the dark somewhere. We have to find him."

"Great Scott! Such a possibility never occurred to me. Certainly we will examine his papers — together. What you are suggesting is astounding. Do you mean it wasn't a golf ball that killed Hugh? But, no, his partner saw it all. You — you don't suspect the man he was playing with?"

McLean shook his head a little impatiently. He wanted to get on with the case, and Henry was now displaying a desire to introduce new and groundless theories — such as a sudden brutal attack on his brother with a driving iron. But McLean had seen the fatal wound and knew positively what had caused it.

The papers were subsequently produced, and McLean hunted through them for any correspondence in the nature of threatening letters, but there was nothing of the kind to support his theory. If such things had been received, Templeton must have destroyed them with due contempt. In the blackmailing case he had at once taken steps to put a stop to it, and McLean was inclined to conclude that Templeton's queer attitude prior to the tragedy was not due to any threat to his life, but to some inexplicable sense of pending death.

Development in this direction being barred, McLean started on a new course. The tee on which the tragedy had taken place was in a hollow close to a private orchard, beyond which was a red-brick house of modern design. The front of the house lay on the neighbouring road, but the back could be seen through the trees, and the tee itself commanded an uninterrupted view of what McLean took to be a bath-room window. Armed with a golf club, McLean drew near the barbed-wire fence and, taking a golf ball from his pocket, threw it clean through the exposed window. The glass was shattered to atoms, and a few minutes later a servant appeared.

"I am afraid I have had an accident," said McLean. "My ball went clean through the window. I had better come round to see what damage I have done."

He accordingly made his way into the main road, and rang the bell of the house in question. The door was opened by the servant he had already spoken to.

"Mr. Quayle is out," she said. "But I have been upstairs. It was the bath-room window, and a mirror is also cracked."

"May I see the extent of the damage? Of course I will take full responsibility."

She showed him to the room in question. One pane of glass was completely gone, and a large shaving mirror which faced it was badly cracked. On peering through the window McLean could see the thirteenth tee of the golf course, less than fifty yards away. He drew an imaginary picture of a man swinging a club. The left side of his head would be in full view — !

"Mr. Quayle is the owner of the house?" he asked.

"Not the owner, sir. He took the house furnished two months ago. Mr. Tomlinson is the owner, and my employer. I agreed to stay on until Mr. Tomlinson returns."

"Well, will you tell Mr. Quayle that I will call again? In the meantime you might get a workman up to put in a new pane of glass."

"I think I had better wait until Mr. Quayle returns."

"Very well. Tell him that the gentleman who did the damage will call this evening."

On his way out McLean noticed a bag of golf-clubs in the hall.

"Mr. Quayle is also a golfer?" he asked.

"He plays sometimes, but not often."

The fact that Quayle kept his clubs at home and not at the club-house led McLean to conclude that he was not a member of the club — but merely a visitor. Upon making inquiries he found this to be correct. The secretary did not remember him, but on referring to the visitors' book McLean found Quayle's name on three different dates during the past two months. Quayle gave as his reference the name of a well-known Scottish club, and to satisfy his curiosity McLean rang up the secretary of this club. The man denied all knowledge of Quayle. The club had no member of that name.

Later in the evening McLean called at the red house. He was told that Mr. Quayle was at dinner but would see him in a few minutes if he would be good enough to wait. This suited McLean admirably. He had, in fact, timed his visit with this hope in mind. He was shown into the lounge, and during the few minutes' wait he made the most of his opportunities. The first thing that took his gaze was a cigarette-case with the initials 'A.R.' stamped on it. He recalled Templeton's information. 'A.R.' might stand for Angus Rowden — the brother of the man who was sent to penal servitude. A quick search brought to light an attaché case. This carried no initials, but it was not locked, and McLean had it open in a few seconds. Inside was some fishing tackle, and also a bundle of receipts. The latter bore the name of Angus Rowden!

★ ★ ★

Ultimately 'Mr. Quayle' entered the lounge. He was a sullen-looking man of about forty years of age, with a hard jaw and narrow grey eyes. The eyes were shifty orbs, moving from side to side in their sockets.

McLean catalogued 'Mr. Quayle' at once as a man of ungovernable temper and devilish cunning. The sort of person who would nurture a grievance to the last day of his life.

"Sorry to call so late," he said. "But I wished to get that broken window off my conscience. As I am going away almost immediately, I should be glad to know what the damage amounts to."

"There hasn't been time to ascertain, but if you will leave your card I will have the bill sent on to you. As a matter of fact, I am only a tenant here."

McLean produced a spoof card, lest Quayle — or rather Rowden — should be suspicious of his real name. Rowden took it and slipped it into his card-case.

"Are you staying long?" queried McLean.

"No. I leave the day after to-morrow."

"The owner is returning, I presume?"

"Not for a month. The house was to let for three months, but I only took it for two."

McLean's eyes lighted up at the opportunity vouchsafed him by this admission.

"Would it be troubling you too much if I had a look over the house?" he asked. "My brother is looking for a house in this neighbourhood in which to spend a golfing holiday. This site should suit him quite well. I had no idea there was a possibility of getting this house."

Rowden consented somewhat reluctantly, and showed McLean into the various rooms. McLean's keen eyes missed nothing, but so far they did not discover anything that would help his theory along.

"Quite nice," he said. "But surely there is a garage?"

"Yes — a rather small one, because half of it is used as a workshop."

"A pity. My brother's car is a large one. Might I take measurements? I have a pocket measure."

Rowden inclined his head and piloted McLean to the garage, which was built into the rear of the house. He opened the door and revealed a very disorderly interior. There was a bench on the right-hand side — littered with tools and oddments — a pile of petrol tins in a corner, and a motor-cycle. The exhaust pipe of the motor-cycle was lying on the floor, and that fact caused McLean's eyes to sparkle. He took out a pocket measure and stretched it across the interior — from the right wall to the edge of the long bench.

"Nine feet," he mused. "That ought to be ample. And the length — eighteen feet six inches."

Rowden got impatient as more measurements were taken, but McLean's attention was elsewhere. There was a most interesting object at the end of the bench. It was now partly dismantled, but its original purpose was plain to McLean. It was a long barrel of about an inch and a half calibre, and it had evidently been fixed to an old gun stock, which was near it. McLean managed to slip a finger into the end of the barrel and it came out blackened with powder! In a box were a number of old golf balls, and some of these bore initials that never belonged to Rowden. A few of them were badly damaged — having obviously been fired at a hard target for practice purposes. Everything was now sun-clear.

"That will do, thank you," said McLean. "I will get a letter off to my brother at once. Don't forget to send me that little account. Good evening!"

Half an hour later McLean was with the local chief of police, and what he had to say caused that official's eyes to open wide.

"The evidence is all there if you want it," said McLean. "The man who styles himself Quayle is Angus Rowden, the half crazy brother of Searle Rowden who was convicted on a charge of manslaughter, chiefly as a result of Templeton's pleading. I have only just discovered that during the trial Angus made himself unpopular with the judge by shouting abuse in court. He had to be ejected. I am convinced that from the day of the verdict he plotted to avenge his brother. He struck a quite original idea. It succeeded even better than I should have expected. He made a gun in which an ordinary golf ball could be used as a projectile, and he practised with them until he became expert. The house near the thirteenth tee was admirably suited to his fell purpose. I have no doubt he tried to catch Templeton alone on that tee, but he failed because Templeton hated playing alone."

"Yet he chose the day of a competition on which to carry out this scheme?"

"Yes, because it was necessary for someone to be playing immediately behind Templeton. From his bath-room window he could see the thirteenth tee and also the twelfth fairway, and the players approaching the twelfth green. He pilfered those initialed balls on various occasions, and he used the one corresponding to the player immediately behind Templeton. It was a man named Conington. Rowden saw him coming up."

"But why didn't Templeton's partner hear the report of the gun?"

"Rowden was cunning enough to prepare for that. He started up the engine of the motor-cycle just before he fired the gun. It was that noise which put Conington off his stroke. To make sure the noise of the engine would drown the report of the gun, Rowden removed the silencer of the cycle."

"But we have to prove this. It is not easy — in face of the fact that Conington identified the ball as the one he had played."

"You are wrong. I found the ball which Conington really played and he is now ready to swear to it. Here are the two balls. That one was fired from the gun, and on it there is still a trace of burnt gunpowder. What are you going to do?"

The chief walked up and down his office in a state of considerable perplexity. He had a fine appreciation of McLean's acute intelligence, yet he hesitated because he foresaw grave difficulties in the way of securing a conviction. It had to be definitely proved that Rowden fired that gun with fell intent, and that was not at all an easy matter.

"I've a mind to take a risk," he said.

"If you don't take it at once there will be no evidence left in a few hours. He is leaving the place to-morrow, and will doubtless dispose of all his paraphernalia. Remember he is in an awkward corner. He has to account for his assumed name, the presence of the golf balls — obviously stolen from lockers in the club-house. He has to explain the use of the queer gun. Moreover, he is a border line case, and is quite likely to blunder at the time of crisis. Get him to-night."

The chief banged his hand on the table, and then pushed a bell.

"I will," he said grimly. "I believe you are right. I play golf myself. That shot of Conington's was incredible. Vardon himself couldn't have got that length on a ball. I am going to make an arrest."

An hour later three members of the police called at the red house. They entered without their being announced and surprised Rowden in the act of destroying the gun of his own invention. McLean's analysis of his temperament proved correct. Upon being told of the nature of the charge he laughed wildly, but when the sergeant of police collected the portions of the gun, and the large number of golf balls, the ill-balanced mind of the homicide led him into a fatal error. He struck the officer nearest him with a heavy spanner, and then ran madly across country. The two remaining police officers went after him, and were joined by McLean, who had come as far as the drive to see how matters went.

Rowden shook off the two policemen, but he did not shake off McLean. For two miles the chase went on in the gloaming, and at last Rowden stood on the precipitous cliffs that fringed the wide bay. He was thoroughly demented now — almost foaming at the mouth. McLean approached him.

"Better come quietly, Angus Rowden,"

he said. "The police will be here in two minutes."

Rowden opened his mouth and grinned inhumanly.

"I got him," he said thickly. "I fixed him as I swore I would. He thought himself clever — " He stopped and an awful expression crossed his face as he saw two vague forms in the distance, running towards him. "They'll not treat me as they treated Searle," he muttered. "This will make them laugh!"

Without a moment's hesitation he turned on his heel and jumped right out. McLean ran forward and saw the body meet the jumbled rocks below. They found him later, with his neck broken.

"Saves us a lot of trouble," said the sergeant philosophically. "I guess he'll be judged where all the evidence is straight. A mad family that. Lord knows why they were ever created!"

15

MCLEAN sat at his writing-table, burning the midnight oil. Before him were various documents, newspaper cuttings and photographs, and late as it was these were sufficient to keep him in a high state of wakefulness. All had reference to the memorable day of his life, when he had been compelled to hand in his resignation from the C.I.D. It had taken him the best part of three years to gather together these links in the chain of lying evidence, and only recently had the last one been forged. It had been sent to him by the faithful and loyal Sergeant Brook, and it portrayed a group of men on a race-course. Beneath one of them was inscribed a cross, and under the cross was written 'Jim Lightfoot.'

McLean rubbed his long, strong hands together, and then produced a box of water colour paints. With a small brush he painted out Lightfoot's moustache and beard, and was extremely satisfied with the result. He was still scrutinising it when the bell rang. Tiny having long retired to rest, McLean opened the door himself and welcomed his expected visitor. It was Brook.

"You got my note?" inquired Brook.

"Yes. Come right up."

"Sorry to be so late. We've just raided a place up west. Wonderful haul of crooks. I'm dead tired, but I wanted to hear if the photograph is useful."

McLean chuckled as he led Brook into his study, and gave him a chair.

"Useful! My dear Brook, I wouldn't sell it for a thousand pounds. Where did you get it?"

"A woman carried it in her handbag. We got her for shop-lifting. The second man from the right end of the group is Pelly, who is wanted for forgery. We got her to name the others, and it was only when she mentioned Lightfoot's name that I remembered your request."

"Good! You don't know Lightfoot?"

"No. The rest of them are very well known at the 'Yard.' How is it going to help you?"

"You remember the circumstances in which I was politely requested to resign?"

Brook nodded sympathetically.

"It was proved that I had a banking account in the name of Amos Adams, into which had been paid quite considerable sums. The cashier identified me as the gentleman who came and asked to open an account. Also he stated I had visited the bank on various occasions to pay in money. Most of the money paid in was proved to originate from persons of strange occupations — some from bookmakers, from restaurant keepers, from people who ran night-clubs and so forth?"

"Yes."

"I have proved to my own satisfaction that every one of those persons was known to Arnaud de Wynter. I have evidence that will show that at one time or another de Wynter was associated with every single one of them. Quite recently I forced from the lips of a dying man a confession to the effect that Arnaud was working with a man named Lightfoot. Now Lightfoot was the man in the dark. He never figured in the case. His name — like de Wynter's — was never mentioned."

"Well?"

"I deduced the part he had to play, and which he did play most cleverly, with de Wynter stage managing it. I will show you that part."

He took up the photograph and gave it to Brook. Brook gazed at it and expressed his enormous surprise in a forgivable expletive.

"The substitute!"

"Exactly. Probably you didn't notice his striking resemblance to me under the moustache and beard. But de Wynter evidently did and took steps to use him."

"It was Lightfoot who opened that account?"

"Undoubtedly. De Wynter knew the contents of my wardrobe to the last waistcoat. Lightfoot shaved off his moustache and beard, dressed himself exactly as I might do, and opened that account. Moreover the gang drew on it, in order not to have their money confiscated later. I have here a cheque made out to Benjamin Cozins — the man who died, and who sold it to me for the benefit of his widow. It is signed by Amos Adams, and is a marvellous imitation of my own writing — one of the facts which told against me. But it so happens there are two ways of writing a 'z' and Mr. Amos Adams — or more probably de Wynter — used the one which I have never used in my life. Interesting, isn't it?"

"By Jove, yes. But it doesn't help you much now."

"I agree — not while Mr. Lightfoot keeps his mouth shut. But if I can persuade him to admit that he was Mr. Amos Adams, and that he received his instructions from de Wynter, then I fancy our old friend will be nearer jail than he has ever been in all his adventurous career."

"But can you?"

"I have hopes. My first step is to locate Jim Lightfoot. Can you help me there?"

"Not at the moment. But there is the woman from whom the photograph was taken. She may know. We can question her."

McLean was reflective for a few

minutes, his quick brain working out possible ruses.

"Do that, Brook," he said. "She won't tell you much, but I should like you to press the point — not too subtly. Ask her frankly."

"Won't get much out of her that way."

"I am aware of that. The fact is you won't get much out of her whatever means you employ. Incidentally, try to discover if she was on very intimate terms with Lightfoot, also how long ago it was when she last saw him."

Brook promised to do what he could, and on the following day he saw McLean and told him what had transpired.

"She wouldn't give much away, but she admitted that the photograph was taken just three years ago, and that she only saw Lightfoot once after that — six months later. Tried to kid me that he had gone abroad for good."

"Six months later," mused McLean, seizing on this valuable point. "That means she saw him clean-shaven, for he wouldn't have had time to grow his moustache and beard so soon after his impersonation of me. That makes it easier. Where is the woman?"

"Holloway Jail."

"Name?"

"Rose Bennett."

"What sentence is she serving?"

"Twenty-one days."

"Good. I will see her."

McLean did not experience much difficulty in getting an interview with the prisoner. He fixed a time between lights, to avoid any possible risk of arousing suspicion. But he argued quite logically that if Lightfoot could be mistaken for him, he could very well reverse the tables.

He was shown into Bennett's cell, and found himself face to face with a well-built woman of about forty. She gazed at him for a moment with wrinkled brows.

"The warder said it was a relative," she said. "But I don't know — "

She drew closer to him, and then her eyes lighted up with recognition.

"Lightfoot!"

"S-sh! I told 'em it was Reynolds. I saw the case in the newspaper, and I've come to warn you."

"Warn me?"

"The cops have got a line on me. They may know that you and I were associated. If they ask you anything — you know nothing, you understand?"

"I'm not a squealer," she replied indignantly.

"But they're clever with their cross questioning. Did they ask you anything when you were lugged up — about me?"

"Yes. I told them nothing of any value."

"They've been pestering you since?"

"Yes — Sergeant Brook asked me where you lived."

"What did you say?"

"What do *you* think. Told him I hadn't an idea."

"Good. You got twenty-one days, eh?"

"Yes."

"When do you come out?"

"The twenty-seventh."

"Just in time. There's a good thing on, and we want your help. Easiest thing you ever heard of — no risk at all. As soon as you're free come straight to my place, and I'll explain. Can't stay now. They only allowed me two minutes, and that because I said I was your brother-in-law. Don't forget."

She promised she would not, and McLean kissed his hand to her and made away. He fully expected that she would question him as regards the meeting-place, and since she had not he concluded that she was fully aware of Lightfoot's habitual residence.

The days passed slowly now. McLean could derive no interest from other cases. He felt he was near to vindicating himself — absolving himself completely. For nearly three years he had been working towards this end. It needed but the locating of Lightfoot, and the wringing of a confession from his lips to cause quite a flutter at police head-quarters, and he meant to bring that about by hook or by crook.

At last the great day dawned. McLean made sure there was no mistake, and that Rose Bennett would really be released that morning. Shortly before noon he was reclining in a taxi, in full view of the prison gates. Punctually to the minute Bennett emerged. She began to walk towards the city, and the taxi followed. The shadowed woman was no fool, and ultimately chose the best means of throwing off any possible inquisitive policeman. She entered one of the largest café's and promptly strove to lose herself among the crowd collecting for lunch. McLean, posing as a placid old gentleman, almost lost her, but luck served him at the last moment, and he saw her emerge from an exit in a side street. From there she made for the Tube.

The chase ended at a flat in Battersea. McLean saw the woman enter by the side door, and he waited to see whether she would be fortunate enough to find Lightfoot at home, in which case the ruse would be exploded and immediate action become necessary. But he was hoping this would not be the case, and that he could catch Lightfoot alone and unwarned. Two minutes later the woman emerged, and it looked as if she had been unsuccessful.

★ ★ ★

Mr. James Lightfoot was a gentleman of acute intelligence. Like many another man who preferred easy money to hard work, he had been associated with de Wynter for some time, and had done fairly well for himself. By this time he had completely forgotten the McLean business, in which he had played the principal part. McLean was finished and done for so far as his police career was concerned.

Having been up all night in quest of spoil, Mr. Lightfoot had slept until well past noon, and was now about to sally forth for a meal. Possessing no servant, he answered the knock on his door in person, opening it with the caution of a man who never knows from one day to another when his liberty will end. He blinked to recognise an old face.

"Rose! This is a surprise. Come in!"

She entered and gazed at him curiously as she took a chair.

"I heard you were in jug," he said.

"Are you mad, Jim?"

"I don't get you."

"You saw me in quod, and told me

363

to come to you. Why do you pretend that — "

"Come off it! What's the great idea?"

Now she had some doubts. Breathing heavily, she went to the window and pulled the curtains aside to let in more light. Lightfoot's cunning face was now fully illumined. "Why, you aren't — It wasn't you who came — "

Lightfoot smelt danger. He seized her by the shoulder and glared into her eyes.

"What's this? Someone visited you, eh — someone like me, and you were damned fool enough to lead him here?"

"But I thought — The cell was gloomy and he seemed to know everything. He told me to come here immediately I was free."

"Did he tell you the address?"

"N-no."

"Of course not. He didn't know it, and wanted to find me. I know who it was, too. Here, this is serious. If McLean has got a line on me it means he knows too much. You got to get out of here quick. Get downstairs and act as if I wasn't at home. Wait!"

He went to the front window and gazed out carefully, but there was no sign of McLean. "He's there," he muttered. "He's watching. He won't leave me alone. Go now — quick!"

He bustled her out of the room and then ran to the telephone and rang up a Mayfair number.

"Hallo! Is that Mr. de Wynter? Good! Something has happened. McLean is after me — waiting outside. I'm not staying here. What's that? . . . Yes, I understand — the passage beside the brewery. But that means he will see me . . . All right, I suppose you know best. I'll leave at once."

He hung up the receiver, jammed on his hat, and left the flat hurriedly. Upon reaching the street he turned left and walked hard. As he turned the next corner he caught a glimpse of a form behind him. It was an aged man, but he seemed to walk with surprising agility. Lightfoot scowled, but pinned his faith to de Wynter. De Wynter would not let him down — could not afford to, in fact.

Half a mile farther on he took a taxi and gave an address at Walworth.

Very soon he was aware that another taxi was keeping its distance behind him. At a certain street he paid off the driver, and cut down a narrow passage. It was a dirty thoroughfare, with high walls on either side. The one on the right belonged to a brewery, but that on the left formed the back part of a block of dirty tenement houses. Half-way down the passage Lightfoot saw an open door. It was the spot mentioned by de Wynter, and framed in the opening was de Wynter's face.

"Keep right on," rapped de Wynter.

"Don't look this way. We'll get him as he passes."

Lightfoot heard and strode on. At the bend he turned his head for a moment. What he saw caused his eyes to gleam. A vague form reached the half-open door, and immediately he was collared and pulled inside. The door closed with a bang. Immediately Lightfoot retraced his steps. He reached the closed door and rapped on it. A few seconds passed, and then it was opened. A pockmarked face came to view, and two cruel eyes scrutinised the caller.

"Ah, it's you! Come in, quick. The boss is upstairs."

Lightfoot entered the dingy place, and ascended the stairs in the far corner. In the room above he found de Wynter engaged in taking a long drink.

"Hallo, Jim!" he said. "It looks as if we have cooked McLean's goose — in time."

"Is he — alive?"

"At the moment — but he can't be permitted to go on enjoying that state of bliss. He knows too much. For years he has given me tremendous trouble. Three years ago I reckoned he was as good as dead and done for, but he has a smattering of intelligence, and seems to have used it with some effect. The mere fact that he is on your trail proves that he knows how that job was pulled off. We can't afford to take any risks now. He will have to go."

Lightfoot winced at the significance of this remark.

"You — you mean — ?"

"That is what I wanted to see you about. They have him in the basement as helpless as a trussed chicken. I want

367

to close a certain chapter to-night."

"That means — ?"

"It is your job. There is an old manhole in the basement floor, leading to a disused drain. You have never been seen on these premises, except by Brinter and Bill, and they are reliable enough. Here is something that will act quickly and silently."

Lightfoot gazed in speechless horror at the little pellet in the round box which de Wynter offered him. He had done many abominable things during his adventurous career, but nothing quite so bad as this. He gulped and shook his head stubbornly.

"Nothing doing. Do you think I'm mad? It isn't necessary. All we have to do is to hold him until we can get clear."

"You poor fool! Do you think I am going to permit him to hold this threat over me for the rest — ?"

"Then do it yourself. You've got as much to fear as I have. I only did what you told me to do. It was you who planned it all and financed it. You told me that was all that would be needed

368

of me — that provided I impersonated McLean my job was ended, and my name would never be mentioned."

"But it has been mentioned, and that makes all the difference. Take this, and do as you are told."

"No. I'm going to clear out. I'd rather risk being lugged for the other job, than for what you suggest. It isn't in my line, and I'm through."

De Wynter's face went purple with rage. Lightfoot was making for the door when he heard an exclamation from his rear, and turned to find himself covered with a pistol.

"Take this!" ordered de Wynter. "Quick, or you'll end where McLean is going to end."

The little box was thrust into Lightfoot's unwilling hand, and he was driven down into the basement. The two cronies were sitting at a table under the flickering gas jet. They stood up when de Wynter entered with Lightfoot. The pistol was no longer in de Wynter's hand, but it was still covering Lightfoot from the recesses of a side pocket.

"Where is he?"

The pockmarked man pointed to some sacks in the corner, which clearly covered a human form.

"Conscious?"

"No."

"Good! Shift that rubbish from the manhole, Bill, and take the cover off."

This was done and a yawning pit disclosed. Lightfoot looked at the box which he held, and then at the heap of sacks in the corner. De Wynter pointed to the latter.

"Get it over — quick!"

"No, I'm damned — !"

Lightfoot suddenly turned and made for the basement door. There was a muffled report and he pitched forward. De Wynter went and turned him over with his boot.

"That will teach him a lesson. We'll have to attend to the business ourselves. Pick up that box, Jim — and you, Brinter, take those sacks away. Quick about it!"

The sacks were removed, and a limp body exposed. It smelt strongly of chloroform, but did not seem to be injured in any other respect. De Wynter tried to turn the gas higher, but the burner was old and broken. He walked across to the unconscious man, and moved him so that his face came to view. It was that of a man of about sixty.

"Good God!"

"What's wrong, boss?" asked Bill.

"This is not McLean. That fool has blundered. Take this fellow away, quick, and leave him farther up the passage."

As the two men sprang to obey, the victim groaned and opened his eyes.

"Where am I?" he asked.

"You had a fit," lied de Wynter — "just outside."

"Fit? Why — Yes, I — I remember. A man stopped me at the end of the alley, and gave me half a crown to deliver a letter to a place at the farther end."

"A letter?"

"In — in my pocket."

De Wynter's nimble fingers went through the man's side pockets, and finally he produced a blank envelope. Inside was a small sheet of paper, and embossed on it was a small owl.

"McLean! It means — !"

He was interrupted by a loud banging

on the basement door. Immediately he sprang for the light and turned it out.

* * *

After an interval of several minutes the basement door yielded to force, and McLean entered with two policemen. The light of an electric torch revealed the form of the late victim, blinking at the strong beam.

"There's the gas bracket," said McLean. "Light the gas, sergeant."

The additional illumination came at the same time as the sound of a scuffle upstairs. The two policemen at once mounted the stairs, leaving McLean to interrogate the unfortunate letter-bearer.

"Are you hurt?" he inquired.

"No. I had a sort of fit, and — Why, you are the gentleman who gave me the letter!"

"Yes. I was anxious to see if that enticing little alley was quite respectable. Evidently it wasn't. I fear I owe you an apology and some sort of material recompense. I will discuss that later. What has been happening here?"

"I — I don't know. I lost my senses."

"Hm! You overheard nothing?"

"Not a thing. But there were three men here when I woke up. Oh yes, and a man sitting over there — groaning."

McLean went to the spot indicated, and found traces of blood on the floor. Then the policemen came back — three of them — and brought with them Bill and Brinton, looking very fierce and untidy.

"Old lags," said the sergeant.

"There was another — the most important."

"Yes, but we lost him. Vanished like a bloomin' spectre."

"What have we done?" blurted Bill.

"Criminal assault," said the sergeant. "You can shut your mouth, anyway. Like to ask them anything, sir?"

"Yes," replied McLean. "I want to know where the other two men are — de Wynter and Lightfoot?"

"How do I know," snapped Bill. "They went off just before you broke in."

"They didn't," exclaimed the old man. "The gas was turned off, and then I heard queer sounds — things being removed, and then a thud."

McLean started, and switched his gaze to the pile of stuff on the other side of the cellar. He went to it and lowered his head. From below came a faint sound — a pitiful wailing.

"Help me remove this litter," he said.

The work occupied only a minute or so, the manhole cover was exposed. When it was removed, the human noises were quite audible. He swung round on the two prisoners. Brinton now realised that further concealment was impossible.

"It's — Lightfoot," he said. "But we had no hand in it."

McLean flashed the torch into the pit and saw Lightfoot huddled in the bottom of it, apparently choking. A length of rope was secured and one of the constables was lowered. Lightfoot was brought up, bleeding at the shoulder and gasping.

"He got me," he said, choking. "Forced me to swallow — I'm dying — poisoned."

McLean realised that this was literally true. The two prisoners were removed, and he and a constable conveyed Lightfoot to the nearest doctor with all possible speed. There a stomach pump was employed, and later Lightfoot was well enough to be transported to Scotland Yard.

On the following morning McLean paid him a visit, and at his request Sergeant Brook went with him into the cell. They found Lightfoot bandaged but otherwise well. He was sitting on his bed looking the picture of misery, and his eyes flashed as he recognised his 'double.'

"Better?" asked McLean.

"Not — too bad. I guess you think I am going to make a statement?"

"That is entirely up to you," said McLean.

"But here is Sergeant Brook with a nice new notebook. You owe something to the police — "

"Damn the police!" His mouth curled.

"But I owe something to de Wynter — the swab, and, by gosh! I'm going to pay him. Take this down while I feel like it."

He made a very clear and comprehensive statement, omitting nothing. He had been given a photograph of McLean, and had done his best to impersonate him — in the name of Amos Adams. De Wynter had collected cheques from various persons who had cause to hate McLean, and these had all been paid into the account of Amos Adams. Later cheques were drawn on the account by de Wynter, who imitated McLean's handwriting perfectly, and the donors of the amounts were repaid. The clothes which he had worn to deceive the cashier at the bank were still in his rooms. They were bought and paid for by de Wynter. He gave the name of the tailor.

"Is that good enough?" he asked when he had finished.

"I think that will do," said McLean grimly.

"Better get it typed quick, and I'll sign it while I feel like murder. He thought he had got me, but now I'll get him. I don't mind a stretch of five years so long as he gets ten. He meant to dispose of you good and well, McLean, but he wanted me to pull his chestnuts out of the fire for him. Hurry up with that typed copy. I'll sleep better when I've put my name to it."

Later he signed the statement, and McLean read it through again, with a smile of satisfaction.

"Only one more thing to do, Brook," he confided.

"You mean de Wynter?"

"Yes. The thing now is to get him. He will appreciate the position, and will fight like a cornered rat."

"Leave it to us," said Brook cheerfully.

McLean shook his head.

"This final act is a treat I have promised myself for three long years. We shall see."

16

A WARRANT had been issued for the arrest of Arnaud de Wynter, and for six weeks the London and provincial police had moved heaven and earth to locate that illusive personage. McLean was not in the least degree astonished. Knowing de Wynter as he did, he gave him the credit of possessing acute intelligence, and of the ability to use it in case of emergency. De Wynter knew perfectly well that capture meant jail, and for no mean period. Like a ghost he had vanished from his familiar haunts — a complete disappearance that caused Sergeant Brook at least to gnash his teeth.

"We've tried everywhere," he said. "We got Solomons, Mrs. Galling, old Rodding who used to run the roulette club. They were all in the plot, but not one of 'em knows where de Wynter is hiding. I wouldn't be surprised to hear he's dead."

McLean laughed scornfully.

"Only the good die young," he said. "No, de Wynter will not pine away and die, like some exotic flower. He's very much alive, and waiting for a chance to beat us all on the last lap."

"Have you any idea where he is?"

"Not the slightest."

"Anyway, you're cleared. We've enough evidence to prove that the commission's finding was absolutely wrong. So far as you are concerned, it doesn't matter whether we get de Wynter or not."

But McLean did not take that view. He wanted de Wynter in the dock. True, he might receive a pardon on the strength of the mass of evidence in his favour, but the *dénouement* would be less complete in de Wynter's absence. Lightfoot's confession, though witnessed by Brook, was still in McLean's possession. It was the one thing that would render a new inquiry imperative, but McLean had no intention of putting it in until a clean sweep-up had been made.

"It's de Wynter or nothing," he said. "I have no intention of asking the Home Secretary to reopen the case until I have de Wynter. A foolish sentiment, no doubt, but there it is."

"We may never get him," complained Brook.

"I think we shall."

Action on the part of the police flagged a little as time went on, but it was not so with McLean. He had given up all work on other cases now. His evenings were spent prowling in dark places, among people whose occupations were strange and mysterious. For days on end he laboured as a dock-hand in a vicinity where de Wynter had had business ramifications, hoping to hear that sinister name mentioned. And at last, when he was actually beginning to believe that de Wynter had escaped through the widely spread net, a scrap of news came to him. The purveyor was a gaunt dock-hand who had been carrying frozen mutton all day with McLean. Work was over, and he was sitting on a crate filling his pipe before going home.

"Hell of a scrap here this morning," he said. "Just before we started work."

"What about?"

"Lord knows exactly. The Frenchies

started it — those chaps on the boat from Brest."

"I didn't know there was a boat from Brest."

"Oh, yes; she berthed early in the morning, with a cargo that wasn't worth carrying. I'll wager the freight didn't pay the skipper's wages. They fell foul of Blatchford's crew in the 'White Horse,' and some heads were split open. Had to leave one man behind. He was took away on a stretcher. But the skipper shipped another hand just before he sailed back."

McLean became attentive.

"An Englishman?"

"No; French. Anyway, he spoke the language pretty well. Now the funny part of it is that the new hand framed that fight. The barman at the pub told me he overheard the fellow tell one of Blatchford's men that one of the Frenchies had spat on their deck as he passed along the quay. Anyway, it all ended in a fine scrap until the French mate came and broke it up. Cute way of getting a job, eh?"

"What sort of man was the fellow who

started the trouble?" inquired McLean.

"Dunno. Welby told me all about it. That's Welby standing yonder."

McLean made it his business to see Welby later. A couple of drinks, and Welby became most communicative.

"Cunning little swine to put that yarn around," he said. "I didn't rumble him until I saw him being shipped as a deck-hand. Didn't even know he was French. He's been hanging around here for days trying to get a ship."

"What was he like?"

Welby described him, and the description fitted de Wynter exactly, so far as the physical part was concerned. According to Welby he was dirty and ill-clad, but that was no argument against the possibility of it being de Wynter himself, putting into practice a well-conceived plan to get out of the country unostentatiously. To procure the necessary 'papers' was not a difficult operation for a man with plenty of money in his possession. There was another point, too, which was significant — the alleged ridiculously small cargo brought by the French boat, and its immediate departure. It looked as if the whole thing was planned from the start, and that the captain of the boat had received instructions to come for de Wynter. The free fight was a put-up job in order to get de Wynter aboard in a more or less natural fashion.

"What was the name of the boat?" he asked.

"The *Matilde* — registered at Brest. She's been here before."

"At what time did she sail?"

"Eight o'clock. You're interested, ain't you?"

"Oh, no; I was only just wondering."

He left Welby soon afterwards, and pondered the next move. By this time the *Matilde* was well out to sea. If she was making Brest there was still time for Scotland Yard to act, and to get the new hand apprehended when he reached the French port. He took that step in due course, and the police acted promptly.

Forty-eight hours later unexpected news came. The *Matilde* had foundered off Ushant and her crew had been picked up by a big liner which was now making Cherbourg. Only one man was missing — presumably drowned — a

Jules Lacoste. McLean at once decided to go to Cherbourg, and in order to forestall the arrival of the liner an airplane was necessary. He was whirled across the Channel at close on a hundred miles an hour, and reached Cherbourg just as the liner berthed.

As the survivors came off McLean scanned them keenly, with a French detective at his elbow. But de Wynter was not among them. The captain of the *Matilde* was interrogated. He admitted that the drowned man was the hand he had picked up in London, but at the moment he was not prepared to make any statement in regard to the cause of the disaster.

"How was Lacoste drowned?" asked McLean.

The captain didn't know. It was only when he checked over his men that he found Lacoste was not in the one boat that managed to get away.

The French detective seemed satisfied, but McLean was not. It was too much of a coincidence that the particular man he wanted was the one missing. Later he succeeded in getting one of the crew of the *Matilde* to himself.

"I am related to Lacoste," he said. "I can't believe he is dead. Can you tell me anything about him? Did you see him just before the ship foundered?"

"No, m'sieur."

"You got away in the starboard life-boat?"

"That is so."

"Why did you all crowd into one boat? What happened to the port life-boat?"

The man stroked his chin reflectively.

"That is strange, m'sieur. I did not see the port life-boat about the time of the accident. It must have been carried away. There was a big sea running."

"Lacoste was on good terms with the captain?"

It was a strange remark but it went home. The man pursed his lips and nodded.

"He was a bad worker," he added. "After twelve hours he was set to look after the captain. It is strange he should get drowned, for there was plenty of time to get into the boat."

It satisfied McLean that de Wynter was still alive — that he had, with the captain's assistance, lowered the port boat within reasonable distance of land, before the ship was deliberately scuttled. The plot was quite a sound one, since if he was detected he could plead that the *Matilde* had foundered, and would have papers to prove that he had sailed on it. On the other hand there was an excellent chance of his making land without being observed, in which case he would stand a very good chance of shaking off the police forever.

McLean decided to act on his own, and in quick time was making for the coast in the neighbourhood of Brest. Certainly de Wynter would avoid Brest itself, and attempt a landing where the chances of being observed and apprehended were few. Arriving at Brest, McLean hired a fast car and commenced to scour the coast on the northern side of the city. His first stroke of luck occurred at a small place called St. Pol. On the beach he found a fisherman busily engaged in painting out a name on a boat. But the single coat of paint was not sufficient completely to hide the name *Matilde*. McLean pointed to it.

"Is that your boat?"

"*Oui, m'sieur.*"

"Where did you get it?"

The fisherman scowled, but McLean did not wait for any lying explanations.

"All right," he said. "You are welcome to it. I shall say nothing. But I want to find the man who came ashore in it. Did you see him?"

The man hesitated and then admitted that he had. The survivor had hinted that he might retain the boat, and had also asked him the way to the nearest railway station.

"What did you tell him?"

"I told him there was no railway station nearer than Morlaix and that was ten kilometres distant. He asked me about a garage and I told him there was one two kilometres along the road — in that direction."

"How long ago was that?"

"Two hours, m'sieur."

McLean thanked him and drove furiously to the garage. As he reached it a big car returned to it. He slipped an English note into the chauffeur's hand.

"You have had a passenger, eh — to Morlaix?"

"That is so."

"He catches the train for Paris?"

"I think so."

"When is it due?"

The chauffeur looked at the clock on his dashboard.

"In six minutes, m'sieur."

"Thank you!"

McLean jumped into his car and drove madly along the road marked 'Morlaix.' The railway ran parallel with it, and when he had covered half the distance the train rumbled up behind him. Drive as he might he could not hold the locomotive, and finally it drew clean away. There was yet a hope that it might linger at the station, but it proved to be vain. He reached the tumbledown 'gare' to see the train steaming out. De Wynter had again got the start!

★ ★ ★

McLean made a few inquiries at the railway station and learned that the train to Paris had not arrived, and that the

388

train which had just left was a local one and went no farther than a place called Brieux, on the coast.

"Did a man in seafaring garb just book for Brieux?" he asked.

"*Oui, m'sieur.*"

"Can you tell me the time of the arrival of the train at Brieux?"

The booking clerk looked it up, and McLean realised that with any luck he could reach Brieux by road before the train was due in. He filled up the car with petrol and started off. The road was in a dreadful state, and the car all but broke its back axle a dozen times. McLean drove it like a fiend, knowing that everything depended upon his reaching Brieux before de Wynter — or rather the man he believed to be de Wynter.

Good fortune favoured him, and it was dark when he reached his destination. On inquiring at the small railway station he was told that the Brest train was due in at any moment. Immensely relieved, he took up a position near the barrier, where he could see the arrivals without being seen himself. Two minutes later the train

389

steamed in. The passengers alighted and passed through the gates. At last came a man in seafaring garb — very greasy and generally soiled. One look at the face was enough. It was de Wynter!

McLean thanked Providence for the darkness as he followed his man. The town was passed, and a deserted lane entered. Occasionally the sea came to view, and away to the left were scattered harbour lights. De Wynter took a turning to the right, and McLean had some difficulty in keeping him in sight, for the lane twisted and turned like a snake. Ultimately more lights were seen, from a slight elevation, and these turned out to be the lights of a big villa situated in extensive grounds. McLean saw de Wynter ring a bell at the wrought iron gates, and a few seconds later a man came from inside and bowed before the visitor. Then the gates clanged.

The wolf had been tracked to his lair! The next step was to inform the Paris police. That course was distasteful to McLean, but he was compelled to realise that it was impossible for him to act alone. He hurried along the lane, quite pleased with the termination of his long quest. An extradition order had been issued. It was only a question of time. He was within a hundred yards of the end of the lane when the bright lights of a car appeared behind him. The lane was so narrow it scarcely permitted a car to pass a pedestrian. He promptly drew in very close to the hedge, and just missed being run down. Then, to his surprise, the car pulled up suddenly and three men jumped out of it. Two of them carried pistols and the third a long spanner. McLean had no opportunity to draw his own weapon. A voice ordered him to put up his hands, and he did so because he realised they were in grim earnest. A few seconds later he was disarmed and collared. He was taken to the car and a pistol was pushed into his side, while the vehicle was reversed and driven back to the house.

He was subsequently conducted along a wide hall and into a large room. Still covered, he submitted to being bound hand and foot and was bundled on to a couch. Some minutes passed and then de Wynter entered. In the short time which had elapsed he had enjoyed a bath and a change of clothes. It was the old immaculate, sneering adventurer again, with gleaming shirt-front and plastered black hair. He grinned and waved his hirelings out. Then he lighted a cigar calmly and sat facing his prisoner.

"I happened to see you arrive at Morlaix," he said. "I like looking out of train windows. I commend you on your knowledge of my movements, but on this occasion you have overreached yourself slightly."

"There we differ," replied McLean.

"We obviously do. I will admit that you have given me more trouble than any man I have ever met, but I do not intend that this state of things shall continue."

"I doubt if it will continue much longer."

"You are right. To-morrow we shall part company. I love the sea, McLean. I built this house because it commanded a fine view of the ocean. I love the blue water, its placid quietude, its air of mystery, its secrets that none may plumb. To-morrow I shall add one more secret to it, for I am going on a yachting trip — and you will accompany me — for a short distance. Do I make myself clear?"

"Quite clear. I have never misjudged you, de Wynter. You do not like murder, but you are prepared to engage in it — when the critical moment arrives. But even my silence would not save you."

"I think differently — for the simple reason that you are the only man who knows where I am — excluding my — "

"Your hired assassins?"

"Why be crude? If you had left me alone I would have left you to pursue your career. As it is, I am bound to defend my liberty. I rather value that."

"Make the most of it," said McLean mockingly. "Even now the hounds are hot on the scent. There may be difficulties about starting that voyage."

De Wynter moved a trifle uneasily, not knowing what lay behind the prisoner's remark — if anything. McLean on his part, was indulging in a bluff. Actually, he found the situation extremely serious, and rather regretted not having made an attempt to apprise the police of his discovery before starting out on a dangerous, single-handed quest.

De Wynter apparently had no desire to resume the conversation. He sighed and rang the bell, upon which two men entered the room.

"Put him somewhere safe, and see that he makes no noise. Then tell Gustave to be ready to sail at dawn."

McLean was roughly handled, and placed in a small room at the bottom of the house. It possessed the merest slit of a window, and was stone-flagged and damp. Before leaving, his warders fixed a scarf round his head, knotting it under his jaw so tightly that it threatened to choke him. Another was tied about his mouth, and the door bolted on him.

Suffering unspeakable agony, he lay there all night, unable to sleep, and almost unable to breathe. Shortly before dawn there were noises in the house, and a little later the door of his prison was opened. The same two men entered, and McLean winced to see them carrying a huge sea-chest. Unable to resist or protest, he was laid in this and the lid slammed on him. His head came up against a big cold object — and he realised it was a slab of lead. Followed some grunting and the sensation of being hoisted. A few minutes later he heard de Wynter's voice.

"All right?"

"Oui, m'sieur. Mon Dieu, but it is heavy!"

"The car is outside. Tell Gustave to put the box into the store-room. It contains some combustibles which I wish to dispose of at sea."

Near to suffocation, McLean found himself being bumped about as the car started at a fair speed. After ten minutes of it the car stopped, and he was carried again. His journey ended in a violent bump on a wooden floor. Then a door closed noisily and all was quiet.

After what seemed an eternity the door opened again, and the sound of voices came to him. It was de Wynter talking to Gustave — who was evidently the captain of the private yacht.

"War mementoes, my dear Gustave. I have come to the conclusion that such things are dangerous about one's property. We will sink the whole lot in a safe spot when the night watch comes on. I am anxious to get to my Riviera villa. Is steam up?"

"I am all ready to sail."

"Good. I will breakfast in my cabin."

Again the slam of the door, followed by a dead silence. Then a bell sounded — and again later. There was no doubt now that the vessel was out of the harbour and at sea. McLean could feel the vibration of the engines, and was aware of a slight heaving motion. He realised that a few more hours of this torture would bring unconsciousness. Things were at a dreadful pass.

He managed to twist round, and brought his face up against the side of the chest. A protruding nail jabbed his face and brought a stab of pain. But it proved a godsend in disguise, for he saw a way to make use of the nail. Working his body about, he got the end of the nail into the scarf which prevented him breathing freely, and risking facial disfiguration he tore away the scarf. The one under his jaw proved more difficult, and he gashed himself several times before it was free.

Breathing was easier despite the airless void. Time was of the utmost importance now. It was a fight against suffocation. He bumped his head against the lid, but it was evidently padlocked. There remained but one possible means of exit — pressure. Setting his shoulders against one end of the chest, he put every ounce of his strength into his legs. His feet pressed down upon the end board, and he felt them bulging. Again and again he tried, almost exhausting himself in his titanic efforts. At last the bottom end gave, and fresher air entered immediately. Now he rested for a while, and prayed that no one would take it into his head to enter the store-room.

After a quarter of an hour he felt considerably revived. Fresh efforts were started — and little by little he wriggled his way out . . . He lay in the open now, staring at the sun-shine which filtered through the port-hole. Then he switched his gaze to the contents of the store-room. There were many cases and trunks piled one on the other, and at the bottom of one of them was a brass bank, broken in one place. He sat up and bumped his way towards it. In a few minutes one hand was free, and that was all that was needed to ensure complete liberty. Numbed and bruised, he tottered towards the door and bolted it on the inside. Now he could rest awhile and recover his full strength!

★ ★ ★

De Wynter, with all his cunning, had overlooked one thing — McLean's pistol. So sure had the scoundrel been of his victim he had not even troubled to search him. McLean produced the weapon and smiled contentedly. But still there was much to be done. The damaged sea-chest told its own story. That must be attended to. He found a quantity of heavy articles and packed the chest with them, then he gave his attention to mending the broken end. The nails he pushed out with a wedge of wood, until he could place the several boards into position. Then the nails were pushed home one by one. Only the closest investigation would have revealed the fact that the chest had been broken open.

Behind the piles of gear there was ample room to hide!

He searched around for something in the shape of food, but found nothing more substantial than a case of red wine. It was necessary to break the neck off before he could drink this, but after a long draught he felt a hundred per cent. better. He reclined behind the cases and waited eventualities.

Soon after darkness fell the store-room was entered. Voices fell on his ears, and he heard instructions given to at least two men. When at last the door closed he peered round the pile, and saw in the dim light an open space where the big sea-chest had rested. He climbed to the port-hole and listened intently.

Some minutes passed and he heard a deep splash — but saw nothing.

"Exit McLean — perhaps!" he muttered to himself.

So far as he could see, there was nothing to be done but sustain himself on wine until the yacht reached some sunny port in the South of France. It was not a pleasant outlook, but far better than the interior of a locked box, fathoms deep.

★ ★ ★

For two days McLean managed to keep concealed, despite periodic visits to the store room on the part of members of the crew.

All he had in the way of food was the wine, and this very soon began to sicken him. At times he listened at the door and scraps of conversation came to him. He learned that the port of destination was Nice, but that the yacht was putting in at Biarritz for a few hours. This information caused him to change his plans.

At Biarritz the yacht lay a mile or so off the shore, and de Wynter put off in a motor-boat for the day. When he returned it was getting dark, and McLean hastened to put his plan into operation. He had satisfied himself that he could squeeze his body through the porthole at a pinch, but he preferred the vessel to be moving, despite the danger of being hit by the propeller. When he heard the engine-room bell go, he climbed on to a box which he had placed close to the port-hole, and prepared to take a considerable risk. The yacht began to move. It was now quite dark. McLean got his feet through the round orifice, then his hips and shoulders. Hanging by his hands, he strove to push his whole body forward — and let go. He hit the sea in close proximity to the hull, and was sucked deep. When at last he emerged he was some yards behind the stern of the yacht, amid churning foam. The yacht pulled away, and he started to swim for the shore. Fortunately the tide was running in, and within half an hour he stood on the beach, under the stars.

One fine morning a trim yacht entered the sunlit harbour at Nice. Two men along the quay saw her take up her anchorage. One was a French detective named Daniel, and the other was McLean. The Frenchman read the name of the yacht.

"*Yvette!* I am assured, m'sieur, that she is owned by Baron Carliss — a wealthy Spaniard."

McLean handed him a photograph.

"That is Arnaud de Wynter. I rather fancy you will find the Baron strikingly like that. You have the warrant?"

"Yes."

"Good! Ah, the tender is putting off. I think I will retire behind this wine dump.

How I hate the stuff!"

The motor-boat made for the quay. De Wynter was sitting in the bows, clad in immaculate 'ducks,' looking at peace with the world. About him was a vast amount of personal luggage, and farther along the quay was a big limousine car, sent down from the white villa on the hill. The boat put in at the landing-stage and de Wynter stepped ashore. Immediately the detective approached him.

"I am a police officer. You are M'sieur Arnaud de Wynter?"

De Wynter controlled himself admirably.

"You are under a misapprehension, m'sieur. I am the Baron Carliss. It is the first time I have heard the name de Wynter."

"You deny that this is your photograph?"

De Wynter glanced at the print and raised his eyebrows.

"I certainly appreciate your mistake. It does bear a striking resemblance to myself, but my passport will prove — "

He got no further, for McLean suddenly emerged from behind the great pile of wine casks, and coughed. De Wynter's gaze went to him. All the blood left his cheeks as he gazed at this apparition.

"McLean!" he gasped.

"A case for identification," said McLean. "I thought I might be useful. M'sieur Daniel, need we waste more time?"

The detective was quick to act. A pair of handcuffs gleamed in the sunlight, and de Wynter found himself in custody, with no hope of seeing the interior of that delectable villa on the hill for a very long time. He was led away, with head bowed. Defeat had come at last, and it brought humiliation unspeakable.

★ ★ ★

Some months later a news-boy was running down Fleet Street selling papers as quickly as he could take the money. In front of him was a large news-bill.

REMARKABLE REVELATIONS IN McLEAN INQUIRY.
FAMOUS POLICE OFFICER THE VICTIM OF A PLOT.
COUNTRY TO MAKE FULL REPARATION.

Shortly afterwards a certain slim house in a quiet London street bore the sign 'Excellent Apartment To Let' just above the form of a small brass owl, and almost simultaneously there appeared some new lettering on a door at Scotland Yard:

CHIEF INSPECTOR ROBERT MCLEAN.

THE END

Other titles in the
Ulverscroft Large Print Series:

TO FIGHT THE WILD
Rod Ansell and Rachel Percy

Lost in uncharted Australian bush, Rod Ansell survived by hunting and trapping wild animals, improvising shelter and using all the bushman's skills he knew.

COROMANDEL
Pat Barr

India in the 1830s is a hot, uncomfortable place, where the East India Company still rules. Amelia and her new husband find themselves caught up in the animosities which seethe between the old order and the new.

THE SMALL PARTY
Lillian Beckwith

A frightening journey to safety begins for Ruth and her small party as their island is caught up in the dangers of armed insurrection.

THE WILDERNESS WALK
Sheila Bishop

Stifling unpleasant memories of a misbegotten romance in Cleave with Lord Francis Aubrey, Lavinia goes on holiday there with her sister. The two women are thrust into a romantic intrigue involving none other than Lord Francis.

THE RELUCTANT GUEST
Rosalind Brett

Ann Calvert went to spend a month on a South African farm with Theo Borland and his sister. They both proved to be different from her first idea of them, and there was Storr Peterson — the most disturbing man she had ever met.

ONE ENCHANTED SUMMER
Anne Tedlock Brooks

A tale of mystery and romance and a girl who found both during one enchanted summer.

CLOUD OVER MALVERTON
Nancy Buckingham

Dulcie soon realises that something is seriously wrong at Malverton, and when violence strikes she is horrified to find herself under suspicion of murder.

AFTER THOUGHTS
Max Bygraves

The Cockney entertainer tells stories of his East End childhood, of his RAF days, and his post-war showbusiness successes and friendships with fellow comedians.

MOONLIGHT
AND MARCH ROSES
D. Y. Cameron

Lynn's search to trace a missing girl takes her to Spain, where she meets Clive Hendon. While untangling the situation, she untangles her emotions and decides on her own future.

NURSE ALICE IN LOVE
Theresa Charles

Accepting the post of nurse to little Fernie Sherrod, Alice Everton could not guess at the romance, suspense and danger which lay ahead at the Sherrod's isolated estate.

POIROT INVESTIGATES
Agatha Christie

Two things bind these eleven stories together — the brilliance and uncanny skill of the diminutive Belgian detective, and the stupidity of his Watson-like partner, Captain Hastings.

LET LOOSE THE TIGERS
Josephine Cox

Queenie promised to find the long-lost son of the frail, elderly murderess, Hannah Jason. But her enquiries threatened to unlock the cage where crucial secrets had long been held captive.

THE TWILIGHT MAN
Frank Gruber

Jim Rand lives alone in the California desert awaiting death. Into his hermit existence comes a teenage girl who blows both his past and his brief future wide open.

DOG IN THE DARK
Gerald Hammond

Jim Cunningham breeds and trains gun dogs, and his antagonism towards the devotees of show spaniels earns him many enemies. So when one of them is found murdered, the police are on his doorstep within hours.

THE RED KNIGHT
Geoffrey Moxon

When he finds himself a pawn on the chessboard of international espionage with his family in constant danger, Guy Trent becomes embroiled in moves and countermoves which may mean life or death for Western scientists.

TIGER TIGER
Frank Ryan

A young man involved in drugs is found murdered. This is the first event which will draw Detective Inspector Sandy Woodings into a whirlpool of murder and deceit.

CAROLINE MINUSCULE
Andrew Taylor

Caroline Minuscule, a medieval script, is the first clue to the whereabouts of a cache of diamonds. The search becomes a deadly kind of fairy story in which several murders have an other-worldly quality.

LONG CHAIN OF DEATH
Sarah Wolf

During the Second World War four American teenagers from the same town join the Army together. Forty-two years later, the son of one of the soldiers realises that someone is systematically wiping out the families of the four men.